Old Embers

By Laurel Howe

Cover Art by Laurel Howe

This book is dedicated to my early readers, critics, and cheerleaders:

Jonathon Howe,

Cleo Howe, and

Laurie O'Brien.

They made it better. They make me better.

Contents

Old Embers 1
    Characters 6
        Mammoth Chaga 6
        Ches's Clan 7
        Donon's Clan 7
    Prelude 8
    A Fruitless Wait 15
    Croaker Breakfast 22
    The Earth Mother 25
    The Wanderer 30
    A Feast for All 34
    News From Afar 37
    Mighty Chagama 43
    Bird Song 49
    False Trails 52
    Bull Mammoth 58
    Crossing 62
    The Journey 66
    The Cat 70
    Annual Mouflon Hunt 73
    Winter Home 77
    In the Trench 84
    Others 89
    Strangers Passing 93
    Shelter 95

An Exciting Meeting	97
Angry Voices	105
New Friends	107
Guest Contributions	112
For the Love of Art	116
Chaga Talks	119
Winter Spa	124
New Blood	130
Old Grudge	133
Long Winter	137
Frozen Elk	142
Spring at Last	147
The Herds	151
Welcome Home	153
Change of Plans	157
Introductions	158
The Gathering	161
Wrestling Match	166
Love Story	170
Feast	171
The Bow Show	174
Spear Contest	177
Run	180
Posse	183
On the Run	186
The Trail	190
Chagama's Story	193
Grief	197

Decisions	198
Reta	203
Nightmares	205
Unmasked	208
Decisions Made	211
Bone Hearth	213
Reconciliation	216
Peace	218
Over the Mountains	220
Epilogue	222

Characters

Moto: Mother of Bel and Cob

Bel: Female child of Moto, twin of Cob.

Cob: Male child of Moto, twin of Bel.

The Wanderer: Traveller, Newsman, Musician, Trader. Belongs to all the clans.

Mammoth Chaga

Triven: Chief. Hunter. Mate is Reta, father of Privon, Sola, Fabe, Cark, Tram and Dell. Previously mated to Flin and Brella.

Sele: Hunter. Mate is Flin, father of Olin, Grady, Ponu, Ras, Alli, and Bron. Previously mated to Sarin (deceased), and Brella.

Privon: Young hunter. Mate is Lonna.

Ponu: Hunter, Shaman.

Ras: Hunter. Mate is Brella.

Reta: Gatherer. Mate is Triven. Mother of Fabe, Cark, Tram.

Maret: Gatherer. Mate none. Mother of Ras, Alli. Previously mated to Sele.

Flin: Gatherer. Mate is Sele. Mother of Privon, Sola, Olin and Grady.

Brella: Gatherer. Mate is Ras.

Lonna: Gatherer. Mate is Privon.

Zin: Chagama. Mother of Triven,

Fabe: Young boy. Brink of becoming a hunter.

Sola: Young girl. Brink of becoming a gatherer. Daughter of Flin and Triven.

Alli: Young gatherer. Daughter of Maret and Sele.

Bron: Young boy. Brink of becoming a hunter. Son of Brella and Sele.

Olin: Boy child. Son of Flin and Sele.

Cark: Girl child. Daughter of Reta and Triven.

Dell: Girl child. Daughter of Brella and Triven.

Grady: Boy toddler. Son of Flin and Sele.

Tram: Boy baby. Son of Reta and Triven.

Ches's Clan

Ches: Hunter. Mate is Ono. Father to Frome, Moke, Kor and Cheel.

Ono: Hunter. Mate is Ches. Mother to Frome, Moke, Kor and Cheel.

Frome: Hunter. Mate is Neti. Father to Bene.

Neti: Hunter. Mate is Frome. Mother of Bene.

Moke: Hunter. Son of Ches and Ono.

Kor: Child. Daughter of Ches and Ono.

Cheel: Child. Daughter of Ches and Ono.

Bene: Baby. Son of Frome and Neti.

Donon's Clan

Donon: Hunter. Mate is Tsutse. Father of Ross and Chor.

Tsutse: Hunter. Mate is Donon. Mother of Ross and Chor.

Ross: Hunter. Mate is Mor. Father of baby boy.

Chor: Hunter. Mate is Luco. Father of baby boy.

Mor. Hunter. Mate is Ross. Mother of baby boy.

Luco. Hunter. Mate is Chor.

Prelude

The sun was high and warm. They were on the open grassland, a place they always approached with caution. Pope had signaled they could go after watching from the cool shelter of the trees for a while. Moto was content. Instinct had set a task in front of her, and she set about accomplishing it with complete concentration. She was gathering grasses. They were tough and difficult to pull but she was strong and patient. She took her time. When finally, her arms were full, she looked up and saw that her people had moved on without her. Panic squeezed her insides. It came in a rush and obliterated everything else, but she clung to the grasses, not thinking to let go. She closed her eyes. She breathed deeply, sniffing the air. She spun, inhaling scent as she did. Relief dampened her panic slightly as she caught the scent of her people and ran after them, oblivious to a saber cat hidden in the grass. The cat had eaten its fill and wasn't interested in the tiny person running nearby and she would never know her luck.

Moto stopped to sniff every few steps. Her people's scent was strong, and her panic lessoned but no other thought passed through her mind except to find them. It was dangerous to wander the grasses alone. When at last she saw them, tears sprung to her eyes.

Her people were a small group. Moto couldn't count but she knew each by scent and sight. They were resting in the trees on the edge of the grass. Some were sleeping, others sitting. Their dark forms were covered in fine, thin brown hair everywhere except their knees and bums. It was sparse but dark and long enough to deepen the tone of their skin. The hair on their heads was longer, as was the hair on the men's faces. Each looked much the same as the other. Around four feet tall, brown of eye and hair, jutting brows and receding chins. High cheekbones and wide noses. Their differences were subtle and easy to spot if you were one of them. Pope was the tallest and he had a scar from an accident hunting an aurochs. Moto didn't know this because she hadn't seen it and her people had few words. She had seen the wound though and knew the scar for the mark left by healing. Her mother was smaller than she herself was and her cheekbones were flatter than others, giving her face a soft appearance. When Moto gazed on her face, she always felt a rush of warmth and safety. Her mother was sitting under the tree, chewing a piece of grass and Moto ran to her and sat as close as she could. The anxiety of moments before began to fade and Moto drifted off.

A gripping pain woke her, and she sat up in alarm. She looked down at her stomach, where the pain was coming from, and relaxed. She had seen other women do this and she knew the pain for what it was. The babe was coming. Moto gathered the grasses that had fallen from her arms as she slept, and she laid them in a pile and then squatted above them.

When the pains came faster and stronger, Moto cried out. Her mother who had still been resting under the tree, roused herself and came to Moto's side and patted her face. "Shu shu" she said as she brushed the hair from Moto's face. The sounds were comforting ones and Moto quieted. Moto's legs were strong and used to squatting for hours at a time as she dug through roots and grasses searching for sustenance and this was just as well. The babe was Moto's first and would not come quickly or easily. The first never does. Another woman, her mother's sister Uil, came to look at her. "Shu shu," said Uil, her large lips pursing when she made the sound. And then another woman came. The birth of children was an event, and all the women would visit her as she labored. They would come again, after the babe was born.

A short while later, Moto cried out again, this time in release as her babe dropped to the grass below her. She reached under herself and pulled the babe forward. A boy. With her hands, she brushed away the blood and fluid from around his mouth and then using both her hands and her tongue, she cleaned the rest of the small body. She took a deep breath with her large nose, inhaling the scent of her new babe. That first scent would imprint upon her and allow her to recognize her son even if her eyes failed. A few minutes later, she was startled by another pain. Again, she cried out. The women who had comforted her earlier had left her in peace so that she could bond with her babe, but Moto's distress drew them back and they rushed to her side in concern. Moto was straining, her face warped with pain and fear. This was her first birth, and instinct told her something wasn't right. The afterbirth should come in a gentle shwoop, not twisting pain. She also knew that when things weren't right at birth, the mother often died. Without a mother, the babe would die soon after. These thoughts were abstract. They came to her in images and feelings and Moto clutched her babe in fear. Her own mother put her arms around her and held her while she struggled. With another cry, another twist of pain, a second babe dropped to the ground. Moto was shocked. She had never seen twins before. Instinct drove her and she pulled the second babe, a girl, forward to clean it as she'd done the first.

Over the next few days, the women visited. They brought meat and water, berries, and brassica. They gathered wood and built up the fire beside Moto. The older women looked at Moto with sadness. They had seen twins born before. They never survived and often, the mother didn't either. The strain of caring for two being too much for her body. The younger women were ignorant to the perils of twins and came with the smiles and generosity that were usually a new mother's due. Moto was content to rest and bask in the glow of new motherhood, oblivious to the concern in the older women's eyes. The twins were demanding but the support of the others meant that she could focus on their care.

The men all walked by as well, curious, but feigning disinterest. They weren't very good at pretending and watching them try caused the women to smile behind their hands.

Moto watched her twins grow with interest, affection, and confusion in equal parts. The confusion came when they started to make sounds. At first, it was the sounds that all babe's made. 'Mu' and 'du' vocalizations were plentiful as were gurgles and squeaks. Next, they learned their names, Cob and Bel and her own name as well. Then they started making sounds Moto had never heard before. Moto would tilt her head and listen, but she was never able to grasp why they made the sounds they did or even that the sounds held meaning.

When the twins were of an age to learn, Moto sat them down and gave them each two rocks. She grasped the heavy rock in her hand and showed the twins. When they each took their own heavy rock, she nodded. She then picked up the lighter rock in her other hand and struck it with force. She showed the twins the rocks sharp edge by slicing a nearby stick. She nodded with satisfaction. The twins looked at each other and made sounds and motions with their rocks and their hands but they didn't strike. Moto shook her own head and frowned. She grunted to draw their attention and struck her lighter rock again with the heavy one. Cob nodded and Bel frowned in confusion. Bel made sounds and directed them to Moto and then she grasped Moto's hand and looked at the lighter rock with a frown. Moto felt a little panicked when one of the twins' made sounds at her. She felt she should know something, or they needed something from her. It felt the same as if she couldn't provide for her children. A little desperate, a little sad.

Moto wasn't the only one of the people who felt inadequate next to the twins. Other adults often frowned at them and then looked at Moto with pity and wariness. Only Moto's own mother seemed to accept them as she found them. It didn't matter. The twins thrived, Bel did learn to form tools with rocks, and the people grew used to them and their sounds.

"Go," and Cob pointed. Bel followed his finger and ran into the trees where he was pointing. He ran too, in the same direction but chose a different trajectory. He would hide close to her, but not beside. The other children were after them in minutes. Cob peaked around the bush he was hiding behind and grinned at Bel who was peaking behind her bush. They were playing a game of hunter and prey. Bel and Cob were the prey. The other children the hunters. They played the game often in the warm summer months when food was plentiful, and their tribe didn't roam so often. Bel and Cob always were hunters or prey together and they took full advantage of the words they had taught themselves. "Under, over, run, hide," were a few simple ones that they used often in their games. "Rock," said Bel and moved her arm in a throwing motion. Cob dug around for stone and hurled it away from them. The other children cocked their heads and then chased the sound. The twins jumped from behind their hiding spots and ran to Moto. She was nearby slicing deer meat, and they were hungry. They had won the game and it was just a matter of time before the others realized it.

When they could get away with it, Bel and Cob used their words to play with the adults too. Usually as a form of distraction. One twin might speak to a gatherer, who of course couldn't understand them. They would talk and wave their arms, frown in frustration, force a tear or a grunt of anger, all the while watching as the other would sneak up behind and take some treasure. Berries or meat, a tool or pelt. Then they would hide in a bush and stuff themselves or watch with delight as the adults searched for their lost items.

In every other way, the twins were like the other children. They learned to shape stones for spears and knives. They learned how to hunt and how to gather. They learned which herbs to use for headache and which to use for fever.

Moto's tribe never stayed in one place very long. They would make beds out of grass and leaves and sleep where they found themselves at the end of the day. If it rained, they'd seek shelter under the trees. If they were lucky, and they rarely were, they found shelter in a cave. They carried their fire with them, careful not to let it die out. They used it for warmth and protection and melting bone marrow. Most of their food they ate raw. Occasionally they came across other tribes. The men postured and the women hid shy smiles behind hands and hair. Sometimes, a pair would leave together, either with one of the tribes or off on their own. Other times it looked as though the men might fight but meeting other tribes was such a treat that a fight was rare.

One day, a few summers after Moto had squatted over the grass and birthed twins, Moto's tribe met two tribes. They were in the shadow of a great mountain that looked like an old woman with sagging breasts and wispy hair. A lucky place. A lucky omen.

Cob sought out Bel. It wasn't the first time they had come across another tribe, but in the past, both had turned down the opportunity to mate. They knew how special their bond was. They recognized that losing their words would bring an isolation and loneliness that would be hard to bear.

"Bel," Cob spoke softly. "Mate," he said and pounded his chest. He watched her closely for her response. Bel was not entirely surprised by this, but it felt like he had punched her in the stomach, nevertheless.

Bel nodded and turned away, tears already forming. Cob reached out a hand in comfort, but she ignored it. He let it drop and watched her for a moment before the urge to take a mate pulled him away.

Bel stayed in the trees near their camp for a long while before hunger nagged at her. She didn't want to go back to the fire but then suddenly an image of a young male from one of the tribes flashed through her mind. He had dark eyes that watched with a stillness she found attractive. He walked with sureness where others swaggered. She felt a pleasant rush through her body as she thought about him and then she sat up straight with a startling thought. She would also take a mate! This decision filled her with anticipation, and she made her way back to the fire with hope and excitement.

The three tribes camped in the trees. They mingled, hunted, and gathered together while the young flirted. Their forest site was not sustainable for so many, and the youths were urged on, backs pounded, and nods of approval sent when the elders noticed their love interest.

When the mating game was over, Cob had chosen a mate from one tribe, and Bel from another. Both would be travelling with their new tribes. The three tribes stoked the fires as they shared their final meal together. Bel and Cob weren't the only ones struggling with mixed emotions. The tribes might be forever bonded now but each would lose members and those left behind would miss them. All knew they might not see each other again.

Finally, the chief from Bel's new tribe stepped away from the fire which signalled the tribe was ready to leave. Pope took this cue and did the same. As soon as mating became a possibility, Moto had begun work on a bone hearth for each of the twins. The hearths were fashioned from the small skulls of monkeys and polished with the fat of geese and the grain of swamp grass. Leather thongs were strung through the mandibles for ease of carrying. When the chiefs rose, Moto hunted for the perfect embers to place inside. Pieces that were hot enough to stay lit, small enough to fit inside the skull and big enough that they wouldn't burn out too quickly. She placed an ember in each hearth and handed one to Bel. This was a valuable gift. Moto's tribe did not know of flint and fire and so fire was often a luxury that tribes went without. With tears on her cheeks, Bel accepted the gift that would give her status in her new tribe and embraced her mother for a final time. Moto turned to Cob and gifted him a bone hearth as well. Finally, the twins faced each other for what they suspected would be the last time. They didn't hug or speak. For once, their words weren't needed. And then they were gone.

A Fruitless Wait

Excitement rippled through the *chaga* like wind across a lake. After a long winter filled with dried food, long boring days, and longer boring nights, they were on the move again. It didn't matter that no signs of a herd had been seen or that snow could be found in shady spots or that even fiddleheads had yet to appear. They were moving and they were happy about it. All of them.

They had wintered in a cave carved out of a hill by a bear or some long-forgotten ancestor. It was deep in a woodland forest and close to a stream. The cave was small. It wouldn't hold a large *chaga* which was most likely why it had been available to them when they had claimed it all those seasons ago. It wouldn't hold them much longer either. One more winter. Perhaps two. Triven had looked at the cave critically when they left that morning, and then he'd grinned and shrugged. That problem was one for another day.

At midday, Triven called a halt and the *chaga* dropped their packs and their shelter poles, their hides and everything else they were carrying. They'd been idle for months and their first morning's walk had caused blistered feet and aching muscles in more than one member of the *chaga*. They'd paused by the river. The same river that ran by their cave. They were following it north. The river had taken them to the edge of the steppe where they would spend the next three seasons.

The young boys, without being told, gathered wood, and had a fire going within minutes of arrival. Flin found a flat stone and threw it on the fire and Reta pulled some dried meat from her pack and tossed it on the stone. It didn't need to be cooked but the heat made it taste a smidge better. The meat was old and although preserved it carried a musty taste.

Sola and Alli had headed to the riverbank together and searched for spring mushrooms and last years roots. They found mushrooms but little else. It didn't matter, others searched as well, and people shared what they found as they relaxed by the fire.

Triven smiled at the sight of the *chaga* sitting so happily around the fire. After months of idleness, endless bickering, frayed nerves, and bratty children, it had felt like sitting by a fire in contentment was as likely as a twin horn wandering past their cave and pausing to rest in such a spot as he couldn't fail to shoot it dead from the warmth and shelter of his cave. He shrugged to himself before looking out across the steppe. The grass was short this time of year and in low spots, snow huddled from the sun's rays. He could see the horizon, blue and bright but he couldn't see a herd. The grassland was deceptive though. It wasn't nearly as flat as it appeared and hills and vales could hide herds, even massive ones although a large herd would make noise and be hard to miss. If they were to have a successful hunt, the *chaga* would need to spread out and watch as much of the steppe as they could manage.

"Let's go," he said when everyone had rested a while. They knew what he meant. He directed the younger children, those that didn't need their mothers too much, closer to home. Sola and Alli, on the verge of womanhood were a little farther out. The gatherers farther still, and the hunters farthest of all but each group was in sight of at least two other groups. The *chaga* communicated with signals and whistles when they were spread out like this. Staying low and waving an arm meant a herd, approach quietly. Standing and waving both arms meant head back to camp, or if the waves were frantic, danger of some kind.

Nobody spotted any herds that first day and none were surprised by this. Fresh meat on the first day would have been a welcome gift but they had dried meat to carry them a few days yet. They would move across the steppe, travelling in the mornings, hunting in the afternoons, and gathering before dark. They were making their way to a narrow stretch of grassland between two rivers. Herds of leapers, twin horns, grey horn, and others travelled through the narrows in the spring. It was easy hunting when the herds moved north and then south again in the fall. Both migrations were critical to their survival. The spring hunt shored them up after a lean winter. In the fall, they dried and cured and salted meat to carry them through the winter.

Sola threw herself back on the grass and stared at the bright blue sky. She wrapped her arms around herself, a futile effort to gather some heat. The sky was clear of clouds and looked warm, but it wasn't. When the wind was still and the rays touched her skin, she briefly felt their heat, but the wind didn't stay still for longer than a moment and she was chilled through. Alli was too and Alli wanted to go back to camp and retrieve their warm wraps but if she did that, the rest of the *chaga* would see her and both girls would be in trouble. They were supposed to watch for herds. They had been doing that for days upon days and the excitement they had felt their first day away from the cave had long since waned. People were hungry, cranky, and likely to beat them harshly were they to leave their posts.

"You won't spot twin horns in the sky," scoffed Alli. Discomfort of any kind always brought the worst of her out.

Sola sighed and sat up and looked for movement. The only thing that moved was a few tiny blades of grass on a hill that twitched with the wind. She was getting tired of watching the grass dance.

Alli was the only girl near to Sola's age in the *chaga*, and they were sometime friends. Alli had a jealous nature and a nasty edge when her jealousy was aroused, or when she didn't get her way. Like today. The elders often paired the girls, oblivious to the friction between them, or perhaps they just didn't care.

"You're a baby still," sneered Alli. A reference to the fact that she had had her bloods and Sola had not. She hadn't gotten her way about fetching their wraps and Sola knew that the rest of their time on the hill would be filled with poking words, fishing for vulnerabilities. Since they had known each other all their lives, Alli didn't have to work too hard to find them. Sola gritted her teeth and tried to ignore her.

"Even your own mother hates you," continued Alli. "Probably because you're so skinny." The *chaga* people prized a fleshy appearance. It spoke of health and competent hunting and gathering. Tears sprung and Sola blinked rapidly to hold them off. If she responded, she'd cry for sure. It wasn't the skinny barb that bothered her. They were all skinny right now. It was the jab about her mother. Sola couldn't remember a time when her mother had been anything other than harsh. She wasn't like that with Sola's brothers which only made it hurt more.

In the distance, Bron waved his arms. They were done waiting for herds for the day. Sola jumped to her feet and made her way quickly back to camp without waiting for Alli. She was tall and straight. Her curves, like her bloods, had yet to make an appearance and they likely wouldn't until she started getting heartier meals. Her skin was the color of an oak tree and would darken under the spring and summer sun. Her hair was like her father's, long and almost black but in every other feature, she took after her mother. Her eyes were a light brown with flecks of green. They slanted slightly above her high cheekbones. Her face was narrow and oval. Her lips were full and her nose small and straight. She had been thin after the winter, but the last few days of near starvation had caused her face to lose much of its flesh. A week or two more of this and her features would disappear into the shape of a skull.

Sola went immediately to her shelter and searched out her pack which was leaning against the inside wall of the portable home she shared with her family. The shelter space was cramped, and packs hugged the sides of it. Sola shared it with her mother Flin, Sele, Flin's mate, and her young brothers. The tight space kept them warm and close at night. It was only used for sleeping or huddling in on wet days.

The shelter was made of two long poles. The poles were bent over into a dome shape and the four ends were dug into the ground for stability. Hides were thrown over the poles and tied in place with leather thongs. At times where hides were scarce or too worn, tree branches would serve. The shelters were adequate for all but the winter. Cold, rainy spring days were not much fun either. Fortunately, there weren't too many of those.

Sola withdrew her warm wrap and put it on, tying the leather thongs together. It was made of leaper. The body of it was a single hide that fit over her head. Leather thongs, one at the edge of the wrap, and one at the side held the garment closed. The wrap had sleeves, also made of leaper and these were tied to the body of the garment with leather thongs as well. When the weather was warmer, the sleeves could be detached. She felt instantly better and walked along the river to gather what she could find for a meal.

Triven, the *chaga* chief, was the last one back to camp. He was tall at five feet ten inches. The only one taller was Sele, his best friend and that by only a finger. His eyes were dark and difficult to read as Triven worked hard to keep his emotions under control. His skin was fairer than most and fortunately he wasn't a vain man or that might have bothered him. His hair hung to just past his shoulder blades. Grey was sprinkled through it, and he was almost white by the ears. His people claimed that each grey hair represented a harsh lesson learned. He thought the scars that covered his torso and arms told a better tale of that, but he rarely argued with his wise woman. His was a commanding presence, instantly recognized as chief when met by strangers.

That evening, after they had shared the fish, the boys had caught and the mosses, mallow and nettle leaves the gatherers had found, *Chagama*, their wise woman, stomped her walking stick before sitting by the fire. This signalled a story. The children perked up immediately, hunger temporarily forgotten. Stories were always greeted with eagerness by the children and just a little bit of trepidation by the adults. *Chagama's* stories could bite.

Chagama rearranged her clothing, a wrap similar in design to Sola's and set her stick down by the fire as she folded her lean frame easily into a cross-legged position. Her hair was more white than grey and her wrinkles deep and plentiful, made even more so by the *chaga's* recent meager meals. She watched her people carefully, looking for signs of distress or illness. Her gaze often made people uncomfortable as she missed little, and they knew it. Secrets were almost impossible to keep in a *chaga* in any case and *Chagama* often smiled to herself in triumph when she uncovered one. She enjoyed the secrets, but they were safe with her unless they might harm her beloved *chaga*.

Everybody would come to listen to *Chagama's* story. Sola, still young enough to be wholly eager sat next to *Chagama* first. *Chagama* waited patiently as the rest of the *chaga* found a spot by the fire. Only the children hurried but the elders didn't take long to join them. There was little else to do after all.

This happened to my mother's father's mother's chaga, began the story. All *Chagama's* stories happened to somebody in the family. This beginning could mean three generations back or thirty. Even *Chagama* often didn't know.

My mother's father's mother's chaga and another chaga, were waiting in the trees for the great herd to pass. There was a giant field of grass with trees on either side where the hunters could hide. Every year it passed this spot and often many chaga came together to hunt them. But always my mother's father's mother's chaga and always her sister chaga. When the herd came through, each chaga would take what animals they needed and hang them out to dry in the trees. And while they dried, the chaga's would exchange stories and laughter. Share fires and food, recipes for cooking, or tips for shaping tools. Hunters or gatherers might join a new chaga. Once a Chagama joined a new chaga.

Chagama paused for effect here and was rewarded with gasps and looks of horror. Sola instinctively reached out and took *Chagama's* hand. "But that is a different story for another day."

For many days the two chaga's waited for the herd. And for many days it did not come. The surrounding area and the surrounding area's surrounding area were picked clean. People grew weak.

My mother's father's mother's chaga chief woke up one morning and packed up his shelter. He swung his bow and arrow across his back and held his spear in hand. And then he waited as the rest of the chaga did the same. They would wait no more.

Triven exchanged glances with Sele. *Chagama's* story carried a message this night and they wouldn't like it, Triven felt sure. They rarely did.

The chaga struggled for many days. When a young female lost her baby, the chaga walked on. When a young boy fell behind and was lost, the chaga walked on. When there was no food for many days, and the youngest baby died, the chaga walked on. Many questioned the wisdom of the chief. Waiting for the herd was an important event in their survival and without the meat and fat, they grew very lean. Finally, they came across a grey horn and with much struggle and some injuries, they killed the grey horn and ate well. A long tooth cat tried to take their kill, but they fought it off and ate him too. The laughing ones came, and the hunters stood guard. The chaga grew strong again.

The following year, the chaga returned to the plains between the trees. My mother's father's mother's chaga chief stood for a long time and so the clan waited. Would they setup camp and wait for the herd? Or would they move on? Finally, the chaga chief put down his burdens and began to setup a shelter.

In the days following, my mother's father's mother eagerly looked for their sister chaga. The herds came back but the chaga did not. My mother's father's mother never saw them again.

When *Chagama* didn't say anything after that, Sola realized the story was over. Unsatisfied, she asked "What happened to the sister *chaga*?" *Chagama* shrugged. Nobody knew.

"How big was the grey horn?" asked Olin, Sola's younger brother. He was just past toddlerhood and full of questions. *Chagama* smiled and said, "He was as big as that hill near the huge nut tree on the outside of camp and that's all I know of him."

Sola mulled over the story. The *chaga* had suffered greatly. Did the story mean they should have waited for the herd? But what had happened to the other *chaga*?

The adults talked around the fire that night. Should they go? Should they stay? Sola crawled into the family shelter and fell asleep long before the discussion was resolved.

The next morning Triven gathered up his bow and arrow and slung it across his back. He packed up his shelter and picked up his spear and waited. "Did your mother's father's mother say which way the grey horn was?" he asked *Chagama*, eyebrows raised.

Chagama laughed. "Doesn't matter. He's long dead." Triven only shook his head and headed north, in the direction the herds would have gone had they arrived. Perhaps one would overtake them.

Croaker Breakfast

Moke stirred under his pile of furs. When he opened his eyes, he saw the faint rays of dawn creeping in through the mouth of his families' cave. Most mornings he hunkered down under the blankets and tried, with much success, to sleep just a little longer. But on this day, he felt different. He stretched and rose, grabbing a hide to throw around his shoulders and walked to the mouth of the cave. It would be a clear day, though it had snowed the night before, at least half a finger, and it would take some work to pack it down so he and his family could walk outside with ease.

He surveyed the valley before him. The creek was still frozen but in one or two places he could see the water gurgling up. By tomorrow, those tiny holes would be bigger, and the ice would be gone altogether in a few days if the weather held. Snow clung to the tree branches, dripping already from the warmth of the morning sun. He couldn't see any animal tracks and the day looked much the same as the one before, but it felt different. He had no calendar and even if he did, the concept of a single day denoting the line between winter and spring would have been completely foreign to him. The transition was gradual. A loosening, not a line. Everyone knew that. Nevertheless, he felt the change. He felt light and eager. For the first time in months, he wanted to tackle the day.

The croak of a ptarmigan drew his attention. "Duhhhh, duh ta duh,", a bird called. Another let out a long groaning sound. And then he heard a few birds, competing at once for attention. It was mating season for them. It made them less cautious and easier to catch. He scanned the horizon, looking for them, and spotted a few in the distance. Their feathers starting to come in brown for their spring coloring made them easy to see against the new snow. In a couple of weeks when the snow was gone, and their fall plumage in, they would once again melt into their surroundings.

Maybe they could have croakers for breakfast instead of months old frozen horse, he thought. He returned to his bed, a pile of furs along the wall of the cave and looked for his boots. He pulled them on and then one by one tied the laces. There were five in all and putting on boots was a tedious process. A spear clattered into his back, and he turned startled. Frome was glaring at him. Frome liked to sleep in, especially in the winter. He cringed and tried to be quieter. Unfortunately, if he was going to catch a croaker or two, he needed to find his net. He hadn't used it in months, and it was somewhere in a pile of spears, ropes, pelts, and other detritus beside his bedding. As quietly as he could, which was not very quiet at all, Moke dug through the pile and pulled out his net. Then he had the tedious job of untangling it. This part at least he could do without disturbing anyone else.

Moke carefully made his way down into the valley. The path from the cave was wide but it was also slippery with the new snow and in places the drop was steep. He shuffled his feet as he descended, brushing much of the snow off the path. The path curved gently around the mountain side. The cave was about two hundred feet above the valley floor, and even with his shuffling, he was down in minutes. Moke paused to listen for the croaker. "Duhhhh, duh da duh," he heard. They were still where he had spotted them earlier. If he was quiet and patient, he could catch a few for breakfast. That would make even the grumpy Frome smile.

Moke laid out his net on the uneven terrain and covered it with snow. He had chosen a place where there were large rocks on either side, which he hoped would increase the chances of the birds stepping into his net. Their feet would become entangled and with luck he would have a few in a short time.

Once the net was laid, he circled around the breeding ground and came up the opposite side. The birds had hidden while he laid his net and now, he waited patiently behind a tree for them to re-emerge. When the woods were again filled with croaker calls, he rose and walked slowly forward. The birds were shy and kept their distance. Some went left, some right but a few of them walked towards his net. Six entangled themselves. One managed to get free and flutter away. Moke was sorry to see him go. He scooped up the net quickly so no others would get away and headed back to the cave with his treasure.

By this time, the entire clan was awake. Five croakers would not fill them up, but they were a welcome treat. Cheel and Kor, the clan's youngest females squealed in delight at the sight of the birds. Moke handed them each one to kill, pluck and prepare. Young though they were, they had already learned enough to prepare birds for eating. He handed a bird each to Ches and Ono, his parents, and kept one for himself. For a moment, the cave was filled with squawks and fluttering wings and then it was quiet as the five of them set to work preparing the birds. Moke eyed the fire and then decided he would rather have his raw. Through the long winter, the meat required thawing before eating and so it had been a long time since they had enjoyed fresh raw meat of any kind.

Frome glanced at Moke from his pile of hides. He was smiling now and moving under the pile and so was Neti, his mate. Not even the promise of fresh croaker could keep Frome from mating. Watching them, Moke felt the longing that had dogged him for the last few months. His sunny mood darkened. He wanted a mate and the desire seemed to get stronger and more unbearable with each passing day. By nature, Moke was easy going, generous and full of good humor. He wasn't used to strong feelings pulling at him and he was having a difficult time coping with them. Suddenly, the croaker didn't taste so good, and he stomped out of the cave in an unfamiliar fit of jealousy.

He walked by the creek and thought of mating. He thought of the girls he knew and who he wanted and who might want him. His hair was the color of the sun. A rare shade which he knew girls liked. His eyes were the color of the sky, or so his mother told him. Not as rare but also attractive. He didn't know that his wide smile which lit up his whole face was his best feature, but he did think he might be able to attract a girl. He'd have to be around one first and that thought caused his anxiety to rise. Would there be a gathering in the summer? He didn't know. He groaned as he pushed that thought aside. The summer seemed an eternity away. Anything beyond that was unbearable.

The Earth Mother

It was a relief to be walking again after so many days sitting in the same spot. The *chaga* hugged the river which wound this way and that and sometimes, Sola spotted an otter or a frog. She would point it out to Bron or Fabe and they would try to catch it. They usually failed. The trees were leafing out. They had that bright lemony green that only new growth had. One morning, Bron saw a bear and cubs up ahead and the *chaga* proceeded cautiously, making lots of noise. It should have been scary as bears are particularly dangerous in the spring with new cubs, but Sola found it more exciting than frightening. She stuck close to the middle of the *chaga* though and let herself be surrounded by hunters with drawn bows. Despite their hunger, Triven decided against trying to take the bear. They were thick-skinned, mean-tempered, and notoriously hard to kill.

Most days Sola walked with Alli. She had forgiven her for her meanness and the days passed pleasantly enough.

"I saw Privon and Lonna mating last night", said Alli.

"EWWWW!" Privon was Sola's brother, and she was not interested in watching him mate, or even hearing about it. Her people weren't too concerned about keeping that kind of thing private, so it wasn't unusual to see, and Sola was as curious as any her age, but she drew the line at watching her brother. Or her mother. Once Sola had seen Privon and Ponu mating. They were both hunters and she thought that odd. When she'd asked *Chagama* about it, *Chagama* had just shrugged and kept silent.

"Who do you want for your first mate?" asked Alli.

"I don't want a mate."

Alli stopped walking at that pronouncement. Her mouth hung open in amazement and she gazed at Sola in shock. This was the first time that Sola had ever said that despite the many times that Alli had brought the subject up.

"But what would you do then? Just stay with this *chaga*? Never have babies?"

Sola pulled Alli forward. Flin, Sola's mother, and her younger brothers were walking behind the two girls and Alli was blocking them. Flin was often quick to lash out so blocking her path was inadvisable.

"I want to be *Chagama*," stated Sola with bravado.

"That's silly. You have to be old to be *Chagama*."

Offended, Sola ran ahead. She had just shared her deepest wish and Alli, as usual, had mocked her. Sola idolized *Chagama* and wanted nothing more than to be like her, except for the old part. She wasn't too keen on aching knees, white hair, and wrinkled skin.

Sola quickly caught up to Reta who was carrying a crying Tram. Tram was Reta's baby and the rationing had turned him into a fussy, unhappy one. Reta was currently mated with Triven, and she had three children by him of which Tram was the youngest. Reta nursed him frequently, but he never seemed satisfied and Reta was looking worn and fraught. Reta was a kind woman and Sola felt sympathy for her. She reached for the babe and Reta gratefully handed him over. Sola was often able to win a smile from him when others failed. She made faces at him as she held him in her arms. Tram responded with giggles and reached for Sola's face, pinching it. She didn't mind. She just laughed at him and made another face. When he fell asleep, she carried him for a while before handing him back to Reta.

Each day was like the one before. The *chaga* walked. They walked in singly or in pairs behind Triven. They walked through trees, or grasses or both. They walked quietly, and slowly; conversation non-existent now. They continued to follow the river as it meandered northward. Herds always went north in spring, and they needed water, just as the *chaga* did. Surely, they would find one soon.

They stopped in the afternoons and the gatherers searched for vegetables, pine nuts, spring mushrooms and moss. Often other *chagas* had been there before them and there was nothing to gather. The hunters climbed trees and stole eggs or sat quietly by the river and waited for animals to drink. Most nights they caught hare or otters or fish. It was not quite enough for nineteen people.

Sola was more hungry than tired as she focused on putting one foot in front of the other. She'd felt hunger pains before. All people of the *chaga* had. But nothing like this. Tram had stopped crying yesterday. Reta's milk had dried up two days before that. Sola was not so young that she didn't recognize this was bad. She was too turned inward to dwell on it, however.

A short while later, the sun still in the eastern sky, Reta stopped by a tree. With a single tear on her face, she carefully laid Tram beneath the branches. Sola felt her stomach roll over as she walked up beside Reta and looked down on little Tram. The worst had happened. It must have or Reta would not have set him on the ground. Sola glanced away from Tram and looked at Reta. She looked defeated. Thin and hollow eyed, a solitary track on her cheek where her tear had fallen.

Chagama came forward and bent to examine Tram where he lay. She shook her head and then sat down. Reta collapsed beside her, shoulders slumped, head forward. The rest of the *chaga* sat in a circle around the tree. Around Tram.

The *chaga* didn't have a shaman. *Chagama* or Triven would try to fill that role when ceremony was required. Before they could say anything, Ponu moved.

Ponu pounded the ground with four beats of his fists, then clapped his hands twice. The *chaga* looked to him in surprise. He was doing what a shaman should do but he wasn't a shaman. Was he? Ponu had been a hunter for only a couple of seasons and probably a little young to be shaman. His mother had died in childbirth, and he had been raised with Privon. They were the same age and the best of friends. Sola adored him too. He was short for a hunter at only five foot five. He had deep brown eyes that glowed with warmth and a gentle smile. Always he seemed a little sad. Sola wondered if it was because he missed his mother.

Ponu repeated the rhythm. When the *chaga* joined him, he began to chant. And when they chanted with him, he began to speak.

"Tram, please give greetings from your *chaga* to the Earth Mother when you see her. Tell her of our need and of our love for her. We return you to her and ask that she listen closely to your sweet voice so that no other from our *chaga* need speak to her in person. To the earth now goes your smile and small body but we will hold you in our hearts instead." The *chaga* continued the rhythm while he spoke. He was nervous and his speech was awkward, as he had never done anything like this before. He wasn't sure what should come next and looked to *Chagama* for guidance.

Chagama smiled sadly in return and said, "Goodbye precious child. May the Earth Mother love you as well as your own mother has done." She leaned forward and kissed Tram on the forehead.

"Goodbye sweet Tram," said Sola. "Peace to you child," said Triven. Each member of the *chaga* said goodbye in turn. Reta was last. She lifted her head. Tears were flowing freely by the time her turn came. The little ceremony had reached past her hunger and exhaustion and pulled her grief to the forefront. She hugged Tram one final time and then laid him back down. "Thank-you Ponu," she said.

Ponu nodded and then got to his feet and began to dig a hole under the tree. Ras and Privon, helped as well. Such a tiny hole was needed that it didn't take them long. They laid Tram in the hole and *Chagama* put some herbs in with him, a gift for the Earth Mother. Reta placed a piece of smooth bone that Tram had liked to mouth when his teeth hurt. A gift for Tram. Ponu found a rock, representing the spirit of the mountains, and *Chagama* placed a wetted piece of hide for the water spirit. It was the best they could manage. They covered him with dirt and wiped their tears. The *chaga* turned and started walking again.

Sola stared at the little pile of dirt for long moments as the *chaga* moved on without her. "What could little Tram possibly tell you that you don't already know?" she demanded of the Earth Mother. And then she slapped her hand to her mouth. Would the Earth Mother punish her? Punish her *chaga* for such disrespect? Was Tram's death punishment? Afraid now and horrified by her words Sola ran to catch up to the others.

The run calmed her down and she wondered instead if the Earth Mother had nothing to do with anything. Maybe Tram had just not had enough to eat.

That night as the *chaga*, despondent, quiet, and hungry sat by the fire, Sola asked, "Can I tell a story?"

Chagama tilted her head and looked at her. Sola felt her eyes boring into her very soul and began to squirm. "Of course, you may," she finally responded.

This story happened to my chaga.

The herds who had always found us in the spring, lost their way. Were they distracted by pretty flowers? Chased by hungry howlers? No one knows. The chaga, who had always relied on the herds to come and fill their bellies after a long winter went hungry.

After waiting many days, the chaga decided they couldn't wait any longer as surely, they would starve. They travelled in search of other herds instead. Every day they searched and each night they went to bed hungry.

Soon, Tram, the chaga's youngest member, began calling to the Earth Mother. For hours he cried for her. The chaga looked hopefully to the sea of grass but the Earth Mother did not answer him. They turned to the river and followed the water spirit. Still Tram called and still the Earth Mother was deaf to him. They turned to the mountains and the Earth Mother was quiet. The chaga wondered if she still was. They wondered if they had offended her. But their wondering did no good. The Earth Mother gave no sign and the chaga was hungry.

Finally, one day, Tram grew quiet. He was still determined speak to the Earth Mother, but he realized he must go in person. He couldn't go all the way himself. The chaga would have to help him take the final step. And he would not be able to come back.

He didn't go right away. His mother needed some time to understand his journey. Finally, he grew completely still. He was ready.

The chaga buried him in the ground so that he could at last be close to the Earth Mother's ear. They had a wonderful ceremony to say goodbye, led by their new shaman Ponu.

"Then what happened?" asked Olin when Sola didn't continue. Sola shrugged.

"That's a stupid story," said Alli. Sola rolled her eyes.

Reta was crying and Sola was horrified when she noticed. "I'm sorry!" she said.

Reta shook her head and took a deep breath. "I thought your story was beautiful. And besides, the ending hasn't happened yet. Tram has just now seen the Earth Mother. She will answer him tomorrow."

The next day started as all the others had. Sunny. Chilly. No sign of a herd. And then Triven halted, raised his arm, hand splayed in the universal sign for stop. He motioned the hunters forward and pointed.

The Wanderer

Moke was excited. The clan was packing up. They were moving on to their spring and summer hunting sites and Moke couldn't wait to leave long winter nights, dark caves, and old food behind. Battling with his excitement was a growing impatience. It was already past midday, and nobody looked ready to go. Ches and Frome, Moke's father, and brother, had left early this morning on the pretext of catching some fresh food for the journey. They hadn't packed before they went. Moke knew they just wanted to get away from the chaos. And the chaos was ridiculous. Moke himself had been packed since just after dawn. He had his blankets, spears, travelling jerky, flint stone, net, hides and poles for a shelter and he was set. Neti, Frome's mate, hadn't packed a thing. And she didn't look like she would start any time soon.

Moke looked over at her. Her dark hair sprawled carelessly across the cave floor and her face peeked above the furs. She had deep brown eyes and a wide face. Moke thought her beautiful, but then he thought every woman of an age to mate beautiful. Bene was at her breast and Neti's face was relaxed with a slight smile. She looked more likely to nap than pack.

With a grunt of dissatisfaction, Moke dumped his load in an unruly heap and stomped out of the cave. He headed towards the river and hid behind a big bush. Perhaps a deer would come to drink, and he could take his frustrations out on it. Of course, he hadn't brought his spears. He had a small knife though and if not a deer, maybe a rabbit. He wasn't there long when he heard Ches and Frome returning. He peeked around his bush and saw them carrying a small deer.

Ches was big and burly. His hair was a dark brown that used to be streaked with gold, but the gold was grey these days. He was good natured and somewhat impulsive. Most of their people were. They were given to action more than either analyzing or dreaming. Moke was different in this sense. He was a dreamer and could often be found with a vacant look on his face, telling those around him that he was somewhere else. Ches and Frome were similar in appearance. Both had massive muscles and light skin, deep set eyes, high cheekbones, and receding chins. Frome was taller than his father and his hair was a shade lighter, but the resemblance was hard to miss. Ono, mate, and mother, said they were of the night, her stars, showing the way while Moke was her sun. She thought her girls, Cheel and Kor were like young birch trees, flexible and strong, with the promise of deep roots and sheltering limbs. Ono herself was like Moke, with sunny hair and sky-blue eyes and a wide, welcoming smile. They both had a flatter face than the rest of their family although only a fellow clansman would ever say so.

"Come out of there boy," said Ches. Moke came as bidden and when Ches saw him, he laughed. "When have we ever moved on moving day? Why do you think we left this morning? Come, you can skin and gut this deer and we'll feast on fresh meat and chyme tonight."

By the time Moke finished skinning and gutting the deer, Ches and Frome had built a huge fire in a pit by the river. Once the flames died down, they laid a flat rock over the flames, and then threw the deer on whole. They covered it with warmed rocks, pine branches and a couple of hides and waited. The chyme, which was the partially digested stomach contents of the deer's last meal, would cook with the deer and provide a delicious, cheesy sauce for the meat. They hadn't had chyme since fall and Moke's mouth watered at the thought of it.

It was hours before they could eat the deer and days before they actually left the cave. Once they did, spirits were high and progress slow. Neither Cheel nor Kor walked very fast but that was okay. The need to hurry that Moke had felt, had more to do with leaving than arriving anywhere. They had meat left from the deer as well as the dried jerky that everyone carried. It would take them a couple of days to reach the grasslands. The forest at the edge of the great steppes, by the mighty *Dubbie* is where they would be for the rest of spring and summer. Herds of deer, bison, elk, aurochs, and oxen would all come to graze through the season. And they would all drink at the river. Moke's family would move every few days as the animals grazed out a spot and moved on. Woolly Elephants would come too but they would hunt those with a great deal of caution, if at all. They were big and dangerous. Circumstances had to be right. An animal alone, or another clan to help or a cliff nearby that they could drive the herd over. A herd of mammoths with young calves was the most dangerous of all. Matriarchs and cows were so protective of their young, they would attack anything coming near the herd, dangerous or not. Moke had once seen one attack and kill a rhino just for existing in their vicinity.

The day was cool, a breeze blowing through made it more so. Moke shivered as he lay in the grass. He was barely hidden as the grass wasn't that long yet. Frome was closest to him, only a few feet away. Ono and Ches were there too but he couldn't see them. They were hunting aurochs. The cows had calved not too long ago, but the calves wouldn't have enough meat to bother with although an aurochs calf was delicious. Moke's favorite. They were after an old bull. He limped and was missing a piece of one of his horns. Moke recognized him as the ornery old cuss that had scarred Frome a couple of springs ago. Revenge wasn't their motivation, however. That didn't even occur to them. The old bull was chosen because he was weakened and would be easier to catch.

Moke snaked forward a foot and peered up. The herd hadn't noticed him. He was about to move again when as one, the herd lifted their heads. They were going to bolt! Laying in the grass was not a safe place to be. Moke jumped to his feet and shouted. Ono, Frome, and Ches did the same.

Heart beating fast, Moke looked around, trying to figure out what spooked the herd. On a hill, just above their camp on the edge of the steppe, Moke could see Kor and Cheel running to camp. They were yelling but he couldn't make out what they were saying. He sprinted towards them, the aurochs forgotten.

As Moke got closer, he could make out what the girls were saying. "The Wanderer, the Wanderer!" they screamed with happy voices. And then Moke heard the notes that always signalled the Wanderer's presence.

The notes were high, the melody happy. Moke's pace slowed and so did his heart. He knew the song well although he couldn't play it nearly as competently. The Wanderer travelled all over the known world gathering news and stories from clans he met during his travels. He played the bone flute exquisitely. He would be fed, clothed if needed and welcome to stay as long as he wanted. He brought his own shelter with him, and if it needed mending or replacement, his hosts would happily tend to that for him as well. His mother had given him a different name Moke supposed but he was only ever called 'The Wanderer' as far as he new.

Neti, who had been with the girls, followed at a more sedate pace. When she reached the camp, she stoked the fire. The aurochs may have run off but there was plenty of bison left from an animal they had taken a couple of days ago. They had smoked and salted it and it had lovely flavor. They also had lots of bones and Neti threw some on the fire. Warmed bone marrow would be the perfect welcoming treat.

The Wanderer played his song until he reached the camp. Wide smiles were on everybody's faces as they waited for him. A long final note that evoked longing signaled the end of his song. The Wanderer removed the flute from his mouth and spread his arms wide. Cheel and Kor ran and jumped into them with the abandonment only children can show. The rest of the clan members waited their turns with good cheer.

A Feast for All

Triven kept his arm raised and pointing until the entire *chaga* had come up beside him to have a look. Ahead, just visible between the trees was an expanse of horns that had to belong to a Great Horn. No other beast was large enough to carry such a rack. The horns swivelled slowly and then bounced, likely indicting chewing. These beasts wandered the forests alone during the spring and they were massive as were their horns. This one was at least a head taller at the shoulder than Triven or Sele, the tallest of the hunters. His head and neck soared above, and his mighty horns stretched the length of Triven easily. He would feed the *chaga* for days. If they could catch him.

Triven checked the wind. Luck was with them. They would be able to get into position without the beast smelling them and charging away. If, that is, they could contain their excitement enough to get into place calmly and quietly.

With an animal this size, the whole clan would help although the gatherers and children would have supporting roles only. The hunters, five of them, would move to encircle the beast. The gatherers would be a fence, to block him if he came towards them, and towards them was where the hunters would drive him if they could. Sele and Privon would travel around and place themselves to the side of the animal. They couldn't get right behind him until the last moment as the wind would carry their scent. Ponu and Ras would travel to the sides as well, but not as far. Triven stayed in front of the animal and the gatherers waited a few hundred feet back. From Triven's spot, he could see the other hunters and the gatherers and signal all of them.

The plan decided, the hunters jogged ahead. The closer they got, the slower they went. They must be quiet so as not to startle the great horn. Adrenaline kept them alert. Desperation kept them careful.

While the hunters were getting in place, the gatherers made small piles of brush and branches. They held their flint stones ready to ignite the pile at Triven's signal.

Once the gatherers were ready, Triven waved his arm in a forward motion. Sele and Privon crept forward and moved into place slightly behind the beast. When ready, they raised their arms, circling above them. Triven rose, the signal for everyone, and arrows flew from all directions. Four landed on the great horn and two flew by. The great horn jumped in the air as he was struck. Sele ran forward and threw his spear but missed. With Sele running towards him, the great horn ran towards the gatherers. Triven stepped forward and threw his spear into his neck. It struck and the beast stumbled but regained his footing and ran on.

To Sola, it seemed to take forever for everyone to get into place. She was waiting and hungry and then suddenly there was shouting, and chaos and she lit her branch and waved it around. The smoke made her eyes water, and she couldn't see what was happening, but she could hear the thunder of hooves and the sound of crashing brush and then the beast was in front of her, huge and, menacing. She froze as it came directly towards her, arrows and a spear sticking out of his hide, blood streaming from the spear wound in his neck. His eyes were crazed, and she was sure he was going to run her down but at the last second, he reared up. He seemed to pause in the air and then he crashed over onto his side. He struggled to rise, feet flailing madly and then he lay still. He breathed, but he was dying. Sola gingerly approached, eyeing his antlers warily and kneeled beside him. She reached her hand out and laid it on his neck. This was not a prayer. Nor was it a thank-you for giving his life. He clearly hadn't done so willingly. They had taken it. Brutally and without remorse. It was an acknowledgement of his spirit. 'I see you,' the gesture said. 'You are not nothing.'

Chagama found a large rock and threw it onto the fire. She then sent Olin, Cark, and Dell to gather more firewood. The other women and older children set to work skinning the Great Horn while the hunter's gathered saplings that would be used to hang the meat out of reach of predators and set it to drying.

Sola's mouth was watering as she helped carve up the meat. *Chagama* grabbed the first few pieces and threw them on the stone to cook. She didn't leave them there long. Nobody would be eating well done meat this day. The children hovered and she gave them pieces which they greedily gobbled up. She then instructed them to bring pieces to everybody still working. The mood of the *chaga* was lighthearted. There was laughter and teasing while everybody worked. The work had to be completed as quickly as possible so that the carcass could be carted away, and the meat safely hung. Predators and scavengers would be drawn to the smell and the *chaga* had no interest in sharing.

When the work was done and bellies full, the *chaga* stayed by the fire. Ponu gave thanks to Tram, and they were quiet as they thought of his sacrifice. To lighten the mood again, Triven told a story of a great horn that he had hunted with his childhood *chaga*. He had put a spear into the beast but neglected to let go. The great horn, far from mortally wounded, dragged him for a good kilometer or more before he thought to release the cursed spear. By the time he returned to the base camp, his mother was wailing mournfully. It didn't stop when she saw him as he was covered in abrasions, clothes rubbed off, blood everywhere. She thought he was a monster sent by the Earth Mother to punish the *chaga* for letting the great horn suffer. She screamed and ran off into the bush. It took him another hour to catch up with her. He had, however killed the great horn and the *chaga* feasted the next day. Sele clapped him on the back while the *chaga* laughed at his expense. Even Reta found a smile.

Ponu struck up another rhythm. This time, it was upbeat and joyful. The adults joined in song and beat. The children jumped to their feet and danced around the fire. Privon and Lonna took a turn as well. They all slept well that night.

News From Afar

The Wanderer had settled comfortably by the fire when he arrived, sure of his welcome. He was about the same height as Ches but where Ches was barrel chested, he was much slimmer. His legs had huge muscles from climbing and walking so much more than other clans' people. He was a friendly man but serious. He loved his role and performed it diligently. There was only one thing he loved more and that was his bone flute. Flutes actually. He had a few of different sizes but the one he had played on his arrival was the one he played the most often. His hair was a light brown, crinkly and sprinkled with grey. It sprouted out from his head in a thick mess. Deep wrinkles lined his eyes, caused from constantly scouting the horizon as he wandered.

The Wanderer began to share his news while licking his fingers after he had finished sucking the marrow out of a bison bone.

"More?" offered Neti. He shook his head. Neti felt a tiny twinge of guilt for feeling relieved that he had had enough. There was plenty of food to share but she was eager for news.

"We will not have a clan gathering this year," he started with. Moke groaned inwardly, devasted. He would have crawled into his shelter and wallowed in despair had this news not come from the Wanderer. This was not a complete surprise. There had been a gathering last fall and rarely was one held every year as it would put too much stress on the clans. However, Moke had hoped anyway. He regretted not choosing a mate when he had the chance but he had been more interested in spear contests than mating.

"Donon's clan has new babies. Luco and Mor each had a son. Both healthy. Luco's boy has blue eyes and brown hair. He was very big and the labor long. It took many days for Luco to recover… but she's fine. Mor's boy has brown hair and brown eyes. He was much smaller, but the labor was hard anyway because he is Mor's first." Mor was Neti's sister and older than Neti. She had lost babies in the past and Neti was relieved that she managed to carry this one to term. She couldn't wait to see him.

"The girl Frenie, fell from the path near her clan's cave in the winter. She slept and didn't wake up for many days. Tsutse gave her yarrow to stop the bleeding into her head. Tsutse shook her head every time she looked at Frenie as if to say there was no hope, but she did wake, and the clan celebrated with music and song. The noise caused Frenie to yell at them to be quiet because 'they were hurting her head.'" Everybody laughed at this. The wanderer's words were matter of fact, but he added gestures and inflections that brought them to life. When Tsutse shook her head in the telling, the Wanderer shook his own and he pinched his lips and looked mournful. His listeners lost themselves in his news. They likely would have, even without the added drama for there is little else to entertain in their world.

The Wanderer had an amazing ability to recall details. He knew that women would want to know baby's sizes and labor details and he recalled them all. He remembered illnesses and treatments, hunts and mishaps, fights, and reconciliations. It would take him many nights to recount it all. And then it would be his turn to listen to the minutia of Ches's clan.

The Wanderer didn't only bring news, he joined the clan wholeheartedly while he was there. He hunted with them, tanned hides, gathered berries and generally participated in all aspects of daily life. While he was with a clan, he became part of the clan.

On his first night, the Wanderer laid out his trade goods on the ground outside of his shelter. On this visit, he had bone flutes, of course. They were of different sizes and shapes and were his specialty. There was salt, blue stones, crampbark berries, bark, and ointment. He had dried calendula, goldenrod, and valerian. He also had some dried thyme and parsley and a beautiful cave bear pelt that Moke wanted desperately. He thought it would make a dashing coat and help him attract a mate. It was big enough to make boots with too.

The next morning, Moke woke early and gathered up his net. It was tangled again so he spent some time untangling it while chewing on bison. Then he was off to the bison kill site. Cautiously he approached. There would potentially, probably, almost certainly be dangerous predators at the site. On a slight rise, still some distance from the kill site but with a good view of it, Moke sat to wait. It wasn't long before he saw some hyenas sniffing around. They squabbled over bones, snarling, and chasing each other. Moke was confident he could scare them away, but he waited to see what else might come. Eagles and vultures flew overhead, landing briefly before being chased off by one of the hyenas. After an hour, he made his way to the site, a spear in each hand. The hyenas snarled at him, and Moke snarled back. One charged him but Moke didn't back down. He snarled louder and charged back at it, arms spread wide, face warped into a vicious scowl, teeth laid bare. The hyena whined and ran off. Moke watched his back. If they were hungry enough, they might decide to surround him and take turns nipping at him. Fortunately, they weren't, and they didn't.

Moke laid his net over the carcass. His net had a long string which he could pull to tighten the net once a foot was ensnared. He laid the string out too and then retreated to hide behind some rocks in the tall grass. The birds could see him, but they wouldn't care if he was still and far enough away. Patience was required as it would take them some time before they relaxed enough to come down to the site after his visit.

Moke let his mind wander. He had hopes of seeing Genu at the next gathering. He liked her quite a bit and he knew she liked him too. They had spent time gathering St. John's Wort together at the last gathering. They'd traded it for fish, a rare treat for them which they had gleefully eaten together. He liked her. She was an easy companion, calm in a way that other young men weren't. He had been too inexperienced to realize that the edgy energy he had would have been better released with her than with the posturing and competition of his peers. It was only watching Frome and Neti in the time since that what he really wanted had become clear to him. He would not make that mistake again. Assuming he got the chance.

And then there was Sout. Moke, and all the other young men, thought she was beautiful. She had the prized yellow hair as well as a particularly narrow waist and large rear. Competition was fierce for her attentions and Moke didn't think he could resist if by some twist of fate, she chose him. He, himself was handsome. Lots of the girls liked him so he supposed it wasn't out of the realm of possibilities. He liked Genu better though. She worked hard and liked to laugh.

A piercing scream disturbed his reverie. With a start he looked towards the carcass. He had caught an eagle. He pulled on his lead to tighten the snare and then he ran down. Carefully, he wrapped the eagle up in the net before daring to bring his hands anywhere near its claws or beak, both of which could give him a nasty wound. Once it was wrapped, he gingerly placed his hands around the bird's neck and twisted expertly. The meat of the eagle was inedible and smelled nauseatingly rancid. He wasn't after that though. The pin feathers were a valued adornment for the clans. The raptors claws even more so.

He pulled the bird free and straightened out the net to lay his trap again. Once done, he returned to his hideout and set to pulling out the pin feathers and claws. It took longer for a second bird to get trapped. Although he would have preferred another eagle, a vulture is what he got. The feathers weren't as prized, he may not even be able to trade them at all, but the claws were still valuable.

It was almost dusk by the time he finished with the vulture, and he headed back to camp at a quick jog. Dusk was not a good time to be out alone on the steppe. Full dark, even worse.

Moke was starving by the time he got back to camp. The Wanderer was well into his news and Moke helped himself to some bison as quietly as possible. Next, he dug through his pile of things in his shelter. There weren't many items there but what was there was in a heap. He found a bone borer and went to sit by the fire where he lay his treasures by his feet. The Wanderer paused his news while Moke went about his business. Although he tried to be quiet, he wasn't successful, and his family watched him with amusement and waited for him to settle. With a great deal of care and concentration, which some could be excused for thinking him incapable given the state of his possessions, he began to carefully bore holes into the talons he had collected. It was time consuming work and would take him an hour or two to complete each talon. The bearskin was valuable so Moke knew a simple talon necklace would not be enough. He would increase the value of the piece by carving intricate designs on each talon. Diamonds to represent mountains. Intricate curves for the river. Spirals represented the unknowable design of life itself and ovals for birth, or rebirth, the luckiest of symbols. The necklace would bring good fortune to any who wore it as represented many aspects of the knowable world. He would also carve cave bear claws on two of the talons to represent the trade he hoped to make. Not many could carve as well as Moke and that would help to make the trade he hoped.

A few days later Moke strung his talons together on a piece of hide. The end result was an intricate and beautiful piece of art. He had also made a hair band with carefully arranged feathers. He had used a few of the vulture feathers in his piece and it had come together nicely. He laid his work out in front of the bear pelt and then stood back and looked at it. He hoped it would be enough.

Ches came up beside him as he looked down on his treasures. "The clan needs salt." Nothing was more worthless than salt when you lived near a supply and nothing more valuable when you didn't. With his heart breaking just a little, Moke picked up his treasures and laid them by the salt instead. If the amount was acceptable, then when he went by the shelter the next day, his treasures would be gone.

The next morning when Moke arose and looked outside the Wanderers shelter, he saw that all the trade goods were gone except for the salt. Moke's necklace and hairpiece were gone as well. The Wanderer was busy taking down his shelter, his pack on the ground beside him.

"You're leaving," said Moke, disappointment easily seen in his manner and voice. He had hoped to catch more birds and trade for the cave bear pelt.

"I am," The Wanderer stopped what he was doing to face Moke. "You are very talented, young Moke. The bear pelt will likely still be available by the next gathering time. You could make another necklace and trade for it then." Moke had wanted it cut, sewn and worn by then so this was not as much of a consolation as the Wanderer might think. He nodded anyway.

The entire clan came to say goodbye to the Wanderer and help him pack. Each brought a hug and a small gift. Mostly pieces of dried meat for his journey, a couple of pretty stones and young Cheel gave him a flower which made him smile as he tucked it in his hair. The clan stood together and watched as the Wanderer began his journey to the next clan.

Ches put his arm around Moke's shoulder. "What do you say we go cave bear hunting?" he asked with a grin. Moke looked up in surprise and happiness. He nodded, unable to speak. With one final glance at the Wanderer, Moke headed to his own shelter to get his spears and travel pack.

Mighty Chagama

At the very edge of the map that Triven held in his head, the same map the entire *chaga* held in fact, lay the Mighty *Chagama*. It rose out of the landscape like a grand dame, standing proud. Her wrinkled breasts, the jutting rocks. One sagged and the other pointed a little too far to the east. The clouds her wispy whitened hair, wild and uncombable. She was mishappen, grey and brooding as she watched over the steppe. A delegate of the great Earth Mother, some said.

It was rare for them to travel there and when they did, it was in late summer, after trailing a herd of galloping ones or twin horns or leapers. It marked the end of the steppe. The place where the herds turned back for the winter. Never had they come so early in spring.

Sola was quiet as they approached the mountain. It seemed to her that she was a warning. 'Don't go past me,' she said. 'For danger lies there. Don't climb up me for I am not a toy for you to play upon.' *Chagama*, who had been walking ahead, paused, and waited for Sola to catch up.

"My mother's mother's mother's *Chagama* says we all come from here," said *Chagama*. "She told me of this place long before I ever saw it." *Chagama* turned to Sola. "Can you feel her?" she asked.

Sola nodded. "Yes. But she isn't like you. Wise and kind. She frightens me."

"Me as well. We will ask for her blessing for she is very powerful."

They continued to walk in silence, watching the mountain get bigger, closer, and more overbearing.

At Mighty *Chagama's* feet, Triven lay down his shelter poles and spears, his water bag, and pelts. "Let's shelter here tonight," was all he said.

"But it's still morning!" protested Maret.

"I know. But we'll have much to discuss this afternoon so we'd best hunt and gather early."

The hunters shared glances and so did the gatherers. The children whooped and ran to play. This was a rare treat for them.

"Get some firewood!" yelled Flin, too late. They had disappeared into the trees.

"I think we should go over the mountain," began Triven. He thought it best to just blurt it out and was almost amused at the shock and outraged chatter that broke out. With patience he waited, aware that *Chagama* watched him closely.

"It is still spring and here we sit in Mighty *Chagama's* lap. The herds are scarce. If we wait, enough of them might not come. And we already know that there isn't enough where we came from."

People were quiet. Tram's loss was still close. None were keen on facing that kind of hunger again.

"Across the mountains, we might find new lands. Food. Hope."

"We will get lost in the mountains," protested Sele.

"Look!' interrupted Olin. "Galloping Ones!" It was still early afternoon. Plenty of daylight and lots of time to hunt. The *chaga* turned eagerly. As they watched, the gallopers disappeared into the mountain as if they'd never been. The *chaga* sat in stunned silence for a long while.

"Come!" yelled Triven and just like that the hunters were gone.

Hours later they returned, panting but glowing with excitement. "The galloping ones have shown as a path through the mountains!"

When the discussion continued, in the dark this time, the sun having set, the mood was entirely different. People were eager and excited.

"Perhaps *Chagama's* sister *chaga* went through the mountains and are living on the other side," said Olin. *Chagama* was amused but just said. "Perhaps."

When it was clear that the hunters and gatherers were all agreed on going through the mountains, Triven turned to *Chagama* who had yet to speak. "What do you think *Chagama*?"

Chagama looked at him and then smiled. "Sola and I said a prayer to Mighty *Chagama* when we arrived. We asked her to show us a way through the mountains if that is what we should do." And then she grinned while the *chaga* cheered.

The galloping ones showed a trail along a river. It was close with trees and large rocks, and it climbed, slowly and relentlessly but at the end of a days travel it opened onto an alpine meadow. The gallopers were still there but the *chaga* was superstitious. They were guides sent by the Mighty Chagama. Not food. The gallopers lingered for three days before continuing north on a mountainside trail. The *chaga* waited with them and only left the meadow when the gallopers had their fill. The gallopers travelled faster and were quickly out of sight but for people whose lives were the land they travelled, easy enough to follow.

Triven led and for the first time since they'd begun their journey through the mountains, he felt nervous. They had been on the narrow path all day. It wrapped around the mountain side and in many places, the edge disappeared into nothingness. Dusk was approaching and the path showed no sign of widening. Where would they rest, he wondered. And then he came to a spot where the path just didn't exist. He looked ahead. He could see the path, an easy leap for a galloper, not so manageable for people. His gaze travelled downward and saw a galloper far below. Triven guessed it had misjudged the jump or been pushed by an eager companion.

Sele, who had been in the rear, negotiated past the travellers to lean over Triven's shoulder and assess the situation.

"If we lash our shelter poles together, we could build a bridge," he suggested and Triven sighed in relief.

"That will work!"

The *chaga* passed their poles forward where Sele and Triven used thin pieces of hide to tie them together. Any that seemed weak or thin, they passed back to be carried. They set the poles across the path and nodded in approval. They were long enough. And there was enough of them for the bridge to be sturdy. The biggest challenge was for the first person to cross. There was nothing to anchor the bridge on the other side and a rough step could cause it to shift. That would be bad. For everyone.

Sele went first and the *chaga* held their collective breath. Sele wavered once and Flin gasped aloud. But the bridge was short, and he took a couple of quick steps and was across in a moment. He sat on the other end, took a moment to steady his hands and slow his heart before anchoring the bridge for the others who crossed without issue. Triven went last and he faced the same problem as Sele in reverse. He stepped quicky and surely and retrieved the poles with relief.

Dusk was upon them, and they still had no place to rest. Quickly, Triven and Sele unwound the ties and distributed the poles for hunters and boys to carry. "We must keep going," he said nervously, and started walking. Although he had tried to hide it, his concern had been plain for the others to hear, and it was a quiet *chaga* that followed in the growing dark.

Triven was just about to stop and tell everyone to just sleep on the path where they were and hope that they woke in the morning, when he took a step that allowed him to see around a jutting rock. A meadow. Tears came to his eyes as he called them forward. They would be safe. For the night anyway.

And so, it went. Around the mountains, through the valleys and meadows, they followed the gallopers. The gallopers always lingered in the meadows and when that happened, the *chaga* setup their shelters and explored the mountains. They found plenty of deer, rabbits, and otters. The younger boys fished in the streams and delighted in their daily catch. There were also birds that were unfamiliar. Ponu caught one with an arrow one day, but it fell in a gully, out of reach and so they didn't bother trying to catch more. Arrows were precious. The women found flora they had never seen before. Little blue flowers, black, misshapen mushrooms that smelled delicious, trees whose leaves smelled of earth and rain and life. Although they were tempted to taste, there was plenty they did know, and they decided it wasn't worth the risk.

One afternoon in a meadow the gallopers had paused at, Sola was filling bladders with water from a stream. A noise behind her startled her and she stood and turned in one fluid movement, her hand grasping her knife as she did so. It was the stallion. He was a bay color and had three ochre stripes across his back. He shook his head at her and snorted. Sola smiled. "Well, you've told me, haven't you," she said with affection. At her words, he stomped a foot. "Ok," she said with a nod. He rose up on his hind legs and Sola was momentarily afraid, but he turned and galloped away.

"Do you think it was a messenger from the Earth Mother?" she asked *Chagama* later. "Or was it Mighty Chagama, maybe:"

"Mighty Chagama IS the Earth Mother, child," replied *Chagama*. "And when she speaks to you, the very blood in your veins will keen in response." Sola thought back to how she had felt. Electric. A little afraid. A lot alive. She nodded at *Chagama* and said no more.

One afternoon, they passed a cave. Sola looked at it and wondered if it would be a good place to winter. But then she noted the steep slope they were on and the valley far below where they would have to get water from until there was enough snow on the mountain. It was shelter but it would probably be a dangerous place to live in the winter.

The days flew past. They were happy days and the most interesting of days as well. Life in a *chaga* had a pattern to it. One that followed the seasons but didn't alter much otherwise. Travelling through mountains was new for all of them and most of them loved it. Maret was nervous and would have rather not travelled through the mountains. Fabe, Reta's oldest boy was often fearful. Sola suspected he would have preferred the steppe to their trek as well.

And then one day, they rounded a bend and looked down on a vast grassland with a river running through it, trees growing along side it. The gallopers ran down the slope and into the grass. The stallion paused at the bottom of the hill, looked back to them, nickered, and then ran at a full gallop into the grasses where he disappeared from sight.

Sola knew at that moment, right to the center of her being, that the Earth Mother was telling them they were home.

Bird Song

Col was dreading the upcoming gathering for many reasons, not least of all the wrestling matches. If that wasn't enough to fill his stomach with gristle and bone, the obvious hints from Trot about mates would do the trick and then there would be hunting and spear throwing, dancing and worst of all, the disparaging looks from the people. Col groaned in despair. He couldn't bear to think of it a moment longer and so he wandered off into the trees where he could fiddle with his songs and have some respite from his father. Col was old enough to mate that summer or so said his clan. He wondered what made them decide when someone was old enough. Was it height? Bet was bigger and he hadn't been told he was old enough to mate so that couldn't be it. He guessed that it was the new body hair, and larger appendage he woke with most mornings. It was hard to hide, not that his people were shy about things like that anyway and it was the only thing he liked about getting older so far. Being a child seemed easier. His mother doted on him and the tasks for a child were ones he could manage.

Col made his way to his favorite tree. A giant oak that curved inward at the base in such a way as it seemed made for his back. He settled in under the sheltering branches and blew through his bone. A pleasing sound was released. His clan used a bone with a hole drilled in it to signal each other. Col had discovered that you could drill more than one hole and if you were careful about the placement of the holes, the sounds could be strung together for a song, much like some birds made. He practised this in the trees when he was alone. He had yet to play for his family. His father berated him about many things already and he was reluctant to have him spoil his bird song.

Col shook his head dashing thoughts away and just played. He had been working on a string of notes for the last two weeks and he was finally happy with how they sounded together. He played them again and again so that he would remember the order. A thing that didn't come naturally but was well worth the effort. When he had played the song a fourth time through, a sound from the trees drew his attention and he sat up straight and scanned the trees. A tuft of hair, standing straight up was his clue to the identity of the intruder. Bet. He groaned inwardly and braced for mockery. But Bet just turned away. Later, by the fire, he still said nothing. Col was confused but grateful.

Two days later, the gathering site was in view. Col felt his feet drag and forced himself to keep up. If he didn't, Trot would clout him, he knew. To his surprise, Bet slowed, turned, and waited for him.

"You should play that bird song tonight. At the fire," was all he said before he jogged ahead again. Col was surprised. Did Bet mean he liked it? Or would it be another opportunity to tease him? Bet was his best friend and his worst competitor by turns. The competition was all on Bet's side. Col wasn't normal and he knew it. He didn't want to be the best hunter or wrestle the strongest man to the ground. He wanted to make music. That's all he'd ever wanted. He *could* hunt. He just wasn't great at it, and he didn't love it like the rest of his family did.

After much thought, Col decided to take Bet's advice and play the bird song that night by the fire. When the chatter quieted for a moment, he took out his bone and played a note. Everyone turned and looked at him. "Why is he signaling?" someone said. Someone else wondered in a panicked voice "What?! Is there a cave bear? A big cat?" Others jumped up in panic and took out their weapons and scanned their surroundings, peering into the dark. Trot too got to his feet and when he determined there was nothing to be alarmed about, he clubbed Bet and told him to, "Put that stupid thing away."

Bet tried to talk over the voices, but nobody was listening. Col's eyes met Bet's, and then he shrugged. The two started laughing. The panic was extremely amusing to two young boys after all.

The gathering was every bit as bad as Col expected. Maybe even a little worse. When Trot pushed young female after young female in his direction, Col cringed. He had no interest in taking any to mate and they were even less interested than he was. It didn't matter that Trot's clan was strong and respected. The females wanted mates who could wrestle well, who could kill a colt with a single spear, who could run fast and throw far. That wasn't him.

When the clan's packed up their shelters and said goodbye, Col did not have a mate. Trot wouldn't even look at him. As they began the long journey to their winter site, Col trailed behind. Pretty soon, his clan was far ahead. Bet turned once, paused, and looked at him. Col shook his head and waved him on.

As soon as they were out of sight, Col felt as if he had been carrying an aurochs on his back for as long as he could remember and had finally lifted it off his shoulders and put it on the ground. He didn't know what would happen to him, but he knew this was right. He paused and looked around. Maybe not quite right. He needed to set a fire for the night. He needed to choose a direction for the morning. It was to be a pleasant evening so he decided to forgo the shelter and he sat by a fire and played his song until he couldn't keep his eyes open any longer.

False Trails

The chaga of my father's father's sister had wandered far from their normal routes. They were following a herd of Twin Horns. To find such a herd in such a place was unusual and exciting and meant full tummies. The hunt was successful and my father's father's sister's chaga was very happy. They dried much meat and celebrated with dancing and singing by the fire for many days. And then my father's father's sister's chaga chief noticed the sun was low in the sky early in the day. The next morning, he packed up his shelter and gathered his spear and his bow and arrow and he waited.

The chaga was far from winter camp and fall had begun. They walked for many days. Because the days were growing shorter, they didn't forage, and they didn't hunt. They ate the twin horns meat they had hunted days past. Many nights the hunters argued, and the Chagama told stories, but every morning was the same. The chief gathered up his shelter and his spear and his bow and arrow and then he waited.

It snowed one day, and they erected their shelters, but they had not yet gathered new branches for their shelters or readied new pelts for warmth. The chaga were cold.

When the snow stopped, the chaga chief again gathered up his shelter and his spear and his bow and arrow and waited. The clan gathered their belongings and soon they were walking again. In the afternoon, although the chief was still walking, a hunter stopped and set down his shelter and his spear and his bow and arrow and he waited. The rest of the chaga did the same. The chief, after some time, looked back and saw that his chaga was not behind him. He knew, then, that the chaga had a new chief.

The new chaga chief decided to make this final stop the winter camp. It was not ideal. The protection from winds was not as good as their usual spot and the stream was some distance away. There were trees on two sides that would break the wind and provide firewood as well as resources for strong shelters. But they were late. They needed to gather and hunt and put food away for the cold days ahead.

The chaga spent hours gathering what they could. They were fortunate and found a great field of parsnips and another of potatoes. They gathered them all. Two of the hunters spent time cutting branches thick with needles for the chaga's shelters. The rest hunted. One day they killed a great horn and sent for the gatherers to prepare and bring back the meat. Often, they caught hare or birds or fish. When the snows came, the chaga had prepared as much as they could. It was a lot, but it wasn't enough.

Two of the chaga died that winter. No babies were born that spring. But spring brought plenty and the chaga chief led the chaga back to their familiar territory.

The *chaga* had been camped for many days on the far side of the Mighty Chagama. Herds were plentiful as were vegetables and berries. Bellies were full and people were happy. They often grinned and congratulated each other for having the courage to come through the mountains.

Sola had listened carefully to the story. She was beginning to understand that some of *Chagama's* stories held a message for the *chaga*. She struggled sometimes to discern just what the message was. Other times it was easy. "*Chagama*, are you saying that we should go back to our traditional winter home? I thought your stories were telling us to come here!".

"Ah child, it is not for the *Chagama* stories to tell people what to do." Sola was frustrated with that answer. *Chagama* never just answered a question directly, not if it was about one of her stories. It would be so much easier if she did. Sola sighed. And then suddenly the answer came to her. The stories weren't trying to tell the *chaga* chief what to do. The story's purpose was to make the chief see possible consequences of actions or inactions. And the *chaga* as well. Sola's face relaxed.

"I see you understand." *Chagama* smiled.

"Well, yes. But isn't it dangerous? Won't some *chaga* chief's think the *Chagama* is telling him what to do?"

Chagama nodded. "Yes, that can happen. If the chief is not a thoughtful man. The *chaga* usually comes to trouble regardless in that case." *Chagama* paused for a moment. "Or chooses a new chief."

The following evening, Triven brought up winter.

"But it's still only summer!" protested Flin. Maret and Reta nodded in agreement. Winter was the dull grey against the bright yellow of summer. A time they survived so that they could dance in the sun. Nobody ever wanted to think about it. And yet, if there was one thing that dominated the lives of these nomadic people, it was winter. Living through it and planning for it took up half the year.

"If we are to return to our winter grounds, we will need to start back before too long. If we're not, then we need to figure out where we will spend the winter. In either case, we need to start preparing."

In *Chagama's* stories, the chief just packed up and waited. Sola had never actually seen Triven behave like that. He always told everybody what he was planning, or more frequently, brought a topic up for discussion and the *chaga* decided. Sola wondered if other *chaga* chiefs acted more like Triven or more like the chiefs in the stories.

"I don't want to go back through the mountains," said Maret.

"I don't either," said Olin.

In Triven's *chaga*, everyone had a voice, even children. That wasn't the case with most *chaga's* and those who came from others struggled with the idea. Flin clouted him. "Quiet," she said. Triven pursed his lips but refrained from rebuking Flin. Olin was her son after all, and even a chief rarely gainsaid a mother.

Nobody spoke for going back. "We must find a winter site then. We can't stay here any longer."

As always, they followed the river. They weren't hungry but all were aware of time ticking by. They had no wish to be like the *chaga* in *Chagama's* last story. Then one day, the river bent back the way they had come. Triven put down his pack and directed the gatherers to spend their day finding what they could. He sent Privon, Ras and Ponu off to hunt with instructions to be back that evening. Fabe and Bron were told to fish and the rest of the children went with the gatherers. Sele and Triven stayed behind. When the rest of the *chaga* was gone the two sat by the river and discussed what they should do.

Sele was Triven's best friend but the two were as different as two hunters could be. Where Triven was thoughtful and considered decisions carefully, Sele was impulsive and outspoken. Triven appeared confident, Sele intimidating. He wore his hair in dreadlocks, and they sprouted from his head in wild disarray. Sometimes, he drew black marks under his eyes and around his mouth with charcoal from the fire. He loved meeting *chaga's* and watching the wariness of strangers. He also loved women and would wipe his face clean and tie his hair back when he met one that attracted him. He would give them a warm smile and a wink, and he often found it effective for a quick romp. Triven valued his council because he was so different and would think of things that Triven might not consider himself.

"Let's see if we can find a place to cross," said Sele, eager for a bit of adventure. Triven nodded and the pair followed the bend in the river and began looking for a safe crossing. They hadn't seen any good winter sites behind them so were not keen to turn back. Crossing a river could be dangerous though, and this was not a small one. It didn't take them long to come to a place where the river widened significantly. Triven tossed a stick in. It moved slowly downstream. He nodded with relief. Being chief in unfamiliar territory was beginning to weigh on him. He needed to find a winter site. Soon. Or all these people that depended on him could be in trouble.

Sele retrieved a rope made of cured leather strips braided together, from his pack and gave one end to Triven who tied it to a tree. He tied the other around his waist. With a spear in each hand, Sele gingerly stepped into the river. He couldn't swim. If he lost his footing, the rope might save his life or, if the water was too deep and the riverbed too slippery, he could be swept under and drowned despite the safeguard.

With a deep breath and a look back at Triven, he stepped into the river. Before taking another step, he used a spear to test the depth. The water was only up to his knees until he got to the middle of the river and then his spear sunk showing a depth of hip height. Gingerly, he stepped forward. The current was stronger, and it was harder to keep his footing. He was grateful for the two spears. Five steps later, the water was knee high again. When Sele reached the far bank, he tied the rope to a tree there. He waved to Triven, clearly relieved to be on the other side and sat under the tree to rest up before the return trip.

A few minutes later, Triven saw Sele tense and peer closely at the ground. Sele started moving towards the riverbank and then he turned to the right. He paused every few steps to peer closely at the ground and then he kept going.

"Sele! Sele!" called Triven as he waved his arms to get the others attention. "Come back!" Sele couldn't hear his words, but he didn't need to. He knew what Triven wanted.

"Long tooth!" he called back. Sele held his fists up to his face, index fingers extended by the corner of his mouth.

Sele's mother had died when Sele was still a boy. He had been found alone by the side of a river. He had never talked about it to anyone as far as Triven knew and nobody knew what had actually happened. Triven had always suspected a predator, probably a long tooth. In any case, Triven had known Sele for a long time and he knew that Sele could not resist going after a long tooth. This, however, was not the time. Triven shook his head and pounded his spears in the dirt. Sele paused and for just a second it looked like he would turn around and leave the cat. But he didn't. In a moment he had followed the tracks up the bank and disappeared into the trees. Triven was furious and his impotence made him more so.

Sele followed the tracks until dusk. He would have kept going had he been able to see. He had no shelter with him and no food. No water either and the river was half a day's hike back the way he'd come. Sele acknowledged to himself that his obsession could very well kill him. He spent an unhappy night, hungry, thirsty, and uncomfortable. When he woke in the morning, he looked at the game trail through the trees that led back to the river for a long, long time. And then he turned his back on it and followed the long tooth tracks.

An hour later, he came to the edge of the forest and peered at a huge steppe. A sea of grass as far as he could see. Empty. The wind blew and the grass moved in waves. It was beautiful and eerie and lonely. He'd lost the tracks a while ago and he couldn't see an obvious path through the grass. His shoulders drooped in defeat. He would have to go back and face Triven empty handed. He turned around and froze. The cat was crouched a hundred feet away from him and ready to pounce. He could just see the stub of her tail swishing side to side, her eyes were focused on him with piercing intent, and every muscle was tense and ready. The wind gusted and blew her scent to him. Musty and sickly. If he wasn't so tense, he might have gagged. One minute she was crouched and the next she had launched herself at him. He brought up his spear just in time. It caught her in the chest, but the momentum of her pounce propelled her forward and him back. He fell with her on him. The claws on her right hind leg sank into his left thigh leaving three long stripes. She continued to struggle, and he was deathly afraid of being clawed again. With all his might, he heaved and pushed her off him. She tried to rise but failed. He tried to rise but couldn't either. His leg screaming in fury and unable to hold his weight. He was fortunate to be on the edge of the forest. There was thick moss under him, and he grabbed handfuls of it and packed it into his leg. and then he lay back, trembling with adrenalin. The cat was still struggling. Her breathing labored. Her feet lashed out every minute or so. He shifted his body farther away. Soon her breathes came a minute or so apart and finally they stopped. Sele didn't move. He was exhausted, dehydrated, hungry and in pain. He'd lost a lot of blood but fortunately the moss had staunched the flow. He slept.

Bull Mammoth

Moke woke to thunder. Crashing thumps followed by shuffling and crunching. He lay for a moment and then felt alarm at the next rolling thump which he felt before he heard. His shelter shook and he scrambled to his feet and threw open the flap to look out. A giant woolly elephant stomped through the steppe grasses a mere five hundred or so feet from their camp. He stared open mouthed at it as it pulled clumps of grass with its nose and shovelled them in his mouth. He pounded the ground with each slow, thundering step. Moke had never seen one that big before. He turned his head and saw Ches, his head poked out of his own shelter, a giant grin on his face. To take this woolly elephant would be a wonder.

They were camped on the steppe, mere feet from the river. A herd of bison had come through a few days ago and meat was drying in trees close to the river or hanging above the fire being smoked. There was no need for them to go anywhere for a while. They had managed to catch three animals, a huge boon for them, and now they were relaxing and enjoying the summer weather and cool river. Life was good.

Ches, Ono, Kor and Cheel crept quietly out of their shelter and walked behind it. Bull woolly's were dangerous. Some, big ones, like this one was, were even more dangerous than a herd. They were cranky at the best of times. A spear in the side wouldn't come close to disabling it but would wake a killing rage in it. Moke tapped the flap of Frome and Neti's shelter and whispered to them. They must have been mating again thought Moke, and he rolled his eyes, if they didn't notice the ground shaking. It took them a few minutes, but they soon joined the others behind the shelters.

"There's no cliffs here," began Ches. You couldn't simply stab a beast like this. Some strategy was required.

"No," said Frome, "But there is one where the river bends to the south. It's only small days from here."

"Humph."

They all thought for a while. Herding him for two or more days would be difficult and dangerous. There was no guarantee it would work either. He could decide to bolt in any direction at any moment.

"It'll be fun," said Ono and she grinned.

Moke felt a well of excitement grow in him. It *would* be fun. And nothing tasted better than a woolly elephant. He looked around. Frome was grinning. So was Ches. Neti glanced at Bene. He was too young to leave but they would need her if they were to be successful.

"Kor and Cheel can carry him, far behind us where he will be safe. You can run back and feed him, when necessary," said Ono. At ten and five, both girls were too young to participate in such a dangerous hunt.

They all looked at Neti, waiting anxiously. Neti looked at their eager faces and then down at Bene and over to the woolly grazing noisily. "Fine."

They wanted to hoot but didn't for fear of startling the woolly elephant. They had to decide what to bring and what to leave. In the end, they decided to bring everything. They could set it down if they needed to at any moment.

Moke was amazed at the speed his clan was packed and ready to go. He couldn't help but compare it to their moving day just last spring and he was astounded at the difference. If he hadn't been so excited about the mammoth, he might have said something. As it was, he shrugged and picked up his pack.

They formed a half moon behind the woolly. Each were a hundred or so feet from each other and a much greater distance from the woolly elephant. They made little noises, sounds that caught the woolly elephant's attention but didn't frighten him. They were designed to make him nervous enough to step away from them but not so nervous that he bolted. On the second day, Ono dropped her pack while she searched for a thong to repair her boot, and the shelter poles clattered to the ground. The woolly elephant raised his head and flapped his ears in alarm. He was poised to run, and the clan froze. If he bolted, there would be no controlling him. He would go in whatever direction he wanted, and he would trample anything in his path. He didn't bolt but he stepped quickly west while they wanted him to go south. They had no choice but to let him wander off course for the rest of the day. He was tense and on alert. They couldn't risk even a small noise.

In the end, it took four days to get him close enough to the small shelf above the river to risk scaring him over. He was a good four hundred feet from it still and the hunters were in their half circle, Ches in the center. Ches drew forth his unlit torch. Each carried one similar. Frome nodded and Ches looked left at Ono. Frome and Ono in turn signalled Moke and Neti.

Moke took his flint stones from the bag that he carried, gathered a handful of grass, and carefully blew a small fire to life. Next, he added wood chips and finally the pieces of wood he had carried with him for this purpose. He looked over and could see that Frome's fire was lit as well. Next, he placed a long piece of wood in the fire, the tip coated in resin and waited as his torch caught.

The woolly elephant paused in his eating. His keen sense of smell had caught the scent of fire. A dreaded scent and he pranced nervously, turning his head, ears flapping, nose waiving in the air as he tried to figure out where it was coming from.

Moke watched Frome. Waiting.

This was the dangerous part. The only way the animal would go over the cliff is if he was too scared to do anything else. The only thing that would bring that much fear was fire. Would five torches be enough? Or would he turn and stampede them instead?

Ches rose, waving his torch. The others were an instant behind him. The woolly elephant trumpeted a sound of primal fear. He was frightened but uncertain of where safety lay. He charged ahead, right at Ches before stopping and running at Moke. He trumpeted again. Moke waved his torch, petrified of being trampled, and at the last moment the woolly elephant turned. Moke tore left as fast as he could. There was an opening there that the woolly elephant could escape through without harm. Moke waved his flame again and shouted too for good measure. Just as the animal was about to slip through, he turned again, and Moke ran after him. He was running towards the river now and Moke harried him loudly to keep him going. Frome joined in and then Ches. The animal ran faster, faster than the hunters, blind now with fear. Moke didn't pause though. He kept after him and then he was gone from sight.

The cliff wasn't high. The fall didn't kill him, and he trumpeted now in pain as well as fear. The sound tore at the hunters. They were feeling beings and neither deaf nor blind to suffering. Quickly, they found a path down and approached him with caution. Even broken, the animal was deadly.

Moke tried to get a spear into his neck, but the nose was whipping back and forth and knocked him down. He would sport black bruises for days. Ches went for the artery in his hind leg. His spear tip was six inches long. It had to be in order to pierce an inch of skin and four inches of fat. It wasn't enough to just thrust either. The spear had to thrown or it wouldn't have enough force to get through the layers. Ches threw his spear, and it pierced the skin, but he knew it wasn't well placed. Frome went for the neck and was successful where Moke had failed. Ono threw hers at the front leg, as near to his underarm as she could manage. A lot of blood sprayed and with relief the hunters thought she had managed an artery. Still, the animal fought, and Neti threw her spear at the neck as well. She too was successful. Eventually, the wailing quieted and soon the animal was struggling to breath.

Crossing

Triven sat by the bank and waited until dusk. With no sign of Sele, he gave up and returned to where he had left the rest of the *chaga*. They camped overnight and made their way to the crossing the next morning.

The *chaga* lined up on the bank and looked nervously at the river. The crossing would be dangerous, but they could mitigate that with the rope and the strength of the hunters. It would have been better to have Sele to help with the deep part of the river, but Triven decided he couldn't wait any longer. He had no idea when and if the hunter would return. He turned his mind away from that. Thinking of Sele just made him angry and he needed to focus on getting his people safely across.

Ponu made signs in the dirt of the riverbank. Squiggles to represent the river spirit. He also threw some meat in the river as an offering. He then asked permission to cross. Sola wondered who had done this for Triven and Sele the day before but didn't ask. Was that why Sele wasn't here? Triven had the closed off look that everyone knew meant he wouldn't welcome questions. Even Olin didn't dare ask where Sele was. Something had happened and they would all find out eventually, she was sure.

Ras crossed the river first. Ras was Sele's first born son and he idolized his father. He wore his hair in the same dreadlocks and painted black under his eyes whenever Sele did. His face was rounder than his father's and he wasn't as tall but that they were father and son was clear to all who saw them. He was anxious as he crossed. Where was Sele? He had a second rope with him and he tied it quickly when he reached the other side. Other's could walk between the two ropes and have a safer crossing. The moment the rope was tied, he started scanning the ground for tracks. He spotted Sele's right away and the cat's right after. He knew then, where Sele went. He wanted to follow but had been given such a stern warning from Triven that he didn't dare.

Ponu and Privon made their way to the middle of the river and Flin and Grady went next. Grady was Flin's youngest child, still a toddler and Sola's brother. Triven carried Grady while walking behind Flin. When they got to the middle, Triven handed Grady to Privon who passed him to Ponu and then finally Ras. Once Grady was with Ras, they guided Flin across the deep part.

Next, they passed across all their packs, holding them high to keep them dry. Then *Chagama*. The hunters carried her across the deep part because of her age and laughed at her loud protests. *Chagama* was very put out but when Ponu kissed and told her how precious she was to them all, she settled down.

After Chagama, Sola went. She sat with *Chagama* while they waited for the others. She suspected they would spend the day and night here. It would take at least another hour to get everyone across and then they all had to dry off.

"*Chagama*, sometimes I feel like that stick there in the water." Sola pointed to a stick lazily making its way down the river. "Pulled this way and that with no say in where I go or which side of the river I end up on."

"All children feel that way, child, although you're not much of a child anymore, are you?" asked *Chagama*.

"Not really," answered Sola. "But it's more that I want to be wise, like you. I want to know the stories and tell the right ones at the right time. I want to make sure little babies like Tram don't suckle on dry breasts and return to the Earth Mother when they haven't even learned to walk yet. But I feel like I can't do anything about those things."

Chagama was quiet for a long time. "No single member of a *chaga* can control those things. They can only try to do the right thing at the right time. But sometimes, there is no right thing that will save the whole *chaga*. Every other year, the herds came and the *chaga* had plenty. Why didn't they come this year? Did they all sicken? Were there too many other *chaga's* who hunted them all before they reached us? Did a chasm open in the herds path, forcing them to choose another? Nobody can foresee those things. They can only make decisions based on what is in front of them. And ask the spirits of the earth and water and wind to guide them. And when the spirits are silent, a *chaga* must send messengers to the Earth Mother. It is our way."

"But couldn't we have given Reta more to eat? If she had larger portions, would her milk have stayed?"

"Yes. If someone else had less, Reta would have more and maybe Tram would not have been the messenger. Someone else might have though, and what would it mean to the *chaga* to lose a hunter? A gatherer? *Chagama*?"

Sola could see the sense in *Chagama's* words, but it didn't take away the pain that twisted inside her when she thought of Tram. She knew Reta felt it more so and she couldn't help but feel that there should have been enough. That the *chaga* must have done something wrong. That if only they were more prepared, had acted sooner or differently, then Tram would be alive.

Chagama watched Sola quietly. She was pleased by her questions and her desire to learn the stories. *Chagama* had been grooming her since she noticed her eager questioning mind at a young age. She was delighted to be proven right. Sola would make a fine *Chagama* one day.

It was late morning by the time everybody was across and reasonably dry but Ras didn't wait for that. The moment everyone was across, he followed the tracks. Triven called him but he decided he wouldn't be deterred and ignored his call. "Where's Sele," he heard Ponu ask.

Triven scowled "He went off chasing a long tooth yesterday afternoon. He should be back by now. Ponu, go with Ras and if you find him, drag his selfish hide back here." The entire *chaga* cringed at Triven's words. It wasn't often that he proclaimed his disapproval so loudly or publicly. Especially of Sele. The two were like brothers.

Three hours later, Ras returned at a run. "Sele, huh, huh, huh, has, huh, huh", he panted.

"Catch your breath Ras. Then tell us what's wrong," said *Chagama*. She was already digging in her bag for herbs.

"Sele has been, huh, scratched by the long tooth, huh, huh. His leg. It's swollen and red and Sele, huh, huh, huh is hot and sleeping."

Chagama nodded. She pulled two herbs from her bag. "Yarrow, for bleeding, marigold for infection". She ground some of each using two stones and added some water to make a paste. She scraped it onto a bit of hide and placed it in Ras's hand. "Rub this on the wound. Make sure he drinks water. Lots of it. Now go."

The rest of the *chaga* followed at a slower pace. When they arrived, *Chagama* examined Sele carefully and cleaned his wound again before applying more salve. "Now, we wait."

The Journey

Col never looked back. He walked south. He walked for days. He walked from first light to last. It was need that finally caused him to stop. He had little dried meat left, and winter was coming. He needed to decide on a course of action that consisted of more than just walking south.

To the west, he saw trees, and far behind those, he saw mountains. He altered his path and walked southwest. Mountains meant caves. Trees meant deer. If he was lucky, he could catch a deer on his own. He hadn't thought of how he would feed himself when he left. At the best of times, he wasn't a great hunter and when a little knot of fear started to form in his belly, he shook it off with a frown. He may not be the best hunter, but he *could* hunt, and he wasn't going back.

He paused to setup his shelter when he reached the trees. Tomorrow, he decided, he would look for deer sign as he walked towards the mountain. He took out his last piece of meat and looked at it and then he put it away. He would have it for breakfast. Instead, he pulled out his flute and started to play his new song. He had finally finished it yesterday and he knew that if he was to remember it, he needed to practice. They song evoked travelling and discovery. It was a happy song with the occasional moment of surprise or fright. He loved his new song as it seemed to describe his journey. His first song had been a little mournful and he played it still, but he preferred the journey.

Tsutse and Donon jumped in surprise when they heard the strange sounds travelling through the trees. They reached for their spears, and their knives and they waited.

"It's not an animal that I've ever heard," said Tsutse, fear notable in her voice. Donon, her brand new mate shook his head in response. They listened for a few minutes and then Tsutse, the bravest of women got mad. She wasn't known for patience. "Let's go see what it is."

Donon looked over at his mate. She was wide of face and body. She had light hair that was almost yellow and deep brown eyes. A scar twisted the side of her mouth and gave her a look of ferocity that wasn't misplaced in the least. He himself was four inches taller than her with brown hair and a deep barrel chest that plenty of women, including Tsutse, found attractive. He might have been happy to never find out what made that sound, but it wasn't in him to deny his new mate anything. He had known her all his life and loved her almost as long. He had reached mating age two winters before her and waited for her. Tsutse, for her part had adored him but never thought of him that way. Donon persuaded her with friendship, respect, and deep affection. Tonight, was their first night away from the gathering where they had mated. They were beginning their life together with a search for a winter home.

Donon picked out a thick branch from the fire and the pair followed the sounds through the trees. They approached Col from behind and listened with cocked heads as he played. They had not heard a bone flute before. Their clans didn't use them for signals or songs.

Tsutse hung back in the trees, spear in hand, ready to throw if need be. Donon cautiously stepped out of hiding and called a greeting.

Col jumped to his feet, dropping his flute, and stared at the stranger wide-eyed. He had never seen someone he didn't know before. He shouldn't be surprised at this turn. He had travelled far beyond anywhere his people had been before. Logic said he would come to people and territories that were new. That's what he had wanted, after all. It startled him anyway.

The stranger came closer and bent to pick up the flute that Col had dropped. Col wanted to grab it from him and hide it away, but he stayed still and watched. The stranger put it to his mouth and blew hard. A piercing wail leapt from the flute and the man dropped it. Laughter came from the trees and the stranger turned and motioned his companion forward, having decided Col was not a threat. How he knew, Col didn't understand but he found himself both grateful and nervous for company and he picked up his flute and sat, indicating that they should also.

"I am Donon," said the stranger. "And this is Tsutse."

"I am….," Col paused. He didn't feel like 'Col' any longer. He was something new. Just born, like a new babe. "I am a wanderer."

Donon thought that was odd but was far more curious about the flute and the song and where Col's family was… he didn't have one was the response.

Col asked about Donon and Tsutse. He listened with intense curiosity. No detail was boring. And finally, he played the Bird song. When he finished, Donon and Tsutse both had tears on their cheeks and thanked him profusely for his gift.

When they had gone back to their own camp, Col, the Wanderer lay in his shelter and reflected on the meeting. It had been wonderful! They liked his music. No, they loved his music! They had regarded him with respect. Perhaps, he thought, he didn't need to avoid people.

Col was surprised the next morning when Tsutse and Donon returned to his little camp.

"We're looking for a winter cave too," said Donon. The Wanderer had told them the night before where he was heading. "We thought it might be fun to travel together?"

The Wanderer wasn't sure what to do with this invitation. He was getting tired of his own company, but he worried that with time, these people would come to see him as strange, as his own family did. He was hesitant but he thought maybe he could enjoy their company for a time and then move on. He nodded with a shy smile.

The three hunted and travelled together for a few days before finding a cave. The Wanderer insisted on sleeping in his own shelter the first night. He understood this night would be special for his new friends and he wanted them to have it to themselves.

A few days later, the first snows came and Tsutse insisted he stay the winter with them. With relief, he agreed, but in the spring, before the snow had melted, he packed up his hides and his poles and he said farewell to his friends. Tsutse put a package of meat into his pack and hugged him fiercely. It was Donon who cried.

Col found he missed his friends sorely. Loneliness bore down on him in a way he hadn't experienced before. As the days passed, he often turned to look behind him, tempted to go back. Fear of outstaying his welcome, of losing his new friends, of them looking at him with contempt instead of affection, always caused him to turn forward again.

Then one day, he saw smoke from a fire. With a deep, steadying breath, he strode forward, flute in hand, notes heralding his arrival.

The clan he approached stared at him open mouthed.

"Hello!" he called. "I'm the Wanderer! I've just been visiting with Donon and Tsutse."

"Tsutse!" exclaimed a mature woman. "How is she? And Donon? Did they find a cave? Where is it?"

The Wanderer smiled as he answered all her questions while he walked closer. His penchant for details served him well as he relayed all he could remember from his time with his new friends.

He spent a week with this clan before moving on again, pack loaded with meat and head loaded with news. As he travelled, he learned the web that connected the people of these clans. Every clan had somebody they loved in another clan. Someone they hadn't seen of spoken to in seasons. His news was welcome, offering comfort to mothers missing their daughters, or fathers yearning for news of sons. His role grew as he travelled amongst them. He carried messages, arranged gatherings, and traded goods. He was welcomed with fanfare and bid goodbye with reluctance. The children especially loved him. He was content. Lonely sometimes but content.

The Cat

The *chaga* setup their shelters on the steppe. Sele's was constructed over him by Triven and Ponu where he lay. Triven didn't speak to Sele or look at him, but he grumbled a great deal under his breath. Those who listened closely might have heard the occasional curse and words like 'irresponsible' or 'selfish' or even 'dumb'. Sele was fortunate to sleep through that.

When Sele woke that evening, he was still slightly feverish but lucid. Flin sat beside him. She held a bladder in her hand and had been dribbling water into his mouth all day. Flin was an older version of Sola. Grey laced her hair, wrinkles lined her face, and curves shaped her body, but it was clear to all whose daughter Sola was. Sola was a little smarter, a lot kinder as well as full of youth and life. Most mothers loved it when their daughters outshone them. Flin resented it though. Sola would never truly understand why her mother barely tolerated her but that was the crux of it. Flin was jealous.

Sele thought they were alone but then a tiny movement caught his attention. Sola was sitting in his shelter, watching him.

"Why didn't you come to help us cross the river?" she asked. She was angry but she was also genuinely curious. She wanted to understand what made chasing a long tooth more important to the *chaga* than helping at the river. Sola assumed that everyone's actions had a motive that satisfied some need for the *chaga*. They relied so heavily on each other for survival, thinking solely for oneself was a completely foreign concept to her.

He shrugged. Now that the long tooth was dead and the chase over, his obsession was quiet, and his reason returned. He had trouble justifying his actions and would prefer not to think about it.

"Why would you hunt a long tooth when we need twin horn? Or leaper? Or great horn? Or anything but a long tooth? And why would you not be there to help us cross that river?" Sola's tone conveyed her curiosity. Her head was tilted, and brows furrowed. She desperately wanted to understand.

Sele had no answer. Her questions were making him uncomfortable, and he didn't like it. Who was she, a child, to question him? A hunter. And not just any hunter. He was the chiefs right hand man and one of the best hunters of any of the *chaga's*, not just their own. His skills kept the *chaga* alive. With each question, his anger grew.

"Aren't we behind preparing for winter? Won't more babes have to go and beg favors from the Earth Mother if we don't get enough?" she asked. Flin's fist lashed out faster than Sola could dodge. It knocked her over and she lay there for a moment, shocked. Children were often clouted by their parents. For insolence or disobedience or just plain bad temper. This was different. It was punch, with power and force. Sola placed her hand over her mouth as she scuttled backwards.

Sele was just as shocked as Sola. He looked to Flin, mouth agape. Flin just glared back before turning to set the bladder down and fuss with the pelts beside her.

Slowly, Sola got to her feet, bent over due to the height of the shelter, her hand to her mouth, tears of pain on her cheek. Her lip was bleeding and already swollen. She would find it difficult to eat for days. But she managed to hang on to the pit of anger that bloomed in her belly. More cautious now, she stepped out of reach of Flin's fists. "I take it that means 'Yes, you should have been hunting meat, not long tooth'". With a final disparaging glance at both of them, she left the shelter. She didn't see the anger blazing in Flin's eyes as she watched her go.

"Sola, take Olin and see what you can find to eat," called *Chagama* without glancing up. Sola, still somewhat stunned by what had happened, was slow to more. *Chagama* looked at her. "What happened!?" she asked.

Sola put her hand to her mouth and tilted her head towards Sele's shelter. *Chagama* sat there for a long moment and just looked towards the shelter. Was she wondering if Sola had earned the abuse? Or if she should or even could do anything about it? And then she got to her feet and with grim determination entered Sele's shelter.

Sola never found out what she said or did. All she heard was a loud moan that could have been from either Sele or Flin, and then *Chagama* exited the shelter, looking less grim and more self-satisfied.

Annual Mouflon Hunt

Every year, at the end of summer, Ches's clan headed back to their cave. If there was a gathering, they went there first, if not, they headed straight back to the cave. The had been gone most of spring and all of summer. Now, it was time to prepare for the long winter ahead. They used the same cave every year and had plenty of pelts stashed inside the cave, but mice and bugs would have done damage, and some would need replacing. The woolly elephant pelts from the bull were a good start but they would need more. Cheel and Kor would need new winter clothes, as they had both grown. Most of the adults would as well. They wore them every day in the winter and by spring, their clothes were rags. They then switched to new ones and wore those every day. They also needed to set aside plenty of meat. They would dry it or salt it and when the weather was cold enough, they would freeze it. They would gather mushrooms and mosses, but vegetables were a tiny part of their diet unless it was chyme from the stomachs of their prey. Fall was a busy time for the clan, but it was also a happy time. Food was plentiful as the herds made their way south. The days were short and full but that meant pleasant evenings by the fire with camaraderie and music and full stomachs.

The first thing they did when they arrived at the cave was pull out the old pelts and shake them out. Away went the mouse droppings and bugs and plenty of hair fibers. Some pelts were salvageable. They could be used to make hide bags or pants or shirts for late spring when it was still too cold to wear just a loin cloth. Others were tossed out with the droppings.

The second thing they did was plan their annual mouflon hunt. Sheep's wool made the best winter boots, and the entire clan needed a new pair. The mouflon lived high in the mountains and were extremely agile. Most of the time, they were difficult and dangerous to hunt. In the fall though, the snow arrived in the mountains early and the mouflon retreated to lower pastures. But the thing that made them easier to catch was that it was breeding season. The males played a dangerous game of butting heads on cliffsides that often resulted in one of the pair falling to his death with amazing frequency.

Moke was reminded of spring as he stood in the cave with his spears, and pack ready to go on the mouflon hunt. Just as in spring, the rest of the clan didn't appear to be in any hurry to get moving. Neti was resting on pelts with her baby, but she wasn't going so that didn't bother him. Cheel wasn't going either and wasn't too happy about that, but she was still too young to keep up while they climbed. Frome and Ches were out, and Moke didn't know where. He wondered if he would be waiting for days to go and with a sigh he sat down.

He didn't have long to wait. Ches and Frome returned with armloads of wood for fire. They didn't want Neti to have to gather it all while they were gone. And then they picked up their spears and empty packs. There was no need to bring frames and pelts for shelters. There were plenty of caves, mostly empty, spotted around the mountain and the clan was well familiar with their location. Ono, Kor, and Moke quickly gathered their spears and packs, and the clan was ready to go.

Kor was beside herself with excitement. She bounced and chatted and laughed and twirled. This was her first mouflon hunt. Moke poked her in the side which made her squeal and laugh. Ono grinned at the pair of them and rolled her eyes with affection. Cheel watched their antics from the mouth of the cave. Tears threatened and Neti took her hand to comfort her.

The clan climbed for most of the morning. Although the mouflon would descend, they would only come down as far as they had to, and the clan would need to climb to meet them. They paused in the afternoon for a rest and a meal of dried woolly. They didn't have much with them as they were counting on getting mouflon.

"Listen," said Ono. The clan tilted their heads as one which made Ono smile. They could hear the telltale sound of butting heads and horns. It was to the west and the clan packed up to search out a path. Within a half hour they spotted them on the side of a cliff. Ches looked up at them and then down to where they would fall if that should happen. There was a wide gulf between them with steep sides. He could see an animal already smashed below but he couldn't see any way to it. He shook his head, and the clan continued west. Where there were two, there would be more.

The path they were following consisted of loose stone. They all understood the dangers of that, and Ches went first, stepping carefully and ensuring one foot was on firm ground before lifting the next. Frome went next and then Ono followed by Kor, and Moke in the rear. Ono was as nervous as a mother hen watching her chicks, constantly glancing behind and cautioning her children. She slipped a bit and her heart pounded. She turned to warn the others and stared mouth agape as the path disappeared from under Moke and Kor. Kor screamed as she fell. They heard the crashing noises of shifting rock and breaking branches, and then there was silence.

Frome turned, expecting to see what, he didn't know but the path and Moke and Kor just gone was not it. Ono screamed and Frome howled in shock too. It was Ches who remained calm. "QUIET," he yelled. "I can't hear them." Frome calmed and Ono managed to cry silently, with just the occasional choked sob. Her eyes betrayed the frantic emotions she felt but Ches couldn't deal with that just then. He wasn't any less upset than his mate but the most comfort he could offer was an arm wrapped around her as he called out and then listened for a response, tears streaming down his own cheeks.

Frome stood and watched for a while. Finally, he said he would look for a way down and he continued up the path.

"Frome," gritted out Ches as he watched him leave at a quick pace. "You won't be helping any of us if you fall off the path too." Frome nodded and stepped a little more carefully.

Ches was hoarse when Frome returned at dusk. He hadn't found a way down.

The three spent the night on the path, uncomfortable and cold and dejected. Ches was afraid to sleep. He thought Frome or Ono might roll off into the abyss like Moke and Kor. He gripped them both by the arm, knowing that if they tumbled, he wouldn't be able to stop them and would likely be pulled over too, but he could do nothing to stop the urge. He spent a sleepless night staring into the darkness. Ono had cried all day and fell into an exhausted sleep beside him. She was restless though and that kept Ches awake as each movement filled him with terror. Frome too, was spent. Of all of them, he slept the most. In the morning, they called again and listened without much hope. Ches now worried about the path giving way under Frome or Ono and insisted they walk ahead. They continued to call and listen. Not even the birds answered.

They didn't find a path down, but they found one that wound around the mountainside and headed north. They followed it until it took them east and towards home. They talked little and had lost all excitement for their hunt. They still need boots however and when they found one dead mouflon, they skinned it and started the tanning process while they dried the meat. They managed to get close to another who was so intent on the females that he didn't see or hear them. Breeding season was never good for male mouflon. They butchered him as well and then they headed home.

Ono was inconsolable when she told Neti of the loss. All the grief that she had held back poured out of her in wails and tears. Neti keened with her and even Ches gave vent to his grief with low moans and large tears.

When their emotions were spent, their loss settled into the space inside them that had been left hollow by their absence. They would all visit that space, from time to time, Ono more often than the others but they would get on with the pressing business of living. A little less joyfully perhaps.

Winter Home

Triven had taken Ponu, Ras and Privon hunting. Sele was still resting in the place the cat had attacked him, and the women and children were nearby, gathering berries which were plentiful and just ripe and delicious.

An hour later, the hunters returned, with happy faces and no meat. The women looked at each other in confusion. Hunters returning without meat was rarely a cause for glee, which these men were obviously feeling.

"We've found our winter home!" said Triven.

"It's a huge cave, with rooms", said Ras.

"And a creek running right by it." Said Privon.

"But the cave is a few feet up. No danger of flooding."

"It looks like maybe that long tooth that Sele killed was living there! That fool did us a favor". Maybe Triven would be ready to forgive him now. Sola didn't think she would.

Sola ran ahead with Privon and Ras while the rest of the *chaga* packed up their shelters and tried to figure out how to carry Sele to the cave. A new winter site was exciting, and she was eager to explore. They would be there for months so she hoped it would have a lot to offer. Winters could be excruciatingly boring.

The ground rose as they approached the cave. Sola could see the stream close by. On really cold days, the water would freeze so they would have to bring in ice chips to melt by the fire. It would be a lot of work, so it was nice that it was close. The cave itself was clearly visible now. Sola looked back the way they had come, and she could just make out their camp on the edge of the forest through the trees. Triven must have spotted it somehow that morning. Because of the elevation, she could also see the steppe beyond the trees. It was vast. A sea of grass that went on until the horizon and probably past that too she thought. In the far distance, she could see shapes moving. A herd of something but she couldn't tell what.

When Sola reached the entrance to the cave, she was blasted with a terrible stench, and she gagged. The cat had left its scent by the door, letting all intruders know that danger lay this way. Stay out. Sola waved her hand in front of her face and then pulled her hair over her mouth and nose before entering. The stench was worse inside. Cat piss combined with rotting flesh, stale air, and feces. She gagged again but kept going. She wished she was wearing more than her loin cloth as then she could have held the clothing to her mouth and nose. Her hair was better than nothing she thought.

The first room was clearly where the cat had spent her time. It was huge. Plenty of room for the entire *chaga* to lay. The ceiling of the cave was high and smoke from the fire they would need to keep warm would rise. There were bones with rotting flesh attached in some cases. Lots of bones. The floor of the cave had dark spots, likely blood stains. At the back of the cave was a wide passage. Sola entered the passage and found it narrowed as she moved through it. At its far end was another room. It was smaller and didn't smell as bad. She hadn't brought any fire and couldn't really see that well. She thought there might be another passage but clearly, she would have to wait to fully explore the cave.

"Sola! Give us a hand." Sola left the smaller chamber to return to the main room. Privon and Ras were picking up the bones and tossing them out the cave entrance. The two young men paused to stare at her.

"What happened to you?" Privon finally asked. Sola reached up to her lip and touched it.

Sola shook her head and looked away. She found she couldn't speak of the mother who cared so little for her. Why she wasn't sure. She felt shame, as if it were her fault. And self-pity which she hated. Angrily she wiped at the tears that came. The two young men continued to stare at her. Privon nodded and they both left the cave.

She glared at their backs as they left her to finish clearing the cave out alone but forgave them once she realized what they had been doing. A short while later they returned with a huge pile of wood and started a fire. The weather was still warm, and the fire wasn't necessary for heat, especially in the cave during the day. The smoke would help clear the stench though and Sola was grateful. She asked them to cut some evergreen branches and she used those to sweep out the smaller bits of bone and feces that remained. By the time the rest of the *chaga* arrived the cave was in better shape. Best of all, Sola was ecstatic to realize, she had burning wood that she could use as a torch to explore the rest of the cave.

There were three other chambers, small and unremarkable. A fourth could only be reached by crawling and the men wouldn't be able to manage it. It was tiny and Sola couldn't think of a use for it. The others would be used to store vegetables, dried or salted meats and hides. The *chaga* would sleep and live in the massive first chamber.

The rest of the *chaga* arrived but didn't move in. Ponu was preparing a ceremony and it would take a few days to get ready. And so, the *chaga* went about the business of preparing for winter while they sheltered outside their new home. Hunting seemed almost too easy with the view they had of the steppe and hunting parties that would sometimes be gone for days at a time were returning with game the same day. The game attracted other predators too, and the women were threatening to banish Ponu if he didn't bless the cave soon.

Sola woke one morning a few days after they found the cave just as dawn was breaking. She had been sleeping in the open air, too proud to join her mother in the family shelter. It would be another beautiful day. It was a little cool and she snuggled under her twin horn pelt for a moment, enjoying the warmth. Cool mornings were her favorite and then realized that things were quiet. Too quiet. Usually, she would hear someone throwing wood on the fire or one of the children fussing, but this morning there were none of those sounds. Had Sele visited the Earth Mother in the night? His leg hadn't looked that sick. Had the food been bad? *Chagama* had a story about that, she was sure. Sola jumped up; her contentment gone.

When she looked around, she saw her *chaga* standing together and looking off into the distance. They were all quiet. Sola joined them. There was a mist over the steppe and the sun hadn't fully risen yet. It made the morning feel muffled and subdued. In the distance she could see shapes moving. Lumbering really. They were of different sizes and had enormous white things protruding from their faces as well as a long, long...limb? The limb swung from their enormous heads and didn't seem to support any weight. As she watched, it pulled great handfuls of grass which it then ate.

Was it an arm? She had never seen anything like them in her life. Watching them, it dawned on her that they were still a distance away, and they towered over the steppe grasses. She had never seen anything that big before. Like the rest of her *chaga*, she just watched them in awe.

Suddenly, Triven became concerned. He had no idea what these things were. Were they dangerous? They were certainly big enough to be. "Ras, Ponu, Privon, get your spears and bows." He paused a moment. "Bron and Fabe, you get yours too." He then went into his own shelter and grabbed all his spears. He gave one each to Flin and Maret as well. Sola had never seen him act like this. Bron and Fabe were too young to hunt and Flin and Maret were gatherers.

"You will only fire on my command" he stated. He turned and looked at each *chaga* member in the eye. This was no time for nervous or thoughtless action.

A long hour passed as the *chaga* waited, alert, a little afraid but mostly amazed. Finally, the herd of beasts passed, showing little interest in them. They brushed close to the trees near their cave but didn't enter the forest.

"What were those?" asked Olin. *Chagama* shook her head. Sola shrugged.

"They were HUGE!" said Bron.

"No. They were MAMMOTH!" replied Triven. "I've never seen anything so big."

"I wonder what they taste like," said Olin. Olin was always concerned with his tummy. Sola punched his arm gently and grinned at him. This hurt her lip and she grimaced.

Ponu ran down to where the beasts had passed and watched them go.

Three days later, Ponu had built a massive fire at the cave entrance and the rest of the *chaga* sat outside the cave waiting with excitement, impatience, and anticipation. Because it was dark and the fire burned bright, they couldn't see inside to where Ponu was. Slowly, they became aware of a beat. It was soft and could barely be heard. The *chaga* joined in, mirroring the beat as best they could. Grady just pounded with his tiny fists and Olin had trouble matching the rhythm. Nobody minded. It was the way of things in a *chaga*. The beat grew louder and the *chaga* pounded louder as well.

Suddenly the face of a long tooth was above the fire. The children screamed and clung to their mothers. The *chaga* members gasped, some scooting backwards, others jumping up in alarm and reaching for knives. Ponu lifted his head and showed his face. He had co-opted the long tooth pelt for the cave blessing and now he peered from beneath it. Ponu lowered his head again and moved with the grace of the cat around the cave. Coming close to the fire and receding into the darkness again. The *chaga* watched, rapt. They had been a long time without a shaman and Ponu was proving to be equal to the job. Finally, Ponu reached out with his hand and carved three long gashes near the cave entrance. And then a spear came from out of the darkness and seemed to pierce the cat. A screeching yowl was heard and then Ponu threw off the pelt and tossed it into the fire. Reflexively, Sele reached for it, but it was already alight. Ponu himself retreated into the dark recesses of the cave while the *chaga* listened to the fading screams of a long tooth dying. The children howled too and then all was quiet except for an occasional sniffle.

The flames whispered and the wood crackled and then a soft rhythm grew out of the darkness. The *chaga* joined in. Again, Ponu came out of the darkness and into the firelight. This time, he took on the shape of the mammoth creatures they had seen three days ago. He lumbered around the fire, moving as the giants had moved. The *chaga* was amazed. Where did he find the fur? How did he make the trunk? Finally, he stopped and lifted his head. "This cave will no longer hold the spirit of the long tooth. Instead, it will hold the spirit of the mammoth. WE will hold the spirit of the mammoth. He reached behind him and drew forward a huge tusk. With the tusk, he slashed a line across the marks he had just made for the long tooth and then he placed it in a hole he had dug by the entrance.

Ponu thundered around the fire and the *chaga* cheered him on. The young ones jumped to their feet and mirrored his movements. Sola wanted to join them, but she was determined to leave childhood and vulnerability behind.

The thundering movements of the mammoth retreated into the back of the cave and the *chaga* quieted as they waited. Ponu again came forward into the light. This time, he was just Ponu, wearing his loincloth and a lightweight skin. There was no rhythm to accompany him as he paused by the fire. A solemness descended on the group. Ponu pulled forward a piece of bark. On it, was an image of all the *chaga* members and he held it up for all to see. Ponu wasn't the best artist in their group and so the people were crudely drawn. No more than stick figures, really. It didn't matter as each member could pick out their image. Triven was plain by his height. *Chagama*, her bent frame. Sola was tall and thin, just starting to curve. Ponu held out the image to each member of the *chaga.* With his knife, he pricked their skin so that a drop of their blood dropped onto the bark. "With your blood on this image, the Earth Mother will know you both inside and out." Grady cried when it was his turn and Olin bravely held back tears for his. Ponu laid the image on the floor of the cave by the entrance. From large hide bags that were close to the entrance, he took handfuls of dirt and sprinkled them at the cave mouth. "Earth Mother, we ask that you live with us in our new home, blessing us and listening to us." When the image was covered, he backed into the cave again, sprinkling dirt as he went. The *chaga* loved this blessing. Tram's passing was still near, and they thought that if the Earth Mother lived with them, they wouldn't need to send another messenger. Reta hoped that the Earth Mother would show Tram the drawing and he would know they missed him and thought of him often.

Ponu came forward one last time. "Welcome to your new home!" he said with a broad grin. The *chaga* cheered and the children jumped up and ran into the cave. They hadn't seen it yet and were eager to explore. Ponu had placed torches around the cave so that it was inviting and warm. He had even put some in the passage and in the smaller rooms. He knew the children would want to see every nook and cranny.

The members of the *chaga* staked out areas for each family. *Chagama* slept alone and chose the spot closest to the fire as was her right as the eldest and the wisest. Triven chose a spot near to *Chagama* for himself, Reta, Fabe, and Cark. Sele chose a spot opposite Triven. The cave was so vast that a wide space was left between them. The members of the *chaga* would work in that space during the long winter. Flin began laying pelts for herself, Sele, Olin and Grady.

"Sola," she called. "You can lay here," and she pointed to a spot near but not quite with them.

Sola looked at the spot and shook her head. She picked up her pelts and chose a spot near the rear of the cave. She would be alone, and likely cold through the winter, but she could not bring herself to share a space with Flin and Sele. As she was laying her pelts, *Chagama* came to inspect. Using a long stick, she lifted the bottom one and frowned. She looked at the one in Sola's arms and her frown deepened. "Those won't do," is all she said. She reached into the store where the other pelts were, and grabbed two thick, warm twin horn pelts. "Come with me" she said. Sola rolled her eyes. She adored *Chagama* but sometimes she was awfully imperious. And then *Chagama* laid those two pelts down beside her own bed and Sola found herself fighting back tears. She gave *Chagama* a hug, something *Chagama* often pretended to hate but secretly adored, and arranged her pelts happily. This new home truly felt blessed.

In the Trench

Moke smacked his head on a tree when he landed at the bottom of the steep hill. He was fortunate that the gravel both carried him down and slowed his descent and that his skull was thick. The bump knocked him out but did no lasting damage. Kor crashed down beside him; the wind knocked out of her. She could just hear Ono and Ches calling but it was a while before she caught her breathe enough to call back. When she did, her calls were weak and faint. She knew they wouldn't hear but she called anyway. Her voice was raw before she gave up. Tears streamed down her face when she finally quieted and looked around. They were in a deep trench. The sides were of loose gravel and steep. There were deep rooted trees, their bases covered in gravel and there were small trees, dead and leaning, taken out by previous slides. A tiny stream trickled at the bottom. It would thrash wildly in a rainstorm, sweeping away trees, rocks, and anything else in its path. It was fortunate that she didn't know that. Seeking to soothe her throat, she knelt by the stream and took a long drink. Finally, she turned to Moke. She had seen him lying there of course but was so sure he was dead that she couldn't bear to take a closer look. She made a final attempt at calling and then crawled up beside him and cried herself to sleep.

The next morning when Kor woke, she was cold and disoriented. She sat up and looked around. The stream bubbled and gurgled at the bottom of the trench calling to her it seemed. A fire was burning, and Moke's body was gone. Moke was alive, she thought with relief. He would get them out of here, she thought with confidence. There was a bladder of water beside her, and some dried meat wrapped in hide. She scurried closer to the fire and took a long drink from the bladder but left the meat. Where was Moke? Had he set the fire so that Ono and Ches could find them? Or was he looking for a way out?

She heard movement behind her, and she scrambled to her feet, terrified. But it was Moke and he smiled gently at her. She ran to his arms, and he hugged her tight. "I thought you were dead!" she said.

"Shhh, It's okay. We're fine. We just have to search for a way out of this trench. Come let's eat and then get moving."

At midmorning, they came across a ram. He was alive, barely, and Moke slit his throat with the knife he always carried at his waist. He thought for a long while as he sat by the ram. How long would it take them to find a way out? They didn't have shelter poles or spears, but both had been wearing their packs when they tumbled into the trench and they had meat, hides and most important, knives. Were they enough? Should he skin and tan the ram? Should he take precious time to carve and dry the meat? He didn't like being in this trench. Kor may not realize the danger of the little stream, but he did. He felt tortured with indecision. He'd never had to make these types of choices before, and Kor was depending on him. He took deep breaths and decided to process the animal while he thought.

Once the ram was skinned, he spent a couple of hours fleshing it. He ran his knife over the inside of the pelt and removed the bits of flesh and fat that remained. This was a tedious and time-consuming task, but the nature of the work calmed him down and helped clear his mind. He washed it thoroughly in the little stream, using ash from the fire Kor had lit to scrub it clean. The water was shallow, and it was difficult to wash thoroughly so he took his time with this as well. Then he sliced narrow strips of leather from the edges of the pelt. Next, he cut two saplings and lashed the pelt between them with the strips he'd cut.

Kor watched her brother working silently for a time before she turned and set herself the task of lighting a fire. Her earlier confidence had gone. Moke was so quiet and so obviously unsure of what to do. Her hands trembled as she struck her flint stones and that frustration brought the tears she'd been fighting. She sighed and looked over at Moke and then just kept striking the stones. Eventually a spark flew, and that tiny light heartened her a bit.

While he worked on the pelt, he was aware of Kor, but he hadn't felt able to deal with her grief and fear as well as his own. By the time he was finished, he felt calm, and if not strong, at least stronger.

Kor had already started slicing the meat into thin slices. She had also found a sapling and cut it down. Thin strips of meat, hung from the sapling over the fire. Kor was quiet and intent on her work. Moke could see the fear in the tenseness of her shoulders and the droop of her head.

He squatted beside her and said, "Good job, Kor. We'll need this on our hike out of here." A tear came to her eye, but she didn't look at him. "We will get out you know. It will be okay. I promise." At those words, her tears came faster but she smiled through them, and Moke hugged her. He was surprised by how much his words made him feel better too. He found that he believed them.

They stayed two days in that spot, drying meat and the mouflon hide. When the hide had dry, Moke found a large stone and cracked the mouflon skull open. He scooped out brain matter and squished it in his meaty palms before slathering it over the pelt. There was just enough brain matter to cover it. He folded the pelt over on itself and left it to cure in the shade of a big rock while they packed their meat and belongings.

Their first day walking was uneventful but tiring. Their packs were loaded and heavy and the loose gravel was exhausting to walk through. Despite that, they only paused for short breaks where they drank from the stream and chewed on a piece of meat.

They walked for days. Moke had chosen to head east and he had no way of knowing if that was the right decision or not. The creek that ran at the bottom of the trench often disappeared underground, so he made sure his water bladder was full whenever he got the chance. Kor's had been damaged in the fall so they shared. In the evenings, he and Kor stretched the mouflon pelt between them. It gave them something to do and kept them from worrying too much.

After a few days, the trench changed direction. It moved south but the sides were still too steep to climb. Larger trees grew up the sides indicating they had passed the slide zone. Moke tried in a couple of likely spots while Kor watched. He looked for places where there were trees they could scramble between but each time, he came to some obstacle he couldn't overcome. A rock face he couldn't climb, a steep and barren area, invisible from below, or loose earth and gravel that sent him tumbling down again. If he got hurt, he worried what might happen to Kor and so he stopped trying.

Finally, the trench opened up, and the creek rolled over an embankment into a river below. Moke despaired. The river was a few feet down and he couldn't see an easy way to it. He couldn't tell how deep it was or how fast it was flowing and neither of them could swim.

The people of the clans were a simple people. They had their ways, developed over thousands of years and rarely did they need to change them. They worked. They had food and shelter. They laughed and loved, slept, and ate. Sometimes they were hungry. Sometimes they fought with other clans. Mostly, they were fine. Moke and Kor had never known real thirst or hunger, the kind that came from days of want. Their brains weren't accustomed to problems like this and so Moke sat by the creek for days and watched the river as it flowed past. Kor tried to talk to him, but he gave her the barest of responses. Their meat ran out and Kor pleaded for more. Finally, Kor grew quiet and sat beside him while he thought. There was a stick beside her, and in her boredom, she threw it over. She liked how it splashed, sunk and rose again and then disappeared around the bend. She got up and found a bigger stick and threw it over. And then a bigger one still. Finally, Moke came to life.

"That's it, Kor! We'll go over on a stick! A really big stick!" He jumped up and the pair began to search for a log big enough to hold their weight. There were plenty around and Moke thought it prudent to throw one over and see what it did before trying it with the pair of them clinging to it. It behaved as expected. It went over, sunk and then popped up again.

He found another and held it upright, Kor in front of him. "Wrap your arms around this and don't let go no matter what," he instructed. When she did, he wrapped his body around hers and walked the log to the edge. They didn't know how to swim but they had been in water, and they knew they needed a big breath.

"When I say, 'take a breath', I'm going to throw us over," he said. Kor nodded. He took a couple of calming breaths and then he said, "Take a breath!". With Kor and the log in his arms he jumped. The log did exactly as he expected. It sunk and then popped to the surface. Unfortunately, he and Kor were on the underside of it, and he hadn't expected that at all. Frantically, he kicked his feet. This made the log roll back and forth, but his movements weren't directed, and he accomplished nothing. Fortunately, it didn't take him days to figure this out and with his lungs burning, he kicked his feet in a purposeful direction and the log flipped over. Kor and he took a long, deep breath. And then they laughed. That had been exciting and frightening and now they were floating down the river and that was fun too.

They had no idea how to direct the log and before long they were cold. Moke was finding it increasingly difficult to hold on. Had he the strength, he would have been terrified for Kor. As it was, he grew tired and quiet, drifting with the log. Finally, the log came to a shallow bend in the river and Moke's feet brushed the bottom. This woke him from his stupor, and he found the strength to pull it to shore. They were both shivering and struggling to move their bodies as their minds directed, but they were out of the trench and Moke would set a fire in no time. "Tomorrow," he said as he gathered wood. "We can figure out how to get home tomorrow."

Others

This story happened to a chaga my mother's father's mother knew.

The chaga chief didn't like other chaga's and he didn't like people and he barely tolerated his own mate. When My mother's father's mother was very young, this chaga and her chaga crossed paths. The chief glared while his mate talked with my mother's father's mate and so they didn't talk long. His mate wore fear instead of a shirt and she begged to trade for salt. My mother's father's mate felt pity for her and so she gave her some of her salt even though she had none to spare. The chaga headed east and soon my mother's father's mother's chaga forgot all about them.

Many years later when my mother's father's mother hair was wispy and her mate was gone and she wore the mantle of Chagama, her chaga travelled east while following a herd of twin horns. The twin horns followed a river that wound over particularly difficult terrain. Rocks and hills and bramble and thick woods. It was very unusual and not a place that chagas would normally go. But. They did like the taste of twin horns. And the difficult terrain would make hunting them easy. If they could just catch up. Chagama thought it was a gift from the Earth Mother and so they went.

After many days of rough travel and good eating, they came to a meadow in the woods where the river slowed, and the trees thinned. It was a beautiful place and the chaga paused to take it in before entering to explore. Before long, they came across some shelters. They weren't built very well, and some were old, the wood rotting, the pelts thin and hairless. There was a giant fire pit in the middle of the shelters, but it had no flames. Not even an ember. The place looked like it should be deserted but somehow didn't feel that way. A bone with flesh by the fire. A smell of feces and urine, too fresh.

My mother's father's mother's chaga wanted to leave but their Chagama thought it was important they stay. She was certain that the Earth Mother had directed them here. She told the boys to gather wood. The girls to search for sustenance. Close by. The men to guard. And so, they waited.

Before long, the people of the meadow returned. Their Chagama was very old but nevertheless, my mother's father's Chagama recognized her. She was the mate of the chief from the chaga that hated people.

The two Chagama's sat together while the rest of the chaga watched.

The chaga was small, too small to even be called a chaga. A band then. Usually, a band was made up of only men and best avoided but there were children, and women. Not many. It was difficult to know just what to call these people.

The chief's mate cried as she told their tale. "We found this meadow shortly after we met you. The chief was ecstatic. It was difficult to get to and they would be free of other people. He was happy. I was happy. We were happy.

We were not a large chaga as the chief preferred us to remain small. We welcomed sons and daughters with delight though. Happy to grow that way.

As each son or daughter matured, they petitioned the chief to leave. Just for a time. So they could find mates. He always refused. And one by one, they slunk away.

The chief passed on and I thought, finally, we will leave. But my youngest son was like his father. He chose his sister to mate, and we stayed. We were a tiny chaga now and even I stopped asking to go. Surely, we could not survive.

My son had sons and daughters. Some died at birth. The ones that lived were like their father. They chose mates among themselves and had sons and daughters."

Their Chagama stopped here and turned away. Chagama looked around.

The children were few. One just stared into space. Another walked funny. One crawled and cried. Another watched them with an angry look. A couple of them seemed okay but most did not. All were thin and naked.

The mother of the crying child bent and picked it up. Her head moved side to side in a continuous motion and she neither looked at the babe nor spoke to him. She put the babe to her breast and when he had barely suckled, she deposited him again and walked away. Her head still shaking. He still crying.

Finally, my mother's father's mother hugged the other Chagama and walked back to us. Both Chagama's had tears on their face.

My mother's father mother's chaga left without looking back. Many days later Chagama spoke. "She asked me to kill everyone in her chaga. She said that they were all wrong, they suffered, and it would be a kindness."

There is no bigger sin against the Earth Mother than to send a messenger she didn't ask for and so Chagama refused her. She didn't pass the request on either. Perhaps though. Perhaps In this case, it was a bigger sin against the Earth Mother to leave them as they were.

There was silence as *Chagama* spoke the final words of her story. The people of the *chaga* were affected deeply. All *Chagama's* stories stirred emotion but this one brought despair and sadness and was as wrong as the children it described. *Chagama* had a tear at the corner of her eye which she let fall for all to see.

"They should have killed those wrong ones," said Ras. His disgust was so plain to see, he even shivered.

"Mother, for the love of the Earth, can you not let us have one night of peace without tales of Earth Mother messengers, woe, and disaster?!" With that, Triven stormed out of the cave into the night. There was no moon that night and the campfire light would only travel a few feet. Triven was not going far.

The others of the *chaga* rose and found their sleeping spots. It had been a long day and they had plenty to think about before they drifted off to sleep.

"Did he call you mother!?" asked Sola, eyes wide in shock.

"Triven is my son. And I have another son, Rost. He stayed with the *chaga* he was born into. Fen and Cas, my girls, mated into different *chagas*."

Sola was quiet for a while as she digested this new information. How could she live her whole life with these people and not know something so fundamental? What else didn't she know? *Chagama* watched her carefully and when she judged her ready, she carried on.

"Triven was a very thoughtful youth, with wisdom beyond his years. This meant that he could often see dangers or benefits in decisions that our *chaga* chief couldn't envision. Because he was so young, the chief wasn't really interested in what he had to say although he did always hear him out. This caused Triven a lot of pain. He was passionate about keeping the *chaga* safe and he couldn't bear it when the chief made a bad choice. He has that in common with you." *Chagama* smiled at Sola as she said this. "He thought the *chaga* was too big in any case and so he asked Sele and Rost to form a new *chaga* with him. Sele agreed. Rost did not. Then he asked me to join him as *Chagama*. My daughters had already mated and gone so I had to choose between Rost and Triven. A very painful time. In the end, I felt that although Triven was capable and smart, he lacked experience and would need my stories. And here we are. He doesn't like my stories, but I tell them anyway."

"I like your stories just fine," grumbled Triven from the mouth of the cave. "I would just like to hear some happy ones for a change." He came in and bent over to hug *Chagama*. "And I will always be grateful you chose to come with me."

"See Sola, he is wise after all!". Sola laughed and then hugged *Chagama* as well before finding her bed.

The next morning Triven sent his hunters out in pairs. They fanned out in different directions. They were not hunting animals this time, although if they came across any they would not ignore the gift. Their instructions were to look for people.

Strangers Passing

Donon was crouched low in the long grass, Tsutse beside him. Chor and Ross were opposite them both. When he looked over at her, for a moment he didn't recognize her. Who was the woman with the rounded limbs and crazy hair that was once brown and now spattered with grey? Then his gaze blurred and he saw again, the girl he'd loved his entire life. The one that the Wanderer had met all those years ago. She was as fierce as ever, never mind the grey. He glanced behind her and saw their two sons, Ross and Chor. They both took after him in looks but Ross was like his mother in temperament. Quick to passion. He shook his head slightly at the thought. There had been no stopping him once he chose his mate. Their daughters hadn't come on this hunt although Genu was certainly old enough. She hadn't wanted to and Ross and Chor's mates had both had babes this year so had stayed at camp to tend to them.

The four of them had been squatting for hours. Hunting with spears was a game of patience and stamina. The clans' people had plenty of both, but Donon's leg was starting to cramp. The elk were close enough now that a sudden movement or sound could cause a stampede or even an attack and their patience would have been wasted. Donon slowly massaged his leg. He shifted ever so slightly, allowing the muscle to stretch a tiny bit. The elk were grazing and slowly moving in their direction. One would walk between them soon enough.

A cow moved nearer, and her calf along with her. Donon pointed to the calf and waited for the others to nod. The calf was large enough to be a worthwhile target and he would be tender and tasty. Older elk were chewy and not as sweet.

When he thought he could stand the cramp no longer, the cow moved forward. A few more steps and they would be right in the middle of them. They were ready. This had to be timed right. If they waited for the perfect moment, the cow could smell them and bolt. If they didn't wait long enough, their spears would never reach. The cow moved forward a couple more steps. She looked relaxed. Donon waited. The calf moved up beside her. She raised her head and sniffed. Donon waited no more. He nodded, rose, and stepped forward to throw his spear at the calf. The cow startled and ran forward before thinking to protect her calf. By the time she did, it was too late. The calf had been speared by all four of the hunters. Donon was thrilled, adrenaline running through him. Often, these tactics failed. There was a substantial sized herd close by though, so this was not a moment to revel in victory. The herd would stampede and Donon needed to make sure they ran away from him and not towards.

He raised his arms and started shouting, "Shoo! Shoo!". The other hunters joined him. The entire herd raised their heads and in a moment were fleeing in terror away from them, the calf's dam with them.

Finally, they could relax. With a grin, Donon turned to the calf, although calf was a loose definition. The animal was more of an adolescent than a calf and had plenty of meat. He heard a loud 'zip' sound and then suddenly felt a sharp pain. He looked down and there was a spear tip sticking out of his abdomen. He looked up in confusion. His clan looked back at him, equally confused. They dropped low to the ground, instinctively recognizing their own vulnerability. Donon fell over, groaning in pain.

Tsutse shimmied over to him, careful to keep a low profile. She looked at the wound and sat still for a moment as she comprehended that the mate who had been by her side all her life wouldn't be there much longer. She blinked her tears away and reached into her pouch. Hops. She would give it all to him. It might make him sleep. The wound would kill him but not quickly and certainly not painlessly. It was best that he slept. Perhaps, if it was enough, he would sleep the sleep of the dead sooner than the wound demanded.

Shelter

Moke and Kor slept the night without stirring. Their clothes were still damp when they drifted off and the fire was mere embers by morning. Moke woke shivering. He resisted the urge to snuggle next to Kor and got up to gather more logs. Kor at least, he thought, would wake to warmth. Should he hunt, he wondered. The snows would be coming soon, and they were far from home. At least he thought they were far from home. He didn't know where they were. He studied the shore of the river, the cut of the mountains against the sky and the trees around him. He had never been here before is all he knew for sure. That was not good. It had been a few days since his last meal, but he knew he could go a few more. Could Kor? He looked at the sky and sniffed the air. It wouldn't snow yet. Moke sighed and decided that heading towards home would be their priority. He didn't have any spears anyway. That thought made him uncomfortable and he decided to look for likely rocks while Kor slept.

Moke found a small piece of flint. He could make a spear tip from it he decided but it would never pierce a woolly elephants hide and probably not an aurochs either. Maybe a deer or a small horse though, if he were lucky enough to get close to one of those. It would do for small game too.

He sat by the fire and held the flintstone firmly in his left hand. In his right, he held a river rock, sturdy and slightly larger. He hefted the rock and slammed it down on the flintstone with precision. A sliver of rock slipped free from the flint. He turned the flint in his hand and repeated the motion. Another sliver slipped free. He continued this process until he had a small, elongated piece of rock left. He knocked out the bottom, to square it off and he was satisfied.

He glanced over at Kor and saw that she was awake and watching him.

"I'm hungry," moaned Kor before she got up. Moke felt bad for her but didn't respond. Kor already knew all the answers.

Moke slipped the rough spear tip into his pack and the two followed the river upstream for the whole day and part of the next until they were blocked by the rising terrain of the foothills. As they neared the mountains, the trees and bush grew, protected from the fierce dry winds by the mountains. The trench they came out of wasn't far. He could just see it ahead. Moke filled his bladder and the pair headed north.

An hour later, Moke started to worry. The scent of the air had changed. The chill had not. Snow was coming. He was torn between the idea of cutting saplings for a shelter and pressing on. He didn't want to stop. He worried that if they did, they'd not be able to move on again. The snow would lock them in, and they were not prepared for that. He watched the ground, looking for anything that could construct an impromptu shelter from if they needed it. When they weren't looking at the ground, they scanned the hills for signs of a cave. So far, they hadn't been lucky in finding small game and now Moke worried about starving as well as being caught in bad weather.

They walked on through the afternoon and Moke was starting to panic. Kor was stumbling a lot. And so was he if he were honest. They were both at the end of their endurance. Was this it? He wondered. He pulled Kor up and fell over himself. He lay there, Kor swaying on her feet beside him. That's when he saw it. A cave. He couldn't tell anything about it, and he didn't care. If a cave bear was in it, then they would likely be killed by it which was better than this he thought. With a burst of energy that lasted long enough to get him to his feet, he pulled Kor along and headed to the cave.

It was farther away than it looked. Or maybe it was just because they were slow and tired, but it seemed to take hours to get there. When they reached the base of the mountain, Moke looked up. They would have to climb to reach it and Moke wasn't sure he could. He was sure that Kor could not. He bent and lifted her up. A tear fell from his eye as he did. He was at the end of his strength. With jarring, painful, slow steps, he made his way up. It seemed to take forever and when he finally reached the cave, he entered the mouth of it and collapsed. Kor beside him. His last thought was that if there was a cave bear, maybe he would be lucky enough to sleep through its anger.

An Exciting Meeting

The fire near the mouth of the cave had gone out. The women and children had been away from the cave all day, gathering what they could. Snow was coming. They could all smell it. They were gathering the last berries from the bushes, the last brassicas, frost bitten a couple of nights ago, but edible still, potatoes, small and hard, perfect for winter storage and parsnips, sweetened by the recent frost. They were also gathering load upon load of dead bush for the fire. This task was assigned to Bron and Fabe. They made a game of it, running to and from the forest with arm loads of wood which they stacked in separate piles near the base of the mountain. At the end of the day, whoever had the biggest pile was the winner and the other would have to serve him that evening. In the morning, they had run at a furious pace but now that the afternoon sun was waning, the nearby brush was gone, and they had to venture further out. They were tired and the speed of their return was more shuffle than run.

Flin and Lonna picked berries all day. Lonna was heavily pregnant, and Flin still carried Grady, so it was a good light task for them. Brella, Maret and Reta kept the children close to them and gathered what they could find. Mostly brassica which was plentiful this time of year. They took turns teaching the children what to do.

Sola spent the day with *Chagama*, her favorite person. They were a short distance from the cave but far enough for it to be out of sight. They were digging up the last of the parsnips and potatoes. She had a large bag made of hide, as did *Chagama*. The root vegetables were heavy, and they kept their bags near rather than carrying them. Sola suspected they would need help to bring them back to the cave at the end of the day. By late afternoon both bags were full.

"Go to the cave and see if any hunters are back," commanded *Chagama*. "And bring new bags. We will have time to pick a few more." Sola dropped a handful of the robin's egg sized potatoes in the bag and started jogging back to the cave. When she got there, all was quiet. The wood piles were larger than when she left but Bron and Fabe weren't around. She couldn't see any hunters or any of the other women. She glanced up at the cave. There was no fire burning and she was sure that had anyone returned, they would have lit it. Sola climbed the path and entered the dark cave. The hide bags were kept in a pile in the tiny cave. A good place to store things like that. Sola took a couple of steps and almost tripped. She paused and waited for her eyes to adjust to the dark.

A body lay on the cave floor. Two bodies. They were clad in ragged hides, fitted to their forms. One was larger than the other. That's all she could discern. She reached over cautiously and placed her hand in front of the larger one's mouth. Air tickled her hand. She watched them for a few minutes and then again reached out and touched the larger one's skin. It was cold. He didn't move at her touch, and she wondered at the soundness of his sleep. None of her people slept like that. She glanced over at the smaller one and saw the body shiver. That prodded Sola to action. She ran down the cave path and gathered up some wood. From the larger room in the cave, she gathered some dried grass and some cattails. She brought those to the fire pit and cleared a small space. Carefully she piled the grass and then laid the cattail fluff on top. She shielded the pile with her body and began striking her flint stone against a piece of shiny stone. After a couple of dozen strikes, a spark lit the cattail fluff. Carefully, she blew on it until the grass caught. She drew in small twigs and dried chips and moss and nursed the fire along. Neither of the strangers moved while she did all this. She was impatient to get a closer look at them but she had enough experience with lighting fires to know that if she rushed, it would only take longer.

When the fire was blazing, Sola sat on her haunches and watched the strangers. Neither moved except for the slow rise of their chests caused by their breathing. She could see better now and yes; their clothes were a little ragged. Well made though and they fit them well. They would keep them warm through the winter if it weren't for the missing patches. Their boots were also worn. She could see the bigger one's foot on the bottom of one of his. But again, she could also tell they were of good quality once. Her eyes travelled up their bodies. It was hard to tell but she thought the bigger one was only a bit bigger than she was herself. But wider. She couldn't be sure when they were laying down and clothed. She looked to their faces. Nothing seemed familiar about them, but it was possible they were from a *chaga* she had met before. She reached forward and moved the dirty matted hair aside from the big one's face and gasped. She definitely did not know this person. The face looked odd. She studied it, a frown on her own face. What was it? She wondered. The eyebrows looked wrong. She reached forward and traced one with her finger. Yes. It jutted out where none of her *chagas* brows did that. She shrugged. People often had differences in their faces. It wasn't a big deal. Was that it? She looked to the smaller one and shuffled forward so she could reach. Again, she moved the matted, dirty hair aside. Yes, this one had the big brows too. Was something odd about the chin? Sola felt her own chin and then reached down and stoked the smaller one's chin. She needed these strangers to wake up so she could look at them properly.

A loud sound behind her alerted her to new arrivals. Bron and Fabe burst through the cave opening, laughing, and shoving each other.

"Shush!" growled Sola. She already felt protective of these strangers who clearly needed to rest.

Bron looked towards her and took in the strangers lying there. Fabe who was still laughing shoved Bron in a continuation of whatever game they had been playing. Bron shoved Fabe back hard and then grabbed his face and pointed it to the strangers.

"Who are they?" Bron asked.

"Where did they come from?" asked Fabe.

"Shush!" growled Sola again. "I don't know anything. I found them like this. Now shush.".

The young boys were as curious as Sola and joined her by the strangers. "Look at his brow," whispered Bron.

"Shush! Or Leave!" growled Sola. She had no real authority, but the boys responded to the sure command in her voice and settled into quietly watching, perched on their haunches, just as she was.

A short while later, Ras and Ponu came in, just as loud as Bron and Fabe had been.

"Shush!" called all three of the watchers. Ponu and Ras were shocked into silence. They took in the tableau of the sleeping strangers and three young ones keeping watch. Ponu prodded Bron and he got up and dragged the hunters out of the cave where he explained what was happening. The hunters glanced in and then decided they would keep watch outside the cave, ensuring anyone else who came would be quiet.

The women and children began to file up the path. The hunters warned them of the strangers, but the women refused to stay out, or to be quiet although in actual fact, they were quiet and shushed the children as well. They joined the watchers in a circle around the sleeping strangers, snacking on jerky and fresh vegetables. This was, after all, the most exciting thing to happen since they found the cave.

Shortly after that, a loudly cursing *Chagama* could be heard approaching. This snapped Sola out of her trance when nothing else would. With a start, she rose to her feet and looked to the cave entrance. *Chagama* was having nothing to do with being shushed and pushed her way through without listening to what the hunters guarding the entrance had to say. She took in the *chaga* members sitting vigil over the strangers and was finally shocked to silence.

"I'm so sorry *Chagama*! When I got to the cave, I found them shivering and asleep, so I lit a fire and kept watch. I completely forgot to come for you!" Sola was deeply ashamed that she had forgotten the old woman in the field, and she blushed and cast her eyes to the ground.

"Never mind. Ras, go collect the potatoes in the field by the hazelnut trees." Chagama moved closer to the strangers and looked them over. She reached out a hand and placed it on first one and then the others forehead. "Sola, bring me those hides there. The smaller one has a fever I think." She threw the hides over the strangers and then moved to the fire. She lifted the smaller cooking stone and placed it over the flames. In a large mammoth skull that she had found shortly after they moved to the cave, she poured some water from a bladder and then waited for it to heat. Once done, she returned the water to the bladder. She fed the warmed water to the smaller stranger in small sips. *Chagama* was incredibly gentle when she was treating illness.

As she was feeding the warm water to the little one, Triven and Sele entered the cave. They pushed past the children crowded around the strangers and stared down at them. Sele was the first to speak.

"What are you doing?" he yelled as he shoved *Chagama* away from the little one so hard that she was knocked over. "These aren't people! Look at their faces! They're wrong. They're like the people in your story." He reached down to grab the little one. *Chagama* was sure he intended to toss her out of the cave but just as he was about to pull, the hand of the larger one wrapped around his arm. The larger one was frowning, clearly angry and obviously protective of the little one. He shifted his body to shield her from Sele's view.

Chagama rose and glared at Sele. "You dare to harm your *Chagama*!" She looked to Triven. This was indeed a crime. *Chagama* knew Triven well. She could read his micro expressions and she could see that he was angry and uncertain. He had never been faced with anything like this before and there were no stories that he knew to guide him. He took a deep breath and looked at *Chagama*. And he realized that she had protested the 'harm' that Sele had done so that he could have some time to think about this very odd situation.

"Sele," he said firmly. "You will leave this night and not return until the sun sets tonight and once again after that."

"You need my strength against these wrong things!" protested Sele.

"Maybe. But I DON'T need them against a small old woman which is where you seem to be putting them to use."

Even with his emotions so high, Sele could see that Triven would not change his mind. Privon and Ponu stepped close to Triven, indicating their support. Although Triven was chief, it was on suffrage. The *chaga* was never obligated to follow orders or even keep him in that position. Triven was grateful for their support and relaxed slightly. "Fine," continued Sele, "but I'm not leaving my mate with these abominations. Flin. Pack some food." With that Sele stomped out of the cave, kicking out at the fire as went.

Flin sighed. She didn't particularly want to go but decided that Sele would never calm down if she didn't. She put some dried meat and fresh vegetables in a hide bag and then grabbed an armload of fleeces. "Olin, come. Sola, carry Grady." Sola looked up, shocked. She detested Sele and had not shared a shelter or a sleeping corner with her mother since they had found the cave.

"No. I won't go with you." Sola and her mother stared at each for a long moment. Flin looked as if she might strike her and *Chagama* stepped in front of her.

"Sola is my child now," is all she said.

Flin wondered when exactly she had lost her. Was it when she struck her before they found the cave? Before that? She knew she had mostly ignored her since taking up with Sele. And then Olin and Grady had come, and Flin had no room in her mind or heart for Sola, except as someone to fetch and carry. Flin forced herself to nod. For a moment it hurt, and then her mind was occupied with gathering shelter poles and pelts, Olin, and Grady.

When things had settled, *Chagama* sat by the fire and pounded the ground.

The chaga hunters walked through the winter storm that had caught them by surprise. They had gone for one final hunt before winter set in. That morning, they had smelled the air and tested the wind and searched the sky. It was clear and sunny. Cold, but cold was as nothing in the fall. Not when you wore new boots and warm clothes. They had followed the trail of a limping galloper. An easy kill they thought. And when the morning turned to afternoon, they said, "surely it will be just ahead," and so they continued on. And when the first flake fell from the sky, they said, "Just a little farther," and they continued forward. It was only when the snow covered the tracks of the limping galloper that they paused and realized they were far from home and a storm wasn't just coming, a storm was here. They constructed a hasty shelter and huddled beneath it for three nights and two days. On the third day, they were relieved to see sunshine. They tore down their shelter in haste and made ready to travel home, all thoughts of the limping galloper gone. As morning turned to afternoon, they heard a whinny and turned around to search out the sound. The limping galloper could be seen in the distance. The hunters were tempted to chase it but then the animal paused and looked at them. It tossed its head and lifted its feet. Then it galloped off and disappeared. No sign of a limp.

The hunters were uneasy now. For the first time. They knew that this was about more than being caught in a snowstorm. Too scared to talk about it, they did the only thing they could. They headed home. Late that afternoon, they realized that Papajon was no longer with them. Frightened, they hesitated before they retraced their steps. He was gone. They couldn't find a footprint or a piece of hide, a hair, or a trace. Again, with nothing else to do, they started home again.

Chagama paused for a long moment. She took a sip of water and a bite of meat. She fiddled with the pelt she was sitting on. It wasn't quite comfortable. Inwardly she smiled at the upturned faces, filled with tension, and barely concealed impatience.

Papajon was fine. He had fallen early in the morning and called to his companions, but his voice was carried by the wind, and they didn't hear him. His ankle had turned and now it was he who limped. A gift perhaps, from the galloper they had been chasing. That thought made him nervous, but he shrugged it off and walked as best he could.

In the afternoon, Papajon chanced to look up. A cave! If people lived there, they could provide him shelter and food. If not, at least he would have somewhere to spend the night. His ankle was very sore by this time and Papajon had been about ready to give up.

A large man came to greet Papajon. We have no food he said. But you are welcome to sleep here. For tonight only.

Now Papajon could smell the meat that had been roasting just a moment before. He could see the trail of juices glittering in the firelight on the cave floor. He could see the plump cheeks of the people around the fire and the way they looked down when he looked at them. But what could he do?

Papajon slept by the fire. They said they had no spare pelts for him and he turned constantly to warm the chilled side of his body. He rose and was on his way before they woke.

The big man opened his eyes and was pleased to see Papajon limping out of the cave. He stretched and searched out the large roast his people had hidden the night before. He tore off a piece and dropped the roast when a "ribbet" sound came from him. He put his hands to his face and discovered that a frog was where his mouth should have been. He screamed in pain when he tried to pull it off. It was firmly attached.

Forever after, the man had to feed the frog on his face before he, himself could eat.

When *Chagama* failed to continue, Olin asked "What happened to Papajon? Did he make it home?"

"Papajon never made it home again. He is seen from time to time by the Earth Mother's people. Sometimes, he brings a boon. Others, well. If they disobey the Earth Mother's laws, then…."

Sola thought it was unfortunate that Sele wasn't around to hear that story.

Angry Voices

Moke woke up to angry voices. He lay quietly with his eyes closed, trying to figure out who was speaking and where he was. He couldn't make sense of the words and then he remembered the cave he had found. And that he was starving. That he had dropped Kor on the cave floor before falling into an exhausted sleep. He opened his eyes in alarm and saw an arm reaching to grab Kor. Suddenly he was wide awake and acting on instinct, he sat up and grabbed the arm in one fluid motion. He glanced up at the face of the arms owner and shuddered. So different a face! But the eyes. They were like his peoples' eyes, and they glowed with disgust.

The arm retreated and angry voices continued. Moke noticed that there were a lot of people in the cave. He saw the warm fire and that Kor had been covered with a hide. They weren't all like angry eyes then. He saw spears, propped against the cave wall behind him. Beside him were his pack and the mouflon hide. He looked over at Kor and saw the redness in her cheeks. He felt her skin and it was hot and yet her body shivered with cold. Fever. He edged closer to her, and he discreetly felt for his knife.

One of the people bent down beside him and spoke but he couldn't understand the words. He thought the person was female, but it was difficult to tell. The features were so foreign! The face was pushed in, he thought as he stared at it. The mouth was small and the eyes flat in the face. The nose was small too, although broad. The skin was dark as was the hair. Brown hair he was used to though. Many in the clans had brown hair. None had skin so dark. He realized the angry voices had quieted and many people were staring at him. So many people! Clans were small. He never saw this many people together unless it was a gathering. Nothing he saw eased the alarm he was feeling.

A giant of a man walked over and squatted beside him. His voice was calm, his eyes unreadable. Moke recognized no words and found his gestures too quick to interpret.

"We mean no harm," stuttered Moke. Absolute silence. "We need shelter. And food if you have it." He gestured to the roof of the cave and then he made as if he was eating. He was terrified but he needed help and he knew it.

Moke's people were without guile for the most part. His terror was easy to see on his face. His gestures for shelter and food were also easy to read. Triven looked to *Chagama* who nodded at him.

"We will give you food and shelter," he said softly. He pointed at the cave ceiling, mirrored Moke's eating gestures, and then pointed at Moke. Before he was even finished, Sola had brought some dried meat and offered it to Moke.

Moke took it politely and then gobbled it up as if he hadn't had a meal in days, which he hadn't. He was so hungry, he forgot about the strangers surrounding him for a brief moment. Their humor brought him back to himself and he grinned shyly. Sola smiled at him and offered him a bladder of water.

Chagama, seeing his hunger, realized that the smaller one would need sustenance too. She heated more water and threw some bones in with it to make a nourishing broth and then she placed the larger cooking stone on the fire and moved aside for the other women to prepare food for the evening.

Chagama handed the warmed broth to Sola who took it to Kor. She looked at Moke who watched intently and raised an eyebrow in question. He nodded in agreement and Sola dribbled some into Kor's mouth.

Moke was still exhausted, and he was nodding off before long. He missed the fight between Triven and Sele, and the story afterwards. When he woke up the next morning, the cave was quiet. The fire was burning but it seemed as though everyone had disappeared, and he and Kor were alone. He might have thought it a dream except for the bladder full of broth lying next to Kor.

New Friends

Moke looked over at Kor. She was still sleeping and when he felt her head, she was hot. She wasn't shivering so he removed some of the pelts from her and then he got up. He needed to relieve himself and find food. He was still starving.

At the cave entrance, Moke looked out to see the valley below. There was a thick forest which would provide firewood, spear handles and shelter frames. A creek ran not too far away and in the distance the steppe. It had snowed in the night, but just a little and the sky was clear now. He could see the footprints in the snow. Some led to the steppe, others the forest. He thought the cave was very similar to the one his family lived in except this one had a better view as it was higher up. It was bigger too, and the steppe was closer. That and the view would be an advantage he thought. They would be able to see herds from a long distance and get to them quickly.

He stepped down the path and took care of business before filling his bladder with water from the creek. He returned to the cave to check on Kor. He picked up the bladder full of bone broth from the night before and dribbled some into her mouth as he had seen the old woman do. He was a little clumsy and more dribbled into her mouth than Kor could handle while sleeping. She sputtered, coughed, and opened her eyes.

"Hi," said Moke with a relieved smile.

 A sound from the entrance drew his attention. The small woman who had given him water the day before threw some wood on the fire before dropping the rest of her load. She smiled a greeting at him and then disappeared into the back of the cave. When she returned, she had meat which she offered to him and Kor and then she sat quietly watching them eat.

Kor greedily ate and then jumped up and ran to the mouth of the cave and heaved her stomach contents down the hillside. Moke laughed at her. "Not so much next time, hey!" as he handed her the broth. He glanced at Sola who was staring at them wide eyed.

"Your eyes are the color of the sky!" she said. He didn't understand and stared back quizzically. She pulled him up and dragged him to the cave opening, pointed at his eyes and then the sky. He was a little surprised at how easily she handled him but found he wasn't bothered by it. He thought he understood what she was saying, and he looked closely at her eyes. He pointed at them and then the cave floor. Her eyes were brown. She frowned briefly and then nodded and smiled. Sola had never seen blue eyes before, and she supposed the cave was too dark to see them clearly the night before. She thought they were the one lovely thing in the otherwise very strange face. It wasn't ugly exactly, but it was disconcerting, and his skin was so pale! None of her people had skin that light. She wondered if it was because he was sick like the other one. His mouth was also strange, wider than she was used to but there was no mistaking the warmth and charisma of his smile.

Kor was still pretty weak, and Moke was reluctant to leave her alone in the cave. The angry voices of the night before were with him still and he suspected that the pair of them were the cause. This warred with his guest instinct which told him he should hunt or gather something to contribute for their keep. He decided he could make a quick foray into the woods for a spear shaft and then sit by the fire and work on attaching the spear head he had made a few days ago. He could hunt tomorrow he told himself. For now, he would stay and protect Kor and maybe learn something from the young, skinny girl who was helping them.

"Moke," he said and pointed to himself. "Kor," he said and pointed to Kor. And then he pointed at the girl and raised his brows.

Those brows are really strange thought Sola. He was making sounds and pointing but she was too distracted by the brows to pay attention. He did it a few more times and she finally caught on. She wondered if he was providing names or genders but decided she would give a name. Once she provided names for the rest of the *chaga*, he would understand. "Sola," she said and pointed to herself.

"Soluh," he repeated back. She corrected his pronunciation but gave up with a shrug after a few attempts. He couldn't seem to make the "ah" sound. "Soluh," she said and smiled.

He walked out into the sunlight and the skinny girl followed him. "*Filo,*" he said, pointing to a tree. "Tree," responded Sola with a smile. She watched as he sawed through the sapling with his knife. He cleared all the branches and chopped the top half of too. He hefted it in his hand and nodded with approval. Sola just watched. She'd seen her own people do similar things of course but a tree could have many purposes and she wondered what he was going to do with this one.

He tilted his head towards the cave and raised his brows. Sola shrugged and he grinned and started walking back.

Moke checked on Kor before sitting by the fire to work on his spear. Sola watched with interest. First, he carved a notch into the top of his spear shaft. He didn't have any pitch, so he made the notch as narrow as possible and then struggled to put his spear tip in it. He wanted the fit to be as tight as he could make it. Next, he removed a leather thong from his shirt. It was a garment made of horse and fit over his head. The sides were kept together with a series of leather thongs that tied the pieces together. It was tedious taking it on and off, but he didn't change his clothes very often so thought little about the design. The arms were attached in a similar manner but if he was careful when he removed the garment, he wouldn't have to untie those. As he had no intention of taking it off, he didn't spare it a thought. The shirt gaped at the side where he'd removed the thong, but it would still serve its purpose.

Moke poured some water over the thong and then wrapped it as tightly as possible around the spear base where it attached to the shaft. When the leather dried, it would shrink and hold the tip in place. He would still likely lose the tip the first or second time he used the spear, but it was the best he could do for the moment.

Sola disappeared for a while and so Moke pulled out his mouflon pelt. He needed boots desperately and he started to cut a pair out. He had no awl, but he would figure that out later he decided. When Sola returned, she looked curiously at the pelt. She had never seen, or felt, one like that. Moke got up and pranced around like a mouflon did, butting his head against the wall and then pointed at the mountains above them. Sola thought he looked hilarious, and she laughed like she hadn't since she was

Olin's age. But she got the idea. It came from some kind of animal who lived in the mountain.

That evening, Brella and Reta prepared potatoes. They were small enough to hide in their hands and didn't take long to roast over the fire. Brella stabbed a potato, slathered it in aurochs fat and handed it to Moke.

Moke had seen potatoes before, but he had never eaten one. Gingerly, he put it to his mouth and took a tiny bite. All he tasted was the fat and he liked fat, so he took a bigger bite. His eyes grew round, and his brows furrowed as he chewed it. And then he jumped up, ran to the cave entrance, and spit it out down the hillside as Kor had done earlier in the day. This caused Kor to laugh hysterically, and that laugh was infectious. Most of the *chaga* joined her and Moke returned with a sheepish grin. Brella stabbed another potato and offered it to him with a grin. He shook his head and turned a little green. Kor also refused. She had spilled her stomach enough for one day.

The women threw some meat on the cooking stone and offered it to Moke and Kor which they accepted gratefully. They preferred their meat raw or cooked very rare but were not about to complain. Kor ate slowly, and not very much. She worried she might get sick again.

When people were finished eating, they loitered around the fire. There was some chatter but all eyes either stared openly at Moke and Kor or focused elsewhere but returned to them so often, they may as well have been staring. Moke felt a little uncomfortable. To distract them and himself, he felt for the bone flute tied around his neck. He often played to soothe his nerves. He drew it out, a little worried as he wasn't as good as the Wanderer, and he knew it. The chatter stopped and all eyes were on him. He took a big breath and blew the first haunting note. The eyes around him were wide with astonishment as he played, and nobody moved until the end of his song.

"More, More!" many of the *chaga* screamed. They also pounded the ground in appreciation. Moke couldn't understand the words of course, but he did understand their appreciation and he began to play again. When he stopped the second time, Bron approached. He was young and curious enough to overcome his fear and shyness.

"Can I try?" he asked. Moke raised his eyebrows in question. Bron pointed to the bone flute and then to his own mouth. Moke smiled. There were four holes in the flute, and it would make different sounds depending on the combination of holes that were covered. Moke quickly showed Bron the sound of the first hole covered versus the second. Bron nodded and Moke passed the flute to him.

Bron blew and the sound that came out was nothing like the sounds that Moke made and the *chaga* laughed good naturedly and covered their ears. Not to be deterred, he tried again, blowing a little less hard this time and met with success. He tried a few combinations and quickly realized that he would not learn to play this in an evening. With reluctance, he passed the flute back. Moke resolved to spend some time in the next day or two showing Bron how to play. Assuming he was allowed to stay.

Members of the *chaga* rose and sought out their sleeping places. As they passed Moke, they patted him on the shoulder. Moke relaxed a bit for the first time since his arrival. There was acceptance in those pats.

Moke lay back on his own resting spot. He smiled to himself. The flute had been such a success. He thought about his need for a mate and realized that this need that had consumed just a few months ago was still there, still strong, but it was no longer all important. He glanced over at Kor who was fast asleep already and then he looked around at the dim shapes in the cave. His sister's health, these new experiences, new friends, were far more important.

Guest Contributions

The strangers warm welcome was destined to be short lived. Sele, Flin, Olin and Grady returned the next morning and Sele was more filled with hate than when he left. He had been stewing in his resentment for the last couple of days. Impulsive and short tempered, he possessed enough wisdom, just, to hide his feelings from Triven when he returned. He bowed humbly to him. To Moke though, all the hatred he felt shone from his eyes, clear to read.

Sola, who was sitting beside Moke enjoying her breakfast had no trouble reading Sele's feelings either. She was overcome with feelings of protectiveness and foreboding. She looked at Moke and placed her hand in his. An instinctive gesture of protection.

Kor was still weak. She had a cough deep in her chest and she was slightly feverish. Although Moke felt that his welcome might be worn out, he was deeply reluctant to have Kor hike for any length of time. On impulse, he jumped to his feet and picked up his spear. He pointed outside and thrust with his spear and then he made his way out of the cave. He studied the view for a while before moving off.

Moke had seen nothing on the steppe, so he decided to hunt in the trees. The clans preferred the forest to hunt in anyway when they hunted alone. Prey could see them too easily on the steppe and it could be difficult to get close. This didn't stop them from trying when circumstances were in their favor, however. Perhaps, if he were lucky, he could find a deer. Or maybe some rabbits. He focused on the ground, looking for tracks in the scattered snow patches as he moved. Eventually, he found deer tracks and followed them.

Moke was concentrating so hard on the ground in front of him that he didn't hear the sounds behind him. The deer tracks were fresh which he knew because the tracks had not yet formed ice crystals. The deer was close, and it wasn't afraid which meant it hadn't sensed him. It was moving slowly and browsing as it went. To bring a deer as a guest contribution would do much to ease Moke's concern about their welcome. He was a lone hunter however, and he knew that bringing a deer down by himself might be difficult. He would have to be very quiet, and his spear would have to find something vital in the first thrust.

Moke was listening intently for the deer. He moved closer and he could hear when it nibbled a branch or took a step. With his ears so engaged, Moke finally noticed the small sounds behind him. A soft tread. He paused. A broken twig. He turned quickly, spear raised, frowning in concentration. He could see nothing. The hair on the back of his neck was raised now and adrenaline was pumping through his veins. Something was there. A cat? A bear? A bird? He didn't know and whatever it was, was quiet now. He turned his attention back to the deer. Or part of it. As he faced forward, he listened behind. He couldn't hear anything.

The deer was in sight now. Still too far for a clean thrust. He inched forward, his attention once again focused on what was in front of him, instead of behind. Another step. He raised his spear. One more step and he could thrust. Suddenly, there was a rush of sound behind him. Startled, the deer bolted. Moke turned quickly and saw the angry one, spear in hand. Triven, his hand on that one's shoulder and someone else next to Triven. Moke couldn't recall his name.

Moke had no idea why they were there. They looked tense. The angry one looked afraid and Triven was talking.

"You would murder a guest? A child?" Triven asked. Moke and Kor were shorter than the people of the *chaga* and so Triven thought him younger than he was.

Sele's eyes widened at that charge. To murder was taboo. To harm a guest was almost as bad. Causing the death of child was the worst of all. "I was going to help with the hunt," he protested.

"Then why were you behind him, spear raised?"

"I only came upon him while he was stalking. I knew if I alerted him to my presence or moved around, I would frighten the leaper." A response that was almost reasonable enough to be true. Triven and Privon shared a glance. Neither believed him.

"He is under my protection. Should harm come to him, I will hold you responsible."

"But he could fall or be kicked in the head by a leaper he's hunting or get ill!"

"You had better make sure none of that happens then." Triven turned from Sele and focused on Moke. "There is something better for us to hunt." He knew Moke wouldn't understand the words, so he pointed back the way they had come and gestured for him to follow.

Privon ran ahead and was gone from sight in a moment. The other three weaved their way through the trees at a more leisurely pace and eventually came to a stop. Triven and Sele sought out dry stones to sit on and Moke copied them. He had no idea what they were about. Would an animal come to them he wondered? If so, he knew nothing of that kind of animal. Triven and Sele weren't talking but neither were they quiet. They shuffled their feet, sighed, coughed, all noises that should be smothered while hunting. Moke shrugged his shoulders and waited.

Privon came running back about half an hour later, two torches in hand. He handed one to Triven and then started climbing the tree that Triven was leaning against. Moke watched intently. What was he doing? He climbed around thirty feet and then took the torch and placed it in a hole in the tree. After a moment, he took it out and slowly put his hand inside the hole. He drew out a chunk of something and tossed it down to those waiting below. Triven caught it and took a bite. He then passed it to Moke. Moke, the potato incident fresh in his mind, took a deep breath and wondered if he could just refuse. Triven was smiling though and making eating gestures so he knew he couldn't. He sniffed. The smell was like flowers but different. He had never smelled anything like it before. He took a tiny bite. His eyes rolled back in pleasure and surprise. He had never tasted anything so good. He took another bite, this time a large one and then he reluctantly passed it back to Triven. Triven laughed and motioned for him to finish it, which he did greedily.

Privon threw down two more pieces and then climbed down. Triven, who had guessed why Moke had left to hunt on his own, encouraged Moke to go up next. Moke had paid close attention to Privon and copied his actions to the point of putting his hand into the hole. Once up there, he recognized the bees and figured this was their hive. Beehives were things he usually avoided. He closed his eyes and put his hand in the hole. He felt around and latched onto a chunk of something that seemed to come away fairly easily. Gingerly he pulled and then tossed it below. They cheered him on and so he put his hand in again. Some of the bees were coming out of their stupor and he gave a loud wail when he got stung. He almost let go of the branch he was clinging to. He looked below and saw three laughing faces below. Privon waved his torch. Oh yes, he needed to put the torch in first. Quickly he raised it up. More bees were starting to waken and were buzzing around him. He got stung again, and then again but the torch worked, and they settled down. He took out a couple more honeycombs and when he looked below, he could see that the three had handfuls of honey each and so he started to climb down.

For the Love of Art

Sola set herself the task of guarding Kor while Moke was gone. Although Sele was not in the cave, who knew when he might return? She worried there might be others who felt like Sele but less vocal about it. The gatherers had all left for the day and it was quiet while Kor rested. Triven had taken Privon and gone hunting. She assumed he had gone in a different direction than Moke and Sele. She didn't normally care about these things and knew she was thinking about them because of her deep distrust of Sele and his ability to master his emotions. She sighed and decided she needed a distraction. Her eyes caught the pile of logs by the fire. A few of them had loose bark. She picked up two and with a stick, dug around the fire looking for some charcoal. When she found two good pieces, she returned to Kor and handed her a piece of bark and a piece of charcoal.

Kor willingly took what Sola offered but she was completely and utterly baffled as to what their purpose might be. She watched Sola with interest to see what came next.

Sola sat across from Kor and laughed at the frown of confusion on her face. Sola decided the best thing to do was show Kor her intention. Carefully, she drew an oval shape on the bark. And then she drew Kor's eyes, looking at the page and then Kor in deep concentration. She drew a nose and her mouth. Sola was a much better artist than Ponu, but her drawing was still somewhat crude. She did however capture the brooding brows and the jutting mouth reasonably well. It was very clear in the drawing that the features of the face were different than those of her own people. When she was finished, she turned the bark around and showed Kor.

Kor stared at the drawing in awe. She recognized that it was a drawing of one of her people. She thought maybe herself but wasn't sure. She had only glimpsed her reflection a handful of times in her life. Regardless of who it was, she was amazed. She stared at the drawing for a long time while her mind raced. Did the drawing hold a piece of her spirit? Was it too poor an image for that? Should she be scared? Should she be pleased? She needed Moke. She didn't know what to think. Kor plucked the drawing out of Sola's hands and rolled it up and stuffed it amongst the hides that made up her bed.

Sola tilted her head. It was clear that Kor wasn't happy with the image, but she didn't understand why. Was she unhappy with Sola's lack of skill? Or was it something else?

Kor looked down at the bark in her hand and the charcoal. Clumsily, she drew a line. And then another. She loved how the color appeared on the bark. She had no purpose to her actions as she experimented with the tool. When there was no more blank space on the bark, she stopped and looked up at Sola, aware of her for the first time since she started drawing. She looked back down at her efforts and saw a black mess. She looked up again at Sola and shrugged. Sola laughed and handed her another piece of bark.

Sola herself drew an image of a mammoth. She had only seen the beast that once, so she wasn't sure that her efforts captured it very well but when she showed it to Kor, Kor said, "woolly elephant," and smiled. Hmm, thought Sola, this image doesn't seem to bother her. Kor took the drawing from Sola and studied it intently. She noted the sure lines outlining the beast and the areas left blank. The next attempt she made with the charcoal, she tried to mimic those lines. Her picture was more a blob than a woolly elephant, but it was heaps better than her previous attempt, and she was pleased.

The women and children had been gathering all morning. They began returning in twos and threes as midday approached. They stored their treasures in the rear cave and returned to the fire for some rest and sustenance. Reta smiled at Sola and Kor as she passed them. Brella ignored them. The children sneaked shy glances at the pair and went to eat. Flin came in and stared at Sola for a long moment. She didn't smile or acknowledge Kor. Sola couldn't tell what she was thinking, and she was uncomfortable under her glare. *Chagama* nudged her aside and sat beside Sola. She had meat in her hands and gave some to both the girls. She had noticed that the guests didn't care for vegetables.

Sola was quiet as she ate. The women began to whisper and not all of them were nice. Although they whispered, they weren't really trying to hide their thoughts from Sola. "That girl is just not right," said Brella.

"You've been listening to Sele," accused Reta. Reta was kind-hearted and loyal to Sola. Sola had always helped her with Tram, and she felt a little sad about how neglected she was by Flin.

"Just look at her. She's been sickly since she got here. Laying around all day." This was from Flin. Sola snapped her head up and looked at her mother. Flin stared impassively back. Sola felt betrayed.

"All people get sick sometimes, and we don't know what happened to them before they got here. Something did though. They were starved and exhausted. That could make anyone sick. It doesn't make them wrong." This was from Maret, who was not the brightest among them, but it sounded so reasoned and sure and this itself captured everyone's attention.

Sola didn't know why she was so protective of the guests. Perhaps it's because it was she who found them. She looked over at *Chagama*, the *chaga's* voice of wisdom. But *Chagama* was frowning, deep in concentration. This worried Sola more than any of the comments made by some of the others. If *Chagama* was against their guests, Triven might be too. And if Triven was against them…

Chaga Talks

That evening, by the fire when all had eaten, there was tension among the people. Even Moke and Kor felt it and retreated to their borrowed pelts for respite from it.

"The *chaga* is divided. Some of you think the strangers are wrong or bad. Others think they are the same as us but just look a little different, sound a little different. Would you say this is a true thing?" Triven looked around. Heads nodded when his glance fell on them. "This is causing tension. Fights." Triven looked at Sele. Then Flin. Sola thought something must have happened with Flin that she knew nothing of. "Flin, what are your thoughts?"

Flin looked startled. She wasn't expecting to go first, and she felt unprepared.

"They bring sickness to us," she finally said.

"Kor has the heat!" protested Sola. "Everyone gets the heat sometimes! Besides. It's almost gone."

"Sola," admonished Triven. "You will have your say at the right moment."

Sola bowed her head.

Triven's gaze shifted right. Olin was seated next to Flin, and he asked him what he thought.

"I like the bird sounds they make," stated Olin and he lifted his hands to his mouth and mimicked playing the bone flute. Flin slapped his leg. She had been expecting his support of her view.

"They are like the wrong ones in Chagama's story. We shouldn't let them stay. They will infect us," said Ras. Triven's eyes narrowed as he looked at Ras in surprise. He was so vehement. Why? Triven frowned in thought. He was normally understanding of human nature and its vagaries, but he couldn't fathom this level of disgust.

"They are not true people," said Sele when it was his turn. Triven wondered where his hate came from. Even if they weren't true people, where was the harm they brought? And then Sele continued, "They will eat the twin horns we will hunt and the great horn we would spear. They will live in the caves our children would have. If they are here, there will not be enough for us."

The entire *chaga* was quiet as they digested these thoughts. They had headed north because there weren't enough resources to support them, and they were too small a *chaga* to fight for them. Was it true, that there was not enough if these strangers were here? The women, who had stayed reasonably close to the cave in the time they had been here, didn't know. There was certainly enough for them. But for their children? Reta shook her head at these thoughts. She was not used to thinking like this. Flin and Brella didn't even bother thinking about it. They just followed Sele's lead.

Triven asked each in turn and then finally Ponu.

"There are no other people here. At least none we have seen. If we do not accept them as people, we cannot stay. There will be no mates for Bron or Fabe. Or Sola, Alli or any other children. Are they people? I cannot say for certain. But they talk, they weep, they care for each other, they hunt, they sleep, they laugh. They do everything that I know people do. If that does not make them people, then what does? The shape of one's brow? Does that make you a person?" He glanced at Bron, who had fallen from a large rock when he was young. His brow was lightly indented still from the event. "If so, does that mean Bron is not a person? And if Bron is not a person, what do we do with him? Do we drive him from our home? Do we deny him pelts for warmth, meat for sustenance?"

Sola slipped her hand in Ponu's. He had lost his mother when he was born and was raised with Privon together by Flin. She had no idea where he got his wisdom. He certainly didn't share it with Privon who was much more the brawny hunter. Ponu had been a comfort to her as she grew, and she adored him.

"Abomination!" yelled Sele. "Bron and Alli will NOT be mating with those things!" He stood and stormed out of the cave. He didn't go far of course. It was dark and it was cold, so he only had the drama of the exit. But that spoke. He was second only to Triven. The only other mature male amongst them. If something happened to Triven, it was assumed that he would lead the *chaga*.

"Who sees merit in Ponu's words?" Asked Triven. He looked around the fire. Heads nodded or shook. Only Bron nodded in support where before he had shaken his head.

"It seems we are still divided." Triven sighed. "We will talk more tomorrow."

The following day was much the same as the one before. The women gathered. The young boys collected wood. The men hunted. Moke went with the hunters and Kor stayed with Sola. Sola though, was anxious throughout the day. Kor wanted to draw so Sola got her some bark but Sola herself didn't participate. When Kor wanted to exchange words, Sola just shook her head. She was worried about what would happen should the *chaga* decide that Kor and Moke weren't people. Would they stop feeding them? Would they kick them out? Or worse, would they kill them? She couldn't concentrate on anything.

Finally, evening came. The *chaga* ate and they sat by the fire expectantly. Triven didn't ask for everybody's thoughts. He asked if any had changed their minds from the day before, and then he asked who had anything new to add. He looked pointedly at *Chagama* who had so far kept silent.

Chagama just shook her head. She was having a crisis of her own. She had been casting around for stories in her mind. She had many, many stories to draw on but only one came to mind so far. It was a hideous story, and she could not bear to tell it and so she searched for others.

Sele cleared his throat and began to speak. "These strangers are not guests. We did not invite them here. They didn't even ask to stay, invited or not. This will be a lean year for us as we were so late finding our winter home. They should leave." Sele spoke quietly and with authority. The people of the *chaga* were more used to his angry outbursts and this gave them pause.

"His words are true," said Maret reluctantly. Sola gasped. Maret had been firmly in Moke and Kors corner only the day before.

Sola felt panic flare. "But what if this were me, in Moke and Kor's family cave?" she asked. People looked down or away but didn't answer.

"You would be lost to us, if they were like us," said Ponu finally. He was disappointed in his people's lack of charity.

"I will think on this. And wait for *Chagama's* wisdom".

The following morning Sola woke up and stared at the ceiling of the cave. It was quiet with the first grey light of morning just starting to filter into the cave. She lay for a while and then she got up and threw logs on the fire. There were embers from the night, and they would eventually catch fire. When she looked out, she could see frost. Soon, winter would be locked in, and their lives would be lived out in the confines of the cave and their immediate surroundings.

Moke joined her at the mouth of the cave and smiled at her before leaving to take care of business. When he returned, he took her hand and looked into her eyes. "Kor, Moke, *fila prent,*" he said. She didn't understand and she shook her head. He pointed at Kor, then himself and then outside the cave, and then he hugged her. She was so shocked she froze. Understand flooded her. He was saying goodbye. Sola felt the tears come and when Moke released her, he traced one down her cheek and gave her a sad smile.

Kor and Moke didn't have much to pack, and they were ready to go in minutes. Sola watched them leave from the mouth of the cave. Suddenly, Kor stopped and ran back up the path. She gave Sola a fierce hug and then ran back down again. Within minutes, the pair had disappeared in the trees.

Sola returned to her bed, tears streaming down her face. On her pelts, was a pair of boots. She picked them up and realized they were made from the mouflon pelt that Moke had brought with him. She took her old boots off and tried them on. The wool was softer than anything she had ever felt. It was like walking on thick mounds of fresh powdered snow only it was warm. No, it was better than that. It was like nothing she had ever worn before. A luxury completely unknown to her. She cried a little more as she realized just how great a gift this was. Moke still had holes in his own boots.

Triven was visibly relieved when he learned their guests were gone. *Chagama*, though, remained lost in the meanderings of her mind.

Winter Spa

It was only a week after Moke and Kor left that a big snowfall came. The blizzard raged for three days and the *chaga* huddled inside. Pelts that had been stockpiled were pulled out. Some were strung across the mouth of the cave, a barrier to the wind and snow. Others, the women began cutting and sewing for new clothes for their children, their mates and themselves. The hunters used the time to make spear heads, nets, and arrow points. The children were willing apprentices, given their own pelts to sew or rocks to hammer. They were also expected to keep the fire going and to fetch when asked. Life was simple though, and the duties light. But even with the drastic change in daily activity, by the end of the third day, everybody was feeling restless.

The sun shone bright on the morning of the fourth day. Sola looked out in wonder. Everything was a thick white and it sparkled and shone in ways she wasn't used to. They had come from the south and although they had seen snow, they had never seen snow like this. She was about to step out of the cave, when Triven pulled her back. He jabbed a pole into the snow, and it sank deeply. He pulled the pole out and showed Sola. Triven stepped out and stamped the snow down before repeating the process with his next step. Sele came up beside Sola and pushed her aside before stepping out to help Triven.

Later in the day, when the rest of the *chaga* came outside, Olin stepped off the path that Triven and Sele had made. He sunk and disappeared. Fortunately, Ponu saw him and called for help. He and Privon and Ras dug frantically for a couple of minutes before pulling out a frightened Olin. By the end of the day, the *chaga* understood that winter would be different here. They needed to learn a new caution. Triven understood more. This snow was earlier than they were used to. It was deeper too. Deep enough to hamper hunting, and he worried that if winter started early, it would also end late. They didn't have enough food for that.

Sola was particularly restless this year. After the excitement of their strange visitors, life seemed dull. And it was really. Even though they were in a cave far away from where they had spent any prior winter, life was pretty much the same. The women gossiped by the fire as they sewed clothes, or prepared food. The men lazed about, or fashioned tools or pulled their mate from the fire to do what mates do. The strangers though. They were fascinating. Different and intriguing. She thought about them often.

Bored, Sola descended the icy path of the cave and decided to explore. The snow was deep, and she didn't get far before tiring and returning to the cave. Her exertions at least meant she slept well. She did the same thing every day afterwards. It gave her relief from the tediousness of winter life and the endless squabbles that would only get worse as the winter progressed.

Her walks carried her farther and farther from the cave. Sometimes, she found some nuts that hadn't been picked, or a tasty variety of lichen and she put them in her bag to bring back with her. After two weeks of this, much to her surprise, she crossed a path that someone else had made. Both frightened and excited, she followed the trail, careful to be quiet and alert. Before long, she spotted smoke from a fire, and she slowed even more. Finally, she peered through the branches of trees surrounding a small campsite. The shelter was very foreign to her. The poles formed a high triangle instead of the round, squat shelter she was used to. It was covered in hides, as her peoples' shelters were and branches as well. Did that provide extra protection, she wondered?

Sola watched the site for at least an hour before she saw movement. Her heart raced in fear, and she thought herself a fool for not leaving earlier but then she recognized the gait of Moke as he dropped wood by the entrance to the shelter.

Sola was horrified. Was this how they were going to spend the winter? It was still early days of the season, and she knew the temperature would drop drastically in the coming weeks. And there would be wind. Wind that could knock that shelter down. Surely, they wouldn't survive. And what about food? They hadn't been gathering all fall like her *chaga*.

Sola stepped into the clearing and called a greeting. Moke turned and stared at her and then his face broke out in the wide smile that changed it from odd to inviting with its warmth and sincerity.

Kor, hearing them, came out of the shelter and threw herself into Sola's arms and then she pulled her into the shelter where Sola was pleasantly surprised. It was warm inside, and the tall shape meant she could stand, in the middle at least, and she found she could move comfortably. Although it was small and there wasn't much call for moving, she thought with almost everything in reach.

The three sat by the fire and Sola tried to understand why they were here and not back to their own home. Communication was always challenging but that was part of her fascination with them. Her brain was engaged, similar to how *Chagama's* stories engaged her mind, but more so and she loved it. So, it seemed, did Moke. His pleasure in her company was plain for any to see. Moke told her that he wasn't sure how far his home was. He had to make a shelter for the journey first. And they needed to hunt for hides and food. For now, they were using both branches and hides for their shelter but when it got colder, they needed to ensure they had enough hides to cover the whole thing and for blankets too.

Sola looked more closely at the shelter. There were only three hides covering it. She guessed they would need at least as many more. When she looked around, she saw that there was only one hide each for a blanket. Their clothes had been torn and needing replacement when the two had been at the cave. They weren't better now and should be replaced before trekking for who knows how long. Moke did, however, point out the location of the shelter. It was close to a steep mountainside that jutted out. It offered protection from winds from the north and from the west. The forest was on the other two sides and so they were reasonably protected. It wasn't a cave, but it was good. Even so, the pair were woefully unprepared for winter.

The three chatted for hours. Laughing at their frequent misunderstandings and mispronunciations. Finally, they tired of that, and sat quietly. A few minutes later, Moke jumped up and said some things to Kor. He grinned at Sola, waving at her to stay put while he and Kor disappeared outside the shelter.

Half an hour later, they returned with armloads of stones of all things. They dropped them in the shelter and then Kor started digging a hole in the ground while Moke disappeared again. He returned with an arm full of wood. They shifted the fire to the center of the shelter and built it up, so the flames were hot. Then they placed the rocks on top and waited for the embers to die down. Moke and Kor stripped off their clothes as the shelter got hot and Sola soon did the same.

This was the first time Sola had seen them naked and she took a good look, noting the differences between them and her own people. Moke was muscular. Far more muscular than any of the hunters in her *chaga*. She tilted her head and decided she liked the muscles. They looked good. Kor was muscular too, but still feminine Sola decided. She was still a child and so lacked curves, but her young body looked strong.

Moke and Kor examined Sola in turn. Skinny, they both thought. Moke loved the way her hips curved away from her small waist. Curves that had only recently come to her. It was very feminine, and something stirred in him. Too skinny though, he thought again and turned away. He didn't really care. He knew she had saved them, and the affection Kor and he felt for her was real and deep.

Soon, they were all too hot to care what they looked like. With a smile Moke pulled Sola to her feet and dragged her naked out into the cold. He collapsed into the snow and laughed at her shocked expression. Then he closed his eyes and let the coldness of the snow be felt over his too hot body. Intrigued by his obvious enjoyment, and then even more so by Kor's enthusiastic roll into the snow beside him, Sola lay down and gave it a try. It was heaven on her hot skin, and she shut her eyes too and relaxed. The moment didn't last very long before she was up and running for the shelter and heat. The other two followed her soon after. The embers had cooled a little and the three of them lay back on the pelts and slept.

Sola woke refreshed and warm in the morning. She stretched with utter contentment. She didn't know when she had felt this good. With the thoughtlessness of youth, she remained with her friends most of the day before heading home. When she got back to the cave, it was dusk and all her *chaga* were inside. The women were wailing and Ponu was dancing around the fire. Something was wrong.

"What's happened!" she cried. The *chaga* was silent as they stared at her.

Sola looked around and noticed wet tracks on a few faces. *Chagama*, Reta, Olin. Shock on others. Ponu and Triven both stared at her open mouthed.

"Do you have a message from the Earth Mother?" Ponu asked, his voice shaking. Sola just stared at him. What on earth did he mean? Why would she have a message from the Earth Mother. Only dead people talked to her. Or spiritual leaders, like Ponu. She frowned. She wasn't one of those and Ponu knew that.

"Can you not speak?" He shuffled around the pile of logs beside the cave entrance and pulled out a small piece of bark. "Perhaps you can draw it?" he asked as he extended his hand with the bark.

Sola shook her head. "Why are you asking me about messages from the Earth Mother?" she finally said.

"Because you are returned from her!" replied Ponu.

"Don't be daft. She's fine." *Chagama* pushed Ponu aside and hugged Sola." Where have you been girl? We thought you had gone home to the Earth Mother."

"OHHHH!" Sola almost laughed but caught herself just in time. The faces around her were grim and she thought a laugh just might make them grimmer. She explained where she had been.

"Moke and Kor don't have enough resources to find their home and the winter is too deep to risk travelling. We should invite them back here," pleaded Sola.

"NO," responded Sele before she had even finished talking. "We've had talks and agreed they needed to go."

Sola was quiet for a moment as she digested his words. Moke and Kor had left before any agreement was made. "No, we had no agreement. They left first."

Triven looked at her sadly. "If they ask for shelter, we will continue our *chaga* talks. They haven't," Triven paused, "and I don't think they will."

Sola thought Triven's argument was silly. "They left because we were all fighting about them, and they didn't feel welcome! Of course, they won't ask!" She turned to Sele, "May the frog on your face ribbit loudly and long!" She retreated to her bed pelts and ignored her people.

"What does she mean by frogs?" asked Sele. He hadn't heard the story. Others had. Those that agreed with Sola just glared at him. None explained. Reta said "Ribbit," and turned her face away.

New Blood

Sola was worried about her friends. She knew they didn't have enough pelts or food. They probably didn't even have enough spears she thought as she recalled the one that Moke had made when he had first arrived. Sola resolved to help them. That evening, when the women brought out the cooking stone, Sola offered to fetch the meat from the store at the back of the cave.

When she went down the passage, she reached in and took enough meat for the *chaga's* meal. She looked around, and then took some more. She made her way to the tiny room where the bags were kept and slipped some meat into a small one.

"What are you doing?"

Sola spun, surprised, and found Alli in the passage behind her. She flushed but lifted her chin, deciding to brazen it out. She gave Alli a look that said, 'what a dumb question' and then replied, "I'm getting meat." She brushed past Alli and into the main chamber where she handed the meat to Reta to heat.

Sola fretted about what Alli had seen all night and the next day as well. Taking more than your share was a grave crime in a *chaga*. They relied on each other for everything and trust, not a natural state for people, was absolutely essential for a *chaga* to function. If people thought Sola was stealing, the punishment would be grave. That she wasn't taking it for herself probably wouldn't matter given how most felt about Moke and Kor. And yet, she couldn't *not* take the meat. Her friends needed it.

The following morning, Sola got up early, retrieved the meat and left as quietly as possible. She didn't see Alli watching her go but that wouldn't have stopped her anyway. Moke and Kor weren't around when she got to their camp, so she left the meat inside their shelter and went back to her cave. They would find it and be grateful, she was sure. Despite the fear and guilt over taking the meat, Sola felt better for having done so. Their need was greater when held up against her guilt.

"We women need the fire tonight," stated *Chagama*. The men stared at her, nonplussed. "Shoo," she said, "and take the children." It was winter, and dark and they lived in a four-room cave with only one room large enough to hold them. A room they were already in. Triven and Sele exchanged glances. Where exactly were they supposed to take the children? And what would they do with them once they got there? *Chagama* harumphed. "Tell them a story."

Sola had never participated in the 'woman's dance' before because, of course, until today, she hadn't been a woman. She'd heard parts of it and glimpsed others, but she was surprised at how new everything seemed. *Chagama* started by pounding a rhythm on the cave floor with a walking stick. The beat was steady and slow, like a heartbeat. "Thump-thum, Thump-thum," it went. She was the only woman standing. The others sat around the fire and when *Chagama* nodded to each in turn, they joined in with their own pounding of the ground, mirroring her beat. *Chagama's* glance landed on Sola last and when it did, the beat picked up just a bit. Sola sat down and joined in. She found her heart raced ahead with *Chagama's* faster beat and it was a little unsettling. *Chagama* got to her feet and began to circle the women sitting on the ground. She paused behind Maret and tapped her with her stick. Maret rose and continued pounding, this time with her feet. When all were standing but Sola, the beat paused. The women all looked at her and Sola slowly got to her feet. *Chagama* started the beat again, faster than before and Sola's heart raced along with it. The women moved now, swaying in their own versions of the ancient woman's dance. They didn't appear to be following any pattern but always, their feet maintained the beat.

Sola found herself lost in the dance. There was nothing but her heartbeat and the fire. The other women receded, and she moved to both in a primal dance. Hands reached for her, but she was oblivious. She circled the fire and felt the beat.

When the beat stopped, Sola kept going for a moment and then she paused, disoriented. She looked up and the women were all around her. Her and the fire. She was naked and she didn't know how she had gotten that way. Just as she was starting to panic, *Chagama* smiled gently at her, and Sola relaxed. Reta and Maret came forward with a bladder of warmed water. They washed Sola from head to toe.

Chagama handed them a leather belt. Each woman had one of these. It was made of thin strips of tanned leather, three, four or five pieces across, braided together to provide strength. Year after year, new pieces would be tied to it. Rope was handy for more than just monthly courses and these belts were a prize possession. Mothers traditionally started a new one for their daughters when they were born and added to them every year until they became women. This one though, this one was *Chagama's* belt, and it was the longest rope Sola had ever seen. "I have no need of it anymore," was all *Chagama* said. Sola glanced briefly at Flin, who looked away. Flin didn't have one for Sola.

Maret and Reta wrapped the belt around Sola expertly. It went around her hips and between her legs before winding back up to her waist. Between the two pieces that sat between her legs, they placed a small rectangle piece of hide. On the hide, they stuffed moss to absorb her flow.

Chagama came forward and rubbed her thumbs across her belly and both her breasts. She left black streaks behind, and Sola realized she must have put charcoal from the fire on her thumbs. "You're a woman now Sola. And we welcome you to us in your new form."

The women cheered and handed Sola back her clothes. Once she was dressed, each woman hugged her. Even Flin gave her what resembled a hug in motion if not in feeling. Ceremony and stiffness seemed to melt away, and then the women sat around the fire, far more relaxed. Sola followed their lead. The rest of the evening was spent telling tales that only pertained to women. Childbirth, mating, periods, loss, and joy. Sola felt as though she had joined a club. One whose very existence she hadn't known about despite living with it her entire life.

Old Grudge

Alli waited until the day after Sola's celebration. Sola would wonder in later times if she waited deliberately. Did she want Sola to be a woman before she accused her? So that the punishment would be harsher? And then she would push that thought aside. It was too painful, and it no longer mattered.

Chagama stared at Sola open mouthed when Alli accused her. Sola felt all the women's eyes on her. The children's too.

"I just took a little!" protested Sola.

Chagama shook her head. "Save it until the hunters are back," was all she said with a great deal of sadness.

"Sola. Did you take meat from the store that was beyond your portion?" asked Triven solemnly that evening after they had eaten.

Sola stared at him, wide-eyed. She had known the question was going to come and that she would have to answer it. She hadn't known how paralyzed with fear she would be when he said the words. She was trembling she realized. She forced herself to nod. She'd thought about lying but she believed so completely that she'd done the right thing that lying about it seemed more an admission of guilt than admitting to it.

Triven nodded and paused a long while before continuing. "Did you know that the meat you took was beyond your portion?" Again, Sola nodded.

The entire *chaga* sat around the fire. All were quiet, even the children. It was a serious matter before them.

Chagama still had not told a story since the strangers came and the *chaga* fought about them. She didn't tell one now either. Others did though.

Reta spoke the story of Tram. The very story that Sola had told all those months ago after he died. When she was done, she looked at Sola with tears in her eyes, "I carry another child. Would you see it go to the Earth Mother as well?" Sola's stomach roiled with guilt. She hadn't thought!

Sele told a terrible story of a hunter in a *chaga* who stayed hale and hearty while the others grew thin. When the food was all gone, the *chaga* accused the hunter of stealing food and then they killed him and ate him. Sola had never heard that story, and judging by the gasps from the others, they hadn't either.

"The punishment for a gatherer or hunter who steals food from their *chaga* is they are forbidden to share in the *chaga's* food. They can stay if they want, but they can never share in the twin horn the *chaga* catches, or the potatoes the gatherers find." Sola was horrified at Triven's words. Would she forever more be forbidden to share with the *chaga*? If he pronounced this judgement, she would be lost.

"I have a story," she said. Triven paused and then nodded his head.

This story may have happened to someone, sometime. People groaned at these words, but Triven shushed them.

A stranger came to visit one day at the end of winter. The chaga turned him away, offering neither food nor shelter. One young girl of the chaga thought that a frog might come to live on the chiefs' face, but alas, that did not happen.

Spring came shortly after the strangers visit and the chaga left their cave in order to hunt twin horns on the vast grasslands where they came every spring. As they walked towards the grasslands, the chaga chanced upon the stranger they had turned away a short time ago. The strangers' hands were blackened and sickly smelling as were his toes. He had not had shelter in the last days of winter and the ice spirits had gnawed upon them. The stranger leaned against tree. He was so thin the outlines of his bones could be seen beneath his skin. No flesh remained. He lacked the strength to walk on and besides, each step was an agony.

The chaga stopped and looked at him in horror. "Would you like some meat?" *they offered. The stranger didn't deign to respond.* "Some water?" *they asked. The stranger ignored them.*

The chaga made to move on, and the stranger whispered, "Please, send me to the Earth Mother. Every moment is agony. It would be a kindness."

The chaga denied him this final kindness for the Earth Mother despised it when messengers came without being bidden.

No matter. The stranger did not have many breaths left in any case thought the chaga and they moved on.

The chaga were correct and the stranger went to the Earth Mother that evening. He feasted at her table, and she cured his ailments, but she grew thunderous when she heard his tale.

The Earth Mother called to the sky spirits, and they created a mighty storm that chased the herds away. The chaga went hungry.

The Earth Mother called up the Sun spirit and she dried the rivers and the streams. The chaga were thirsty.

Finally, the Earth Mother shook with fury. The ground rumbled and roared and buried the chaga alive. When they arrived at the Earth Mother's table, she denied them her feast and the chaga were made to watch as the stranger dined on the finest of her offerings.

For such is the anger of the Earth Mother when those in need are denied sustenance.

"That is not a true story," scoffed Alli. Flin nodded and so did a few of the others.

"It's a good story though," said Reta. The Earth Mother had been known to unleash her fury when *chaga's* disobey her laws. *Chagama* had many stories of that.

"They are not people and the Earth Mother's laws do not apply," said Sele firmly.

Chagama's face turned to thunder at that. "ALL creatures belong to the Earth Mother! And She will punish any who are needlessly cruel. We do not deny a beast water before we kill it or keep them in agony. Always, our laws say that we should take what we need with as little suffering as possible." *Chagama* stood and looked at the people she loved more than anything in the world. She didn't feel love at that moment. "I don't know whether those strangers are people or not, but Sola believes they are, and she acted in a way consistent with that. And," *Chagama* glared at Alli, "the crime took place while Sola was a child still. It is only the accusation that comes while she is an adult. Why is that Alli?" Alli stammered and *Chagama* shook her head in disgust. "Never mind." *Chagama* turned to Sola now. "Go to your bed. You will not have food come the morning."

Chagama turned back to the *chaga*. "It is a cruel thing you contemplated doing to that girl. I am deeply ashamed of all of you. I don't like any of you very much right now. And you Alli. You, I don't care for at all."

Now *Chagama* didn't have the power to pronounce judgement. That power belonged to the group. None were inclined to overrule her and indeed, many felt as ashamed as she had meant them to.

Long Winter

The winter days dragged on. Those who kept an eye on the food stores, worried. Those who didn't, spent their days with lazy carelessness. The children had learned that the path down the hill was a joy when it was slippery and would spend hours climbing up and sliding down. It got so slippery that Triven and Privon spent quite a few hours chopping steps into the side of their hill. This was a mixed blessing. The children were not happy about it and therefore nobody else was either. Olin got quite a few knocks to the side of his head before changing from a rampaging beast to something resembling a human child.

Normally, *Chagama* told stories in winter, more stories than any other time. She hadn't told a story since Moke and Kor left. She was often quiet and difficult to engage. Sola worried about her. Brought her food and water. She asked her questions and *Chagama* always responded but only just. Answers were yes and no if she could get away with that. A phrase or a sentence if she couldn't. Often her responses were difficult to understand. "Will winter be longer here?" Sola asked. "Winter will last as long as winter does," was *Chagama's* response. Sola was often tempted to give up on her and then she would remember how much she loved her.

The winter went on relentlessly. The *chaga* agreed it was time to ration. The children played less, and people lost weight. Flin lost the baby she was carrying. And then Reta started to spot. Sola was worried they would blame her but even she knew the small amount of meat she'd given to Moke and Kor wouldn't save these babe's. Something more was needed.

Triven, after much thought came to a decision. In the evening as they sat by the fire, he laid out a plan to hunt on sunny days through the rest of the winter. Hunting in winter was something they rarely did. It took some convincing. The deep snow worried the other hunters and they felt out of their element. The herds had long since moved south. Although they had hunted in forests, it wasn't their strength. This combined with the snow had them worried. Wouldn't it just make them hungrier? All that effort. And how much success could they expect? In the end, the hunters agreed that they would try.

Moke and Kor were not experts at hunting in the winter either, but they weren't without experience. The clans spent a great deal of time sleeping in the cold months. A great deal of time. Days would go by when a person would get up to relieve themselves, have a nibble of something and fall right back to sleep. As Moke and Kor had nothing to nibble on, hunting was a necessity. Moke scanned the sky. He could see no sign of a snowstorm and when he sniffed, the air smelled of pine and stale urine. His eyes turned to the south, where Sola would come from were she to visit. She came rarely, knowing, without him telling her, that too many visits would be a burden on their resources. The visits sustained them in a different way. It gave them heart and hope and strength. Moke wasn't used to being the adult and when she came, he relaxed. It was good for him, and it made Kor happy in a way he didn't. He would gladly have put off hunting for a visit. There was no sign of her though and if she were to come, she would be here by now. He rolled up some pelts and Kor tied them to his back. He tied some to hers as well.

They had travelled for the morning and into the afternoon when Moke spotted movement. He stopped to watch and then realized it was the hunters from Sola's clan. Or *chaga* as she called it.

The hunters moved clumsily through the snow. As Moke watched, he saw one slip and another step into a deep bank and sink to his hips. His companions struggled to get him out and Moke realized they were exhausted. They sank into the snow after their struggle, which would only make them wet, and then cold and then more tired as their bodies used their energy to keep warm. Moke shook his head at their incompetence.

Moke changed direction so that his path would meet theirs. Kor followed. The hunters arrayed themselves in a line when they noticed them coming. Triven, Ponu, and Privon relaxed when they recognized Moke. Ras and Sele's posture were alert but not threatening.

"Good Morning!" Moke called the greeting Sola had taught him. As she always arrived in the morning, Moke had no cause to know that the greeting should change once the sun was high in the sky.

Triven chuckled before replying "Good afternoon, Moke." Moke heard the new words but decided to ignore them for now.

Ponu was shivering as they stood together, and they all looked lean and tired. Grateful for the shelter he had been given, Moke was eager to repay the debt. Moke pointed to a dead and leaning tree. He started to push it over. It was still far too rooted for him to succeed on his own. He looked behind him and Triven, and Ponu were quick to start helping him. When Sele, Privon and Ras added their strength, the tree fell over. Using his feet, Moke cleared a relatively snow free spot under another large tree and then broke some of the smaller branches off the dead one. The others got the idea and helped. Before long, they had a large fire going and the group huddled around it.

After resting for a while by the fire, the shivering subsided. Dusk was coming and Triven rose and started building a shelter around them. The hunters had brought proper shelter poles and hides and there was just enough room to include Moke and Kor.

Moke was the first one awake in the morning. It was still dark, and it was only his finely tuned internal clock that told him morning was approaching. There was a reason he had gotten up so early. He knew what the deer would do in this deep snow, and he wanted to teach Triven's clan. He warmed himself at the fire and when the first rays of the sun reached him, he shook Triven awake.

With a motion to be quiet, he encouraged Triven to follow him. He walked first, using his spears to pick his path. When Triven started to walk beside him, he shook his head and motioned to the trampled snow behind. Quietly they moved through the trees until they reached the edge of the forest. Moke looked out on the steppe, barely visible in the predawn light and led Triven south a few feet. He paused be a large tree and motioned Triven to wait. Then he moved to another tree a few feet away. They stood quietly as the sun inched over the horizon, giving the grey dawn a pale-yellow cast. Their patience paid off. A deer came to the edge of the forest, eyeing a patch of grass protruding from the heavy snow on the steppe. Triven raised his bow and notched an arrow. He looked over at Moke. Moke shook his head. The deer was too far. It was too far for spears. He had never seen a bow and arrow before and had no idea what it could do. Triven could easily have made the shot, but he waited respectfully as Moke had asked. Another deer came. Again, Moke shook his head. Two more came and still Moke said no. Finally, a deer came and Triven froze in place. It was mere feet from him. Moke grinned and nodded. Triven wasted no time and loosed his arrow into the flank of the deer while Moke closed the distance and thrust his spear a moment later.

Triven thrilled at a successful kill. He hooted to the sky and danced around the deer. Moke laughed at him. Triven took no offense. He recognized the gift the young man had given him. Not only was there fresh meat, Triven had learned something about the habits of deer in this new environment. Impulsively, he drew Moke into a big bear hug. Any debate about Moke's status as a person was forever laid to rest in Triven's eyes.

Moke finally gave in to his curiosity. He asked Triven to look at the bow and Triven handed it over to him. He gave him an arrow as well. He showed Moke how to pull the string back and place the arrow in the notched space. Moke did as shown and loosed his arrow. It flopped to the ground, and it was Triven's turn to howl with laughter. Moke looked down in disappointment and then laughed as well. This morning was too good not to.

Moke and Triven carried the deer back to camp. The others were still sleeping, the sun not quite over the horizon yet. Triven made a lot of noise when he dropped the deer by the fire and that woke them. Delighted at the fresh kill, the hunters set to work processing it.

With Triven's consent, Moke showed Kor the bow and an arrow. All morning, they notched the arrow and it fell to the ground. Moke had one go a few feet but that was the limit of their success.

Triven, glanced at Moke once in a while and chuckled. It took practise to use the weapon and the pair were holding their arms wrong. Once the deer was gutted, he rose and joined them. He took the bow and stood, with the arrow notched for long minutes while Kor and Moke studied his posture and the position of the arrow. And then he loosed the arrow. It travelled far and both the strangers stared open mouthed. Moke had seen Triven use it earlier, but the deer had been close. Moke stumbled through the snow after the arrow to see just how far it had gone. It was so deeply embedded in a tree that it broke when he tried to retrieve it. This was a wonderful tool!

The hunters ate almost the entire deer in that one day. Everybody had been hungry, and they gorged themselves. Moke played his flute as the others lay back and enjoyed the feeling of being full. The hostility that had often radiated from some of the *chaga* hunters seemed at rest. At least for the moment. They camped another night and the following morning, all of them went to the edge of the forest. Four deer were taken that day. The hunting so easy with the bows and arrows. Moke and Kor took one deer back to their camp as well as a deep longing to create and master the tool they had witnessed.

Frozen Elk

Sola's heart had soared with pride when she heard that Moke had helped Triven hunt the deer. Her stomach had soared too. And the water in her mouth had flooded it. It had been months since she had fresh meat and although the deer was lean and old and stringy it was delicious.

The hunters were out again. Moke's hunting method had seemed easy to Triven at the time, but he had since learned how much luck had played a role. He and the others had gone out every day since Moke had helped them two weeks ago but had only managed to catch a deer once. It helped but it still wasn't enough. The people of the *chaga* were in real danger of starvation and winter showed no signs of abating.

Boredom and longing finally got the better of Sola. She filled her pockets with a handful of nuts, a portion appropriate for herself, and resolved not to eat a morsel of their food. She started the long trek to Moke and Kor's camp. Just before she reached their camp, she paused to pull some lichen from a tree and took a small taste. It was a bitter variety and her face scrunched up in distaste.

A laugh startled her, and she dropped the rest of the lichen. Moke and Kor were standing a few feet away. Both were having a good laugh at her expense. She didn't care. Her smile widened as she went to greet them. When she reached Moke, she threw her arms around him and hugged him tight, and then the same for Kor. It had been weeks since she'd seen them, and she was relieved to find them healthy.

"I missed you." She said and found those words were true. Moke radiated good humor and kindness and she really liked him. The business of living was often tedious and lonely, even living amongst so many and she didn't feel any of that when she spent time with him.

Moke stepped back and took her in. She was skinny, he thought. No wonder she was eating trees. Kor and he had noticed jackal tracks weaving through the trees. There was nothing particularly odd about that except that the tracks showed the animals going back and forth in the same direction every day. That meant a meal. Probably a big one. He motioned for Sola to come and the three followed the tracks.

Moke, Kor, and Sola followed the tracks for at least an hour, maybe longer. They heard the animals before they saw them. Yipping and growling would burst forth from the forest and then quiet down. Moke slowed as they got nearer. If the pack was very large, they could be dangerous. Jackals normally fled from people, but a large pack could do damage if it wanted and warranted respect. They peered through the trees, and finally, they saw the pack. There were only a handful of animals. Eight in fact, but neither Sola nor Moke could provide such an exact number. They only knew that eight weren't a danger to them if they were loud and confident.

Still. Moke waited. If these tracks had drawn humans, they might also draw other animals. Whatever the jackals were eating didn't seem to give off a smell and the animals were struggling to get a bite. Finally, Moke deemed it safe enough to approach. He started with a "Yip, Yip, Yip," yelled loud enough to startle Sola. Two of the jackals jumped in fear and tore off through the trees. One gave them a long look before running after his companions and the rest followed suit.

Moke, Kor, and Sola approached cautiously. A large elk lay mostly buried in the snow. It was frozen solid which explained why it gave off only a slight smell and why the jackals struggled so hard. Moke looked at Sola and gave her a jaunty grin. An Elk this size would feed the *chaga* for days. He looked around for deadwood and spotted a likely tree nearby. It was huge and too much for the three of them. He would have liked to light a fire to start the thawing process. The elk was too frozen for his tools. The jackals had been coming for days as far as he could tell and still only managed the most meager of meals.

The three headed back to Sola's cave. She went directly to the small cave and bent down and began throwing bags out to carry the meat in.

"We found a frozen Elk. It's HUGE. We'll need some help carving it up and bringing it back. Bron and Fabe, would you be willing to carry wood out and help us?" She asked, tossing the words over her shoulder as she rifled through the bags.

"I want to come too!" cried Olin. Cark and Dell, chimed in as well. As young girls, they wouldn't normally participate in this type of work, but the long winter boredom was getting to them too.

Sola shrugged and glanced at their mothers. They nodded and the girls started screaming in delight. Sola rolled her eyes and almost regretting agreeing but they were so infectious she couldn't help but laugh at them.

"Alli?" she asked. Alli shook her head no. She agreed with Sele. These strangers weren't real people, and they made her uncomfortable. Sola was relieved. She found that she barely tolerated Alli these days. Alli, for her part, didn't understand how Sola spent so much time with the strangers. She shuddered at the thought.

Bron and Fabe loaded up a large amount of firewood. They could take down the deadwood tree when they got there but would need something to get the fire going. When Olin started to load up, Flin just said "No." Olin glared at her and would have protested but her face was like ice. He found himself afraid of her and went to sit by *Chagama*.

Reta and Brella declined the adventure. Sola was sure it was because they were looking forward to a break from their bored children.

Sola gathered up shelter poles and handed shelter hides to the girls to carry and then they were off. Moke was amazed at the speed in which Sola's clan organized themselves. It would take at least a day, probably two for his own clan to get ready for something like this. And it wasn't because they had more to pack. They just got distracted so easily and, in the winter, especially, they liked to lounge.

The jackals had returned to the elk by the time they got back, and they weren't too happy to be chased away. One charged at Cark and two more at Dell. They were small and the jackals were not afraid of them at all. Sola cautioned them to stay close at all times. Cark and Dell clung to Sola while the rest got the fire going.

Sola picked up a burning branch and waved it at the jackals who were hovering mere feet from them. They yipped and ran away.

"Stay close to the fire and be ready with a stick and they won't bother you anymore," she said to the girls. They nodded in understanding.

From the trees, came growls and yips from the jackals who had fled there. Sola thought they might be fighting amongst themselves or may have stumbled across prey, and then a piercing wail filled the air. It sounded human. The entire group of them froze in horror. Sola reached into the fire for the stick she had just placed back in and ran towards the sound. Moke and Kor followed her. Bron stayed with the young ones and Fabe trailed behind.

The jackals were easy to find. Their yipping constant. It was hard to see what had them excited but it was easy enough to hear. Olin was screaming in terror and pain. Sola ran forward, the jackals so intent on Olin, they didn't see her. She seared one who yipped and ran, and then she could see. Olin was struggling to stay standing. To fall was certain death. The jackals would fall on him all as one and rip him to pieces. One jackal had hold of his leg and was tugging. Another his arm. Sola swung in a wide arc at the one attacking his leg and struck it on the side of his head with all the force she possessed. She heard a crack and was sure she had broken something. "Grey Horn turd!" she yelled as she swung again. The animal let go and staggered away, whimpering. Unfortunately, this caused Olin to lose his balance and the remaining jackals rushed him, too filled with blood lust for caution. "Vulture supper!" Sola shouted as she swung again and again. Moke caught her arm. She had been about to hit him in the face. Kor hit an animal and so did Fabe. The jackals ran and didn't stop for miles, wounded, bleeding and defeated.

Sola dropped to the ground beside Olin. She couldn't imagine how he would survive. She examined his leg. The hide pants he wore were thick and difficult to pull up or down.

"He just bit the pants," said Olin, while she struggled. Sola found the spot. The pants were torn but apparently Olin wasn't.

"What about your arm?"

Olin, with Sola's help pulled his wrap off. His arm had shallow teeth marks. Again, the hide was thick and difficult for the small jackals to pierce. Sola hugged him, tears starting at her eyes. He was fine. Then she yelled at him. For a long time.

It would take a couple of days to thaw and cut the meat. Moke helped them setup their shelter. They had taken one of the larger ones and all would fit inside but it would be cozy.

It was cold but the work was easy once the fire was going and offered delicious snacking while doing it. With a large fire roared beside them, their bellies full and not an adult in sight, the children were happier than they had been in days. It was like a celebration to them.

"Music," was a word that was the same in both languages, having been taught to the *chaga* by Moke on his last visit. Olin started the request and Bron was quick to join him and soon all the children were saying the word.

Moke was happy to oblige and treated them all to a long, mournful tune. He followed this with a happy one and Olin and Bron danced to it. When he finished, Bron brought out a bone flute of his own. He handed it to Moke who examined it closely and shook his head. When he played the flute, the sounds were ugly and disjointed. He patted the spot beside him, indicating to Bron that he should sit and then he held the two flutes side by side. The holes in Bron's flute were not equally spaced and so the sounds were unpleasant when played one after the other. Moke also thought the bone he had used was too large, although that was a matter of personal preference. When he placed his finger inside the flute, the surface was uneven, and this would distort the sounds. Fashioning a good bone flute took time and patience. Moke showed Bron the differences between the two flutes, emphasizing the space between the holes. He pointed to the distance on Bron's and shook his head and then pointed to the holes on his own. He wasn't sure but he thought Bron understood. Then, he took Bron's finger and placed it inside his own flute and then Bron's. Bron nodded. He didn't know how he would make the inside of his flute smooth, but he would figure something out. The music spoke to his very soul. He thought maybe even the Earth Mother could hear it. And if not her, then the sky spirits. It could only bring good fortune to the *chaga* he was certain.

Spring at Last

Although Sola coped with the remaining days of winter, the younger ones increasingly did not. They fought, they cried, they refused to eat and yet begged for fresh food. Normally *Chagama* would tell stories that would provide momentary relief, but she had yet to break her silence on that front. Sola glanced up one afternoon while Olin was tossing pebbles at Grady who was gearing up for an almighty temper tantrum.

Sola cleared her throat and said "Come." She pounded the ground, like *Chagama* used to do at story time and then she waited. She didn't have to wait long. Grady plopped in her lap and Olin sat as close to her as he could. The other children sat around and even Reta joined. Ponu listened from afar.

There was once was a large gaggle of geese that lived close to my mother's father's father's chaga's spring camp. The camp was on the edge of the steppe with a large marshy lake close by. It was a good spring camp as the herds would come to graze and then to drink and the hunters had an easy time of it. My mother's father's father liked to observe the gaggle's behavior. At first, the geese paired up. Then they built nests and filled those nests with eggs. My mother's father's father's chaga feasted on eggs that spring. Goose eggs are delicious.

"What do they taste like?" asked Olin, his eyes round with wonder. Olin could never listen to a story without interrupting. Sola smiled down at him.

"They taste like duck eggs, only sweeter." It had been a long time since Olin had duck eggs and he couldn't remember what they tasted like either, but he thought better of asking.

There was one family of geese in particular that my mother's father's father liked to watch. Probably as it was closest to his observation point and my mother's father's father was just a little lazy when he was young. The goose family had plenty of goslings that year. The first to hatch was the biggest and he was a bit of a bully. While the goslings were little, they stayed close to their mom and dad and the big gosling only bothered his siblings. He would nip at them when their parent's brought food. Most goslings do this, but he did it even when he was full. When they were walking to the lake, he would pull the feathers out of his sibling's rumps. His mother and father honked at him when they saw his behavior, but the discipline had no affect. Pretty soon the goslings were practising flying. Even though the big gosling had plenty to do, he still harassed his siblings. Not content with that, he started harassing other goslings too. And then he started bothering the smaller geese. Everywhere he went there was havoc and he delighted in it. His parents did not. Nor did his siblings. Or the gaggle.

One morning, this big gosling, swam out to the middle of the lake. When he tried to return, a goose faced him and ferociously pecked at him. He moved on and attempted another entry point. The same thing happened. Everywhere he went, he was faced with pecking beaks and fierce honks. He started to honk. His parents would recognize his call he thought and come rescue him. He honked for the remainder of the day and into the night. His parents didn't come.

After a restless sleep, he tried again. This time, the geese were not content to just peck at him. They chased him viciously. They bit him and pecked him and didn't relent until he was far from the gaggle.

The gosling spent the rest of the spring and summer swimming alone, far from the gaggle. Once in a while, he would try to return but the gaggle would not give way. He was not welcome.

My mother's father's father's chaga moved on to their summer hunting grounds and so did not see what happened next, but in the fall, on their way to the winter camp, they passed that way again. They setup shelters for a night as they still had far to go.

That night, the first ice came. In the morning, my mother's father's father saw the big goose on the lake. He was frozen in place. My mother's father's father went down to the lake and set to freeing the gosling who by this time was full grown. He pounded the ice with his spear and soon the bird was free. My mother's father's father picked up the goose and looked into its eyes. Did he see humbleness there? Regret? Shame?

None of the children answered Sola's question. How could they? Of course, Olin had one of his own. "What happened to the goose?"

"My mother's father's father cooked it for breakfast I expect," answered Sola. "Is that not what you would do with a found goose?" And then she rubbed his head.

Olin was thoughtful after that story, and it was quite a few days before the effect wore off for which everyone in the entire *chaga* was grateful.

Moke watched the sky from his shelter by the cliffs. It was clear. This would be the day then. With some sadness and some eagerness, he turned to Kor. "Time to go," was all he said before he started rolling pelts.

He had been putting their departure off, hoping to say goodbye to Sola. She hadn't come since the elk. Winter was loosening its grip and they needed to find their home before the clan moved on. Otherwise, he and Kor would have a difficult spring trying to catch up with them. An hour later, the pair were packed and ready to go. With one last long look south, they turned their backs and began the trek north.

Sola was finally able to get away. Increasingly, she had been expected to keep the children busy but today, Reta had sent her out before the other women stirred and Sola was quick to take advantage. With a hug and smile she was off.

When she got to Moke and Kor's camp, all that greeted her was silence. The ground was bare of snow where their shelter had been. The fire site blackened and cold. Some discarded pieces of pelt and a few bones were all that was left.

She turned away with a shock of loneliness and disappointment so deep she would have been loathe to talk about it. She realized how much the pair had come to mean to her and she cried as she contemplated the idea that she might never see them again. They were as her own family. Only a little different. A little kinder to her. A little more accepting.

She didn't return to the cave until dusk. When she got there, she silently helped herself to some food and lay in her pelts.

"Sola," called Reta quietly. Sola pretended not to hear. She couldn't bear to talk to anyone just yet.

The Herds

The gallopers came through first. Tiny green shoots of spring grass drew them and kept them there for a short time. With stealth and skill, the hunters descended from the cave and walked the short distance through the forest to the edge of the steppe. They all shook their heads as they looked at each other. These weren't the horses that had guided them through the mountains. This stallion had spots instead of stripes. There was no dark colored mare, and the horses were fewer although they couldn't say by how much. They would not touch the horses that led them to their new home but these, if they could catch one, would be good eating.

The hunters spread out, careful to be quiet. A galloper raised his head. The male. He sniffed the air. He knickered and pranced, clearly nervous. The female beside him raised her head and the one next to her too. With a toss of her head, she poised for flight when an arrow caught her in the neck. Another in the stomach and one in the head. The galloper beside her bolted. Another had just enough time to spring back on her hind legs before a flurry of arrows took her. And then the herd was gone with a sudden thunder that faded in mere seconds. A cloud of moldy dust from last years grasses rising in the air, the only evidence of their passing. Except for the gallopers lying in the grass.

The hunters made a fire on the steppe and began to process the gallopers. The gatherers were preparing the cave for their long absence. Edible foodstuffs, they packed to bring with them, just in case. Moldy and rotten food they carted out and left far from the cave. They stacked the pelts they wouldn't be taking with them in the back of the cave. They sorted through their tools. Some would stay. Some would go. It didn't take them long. They didn't have many possessions.

Soon they joined the hunters and took over the processing of the mares. Triven and Sele returned to the cave. They too, needed to sort through spears and knives, axes and arrows and decide what to bring. As a final step, they peed all over the cave. Their scent, they hoped, would deter predators from claiming the cave.

Happy people sat at the fire that night, bellies full of fresh meat. Gallopers were a favorite and there were smiles all around. The cave had begun to feel like a cage and with the arrival of herds, the *chaga* would be on the move. Triven was reluctant to break the mood, but decisions needed to be made.

"Shall we follow the gallopers?" he asked. The animals had gone north.

"Yes! Yes!" cried Olin. Sola shushed him. The question wasn't for him. "Yes, Yes," she cried in echo of Olin. He glared at her in mock outrage but stayed silent. She grinned down at him.

"If we follow the gallopers, will we be able to return south to our normal winter site? I really want to go there." This was from Maret. Her sister lived in a *chaga* that they often met during their travels, and she was missing her.

"We would have another hard winter if we journeyed back there. Once again, we would have barely enough time to prepare for winter."

"I don't care," said Sele. "There aren't any other people here."

"There are Moke and Kor's family." Triven held up his hand. He didn't want to debate their status as people this night. "There were too many people where we came from. Do not forget how close we came to being vulture supper. That will only get worse. We are still a small *chaga*. We cannot fight for territory or mates. And we don't know why the herds didn't come. Maybe they won't come again. All the things that directed us north are unchanged as far as we know."

Even Sele was quiet. They had been forced to come north. Triven's words were true.

"We don't yet know that there aren't other people here," said Ponu. "Other than Moke and Kor's *chaga* I mean. We haven't really explored a great distance around the cave."

"Perhaps we could stay through another winter before making a final decision?" This was from Chagama. She had not participated in any *chaga* decisions all winter and the entire *chaga* was surprised to hear her speak now.

"You are wise as ever, *Chagama*," said Triven. Some nodded. The rest were silent. It seemed the decision was made.

Welcome Home

It took nine days for Moke and Kor to travel to their winter cave. It was easy to find. They followed the mountain range and when they were three days out, they recognized where they were, and excitement grew in their bellies even as those same bellies roared with hunger. As they travelled, the snow melted quickly, leaving their feet soggy and their bodies warm. They had no lighter clothing or boots to trade, forcing them to stop early enough to dry them out by the fire before soaking them through once more the following day. Their food ran out on the fifth day. Something in the air, the ridgeline, the grass, told Moke they were close, even though he didn't actually recognize where he was, and he pushed Kor to keep going.

Finally, the cave was in sight. It was hard not to just drop all their gear and run home, but they didn't. They would need their things. They didn't talk, both too weary for that but they did share one happy glance before walking on. Moke's excitement faded as concern replaced it. There was no welcoming smoke from a fire. Each step that drew him closer, made his view clearer. He could discern no movement. It was afternoon. Even had they slept in, which was extremely likely, they should be stirring by this time.

It was quiet as they climbed the slope to the cave. By then, they knew nobody was there. Their hearts were heavy with disappointment and yet eased by being among their people's things.

They dropped their gear and fell on pelts that smelled of family and smoke and home and slept. They woke before dawn with a gnawing hunger and searched the cave for any meat that may have been left behind. Moke went below to the winter store. Nothing. Moke and Kor looked at each other. "I guess we're hunting today," they both said in unison and smiled.

It was another five days before they caught up with their clan. Days filled with hope and excitement and if Moke were honest, just a little bit of wistfulness. At first, they couldn't find the trail. They knew the clan must have gone north, following herds of some kind but the steppe is so vast, you can travel to the horizon, only to see another horizon far off in the distance of the same endless grass. A herd could go by, and you would never see it. Ches often lay his head on the ground. He would stay like that for hours sometimes. When he got up, he would point north or west or somewhere, and they would go. Inevitably, they would find a herd. He said he felt the thunder. Moke had tried it, but he had never felt the thunder unless the herd was so close, he could see them.

If instead, the clan had travelled the forest, which they often did, new trails would have been lost among the many old ones worn in during the winter.

And so, they travelled north. Sometimes through the trees. Sometimes on the steppe. Finally, they saw shapes above the grass that could have been people. They could have been the heads of a herd animal too, but Moke thought, hoped, they were people. When they got close enough, Moke could see the figures of Frome and Ches and Ono and Neti. A little closer and he spotted Cheel and was that Bene? Walking already! They weren't really close enough to make out features. It was only because their movements were so well known that Moke knew who he was looking at. Finally, Ches looked up. He was still for a long time. Ono bumped into him and then looked to see what he was watching. A hand flew to her mouth, and she clutched at Ches. When Frome and then Neti finally noticed the stillness of Ches and Ono and the figures approaching, they too stood and watched. It was Cheel who reacted with abandonment. She looked to the horizon and recognized the movements of Moke and Kor. Unlike her elders, she didn't disbelieve her eyes, or fear spirits. She ran and she ran, and she ran. She was exhausted long before she reached them, but Ches picked her up and carried her onwards. Tears streamed down his face as at last he stood face to face with the children he had long since thought gone forever.

Ono caught up to them a moment later but was unable to speak. She gazed upon them and then collapsed into the ground. Kor and Moke sat either side of her and each wrapped an arm around her. They stayed like that for a long while, the wind whistling past them, the grass ruffling at its pull. Cheel and Ches sat and waited. Finally, Ono calmed.

Moke and Kor talked for hours that evening as they related their experiences. And for the whole of the next day as well. Their clan listened in rapt attention. Crying and laughing, smiling, and sighing. Ono brought food quietly and unobtrusively while Frome shared water. Never had such a tale been told around their fire.

Weeks later, Moke and Kor had gained weight and Kor at least seemed no worse for wear. Moke had lost his smile. Where before it was wide and full of life, now it was tinged with sadness. He was as kind as ever but quiet. Ches talked of the coming gathering and mating and Moke displayed a twinge of excitement that drained away as soon as Ches looked away. It did however return. No amount of sadness could shake his desire for a mate.

The Wanderer found them in early summer. The clan sat with barely subdued excitement as they held back their news. It would take days for him to give them all his news and tradition said they should not speak until he was done.

On the third evening, the Wanderer was unusually quiet before he began his tales. His eyes were cast downward, and he looked as though he was struggling to find the right words. His brows puckered and his eyes watered. The Wanderer had told this tale three times already. He was a master, and he knew he needed to bring the proper atmosphere to a story like this. With a final deep breath, he began.

"Last fall, I visited with Donon's clan." He gave news about the babies. Who was walking, getting fat, and their names. He shook his head as he talked. His voice cracked often, and his eyes welled. He dropped hints, things like 'if they only knew' or 'life was to change'. His audience leaned forward and listen raptly. Something big was coming and they knew it.

"Donon woke one morning and looked out over the steppe. He could see a herd of elk in the distance. They were moving east of Donon's camp and were on the edge of the horizon so he knew they would need to travel quickly if they were to capture any. Tsutse, Ross, Chor and Donon jogged ahead while Luco and Mor packed up the camp and came more slowly with the children. Their babe's too young to travel fast. Soon the hunters were far ahead of Luco and Mor and with the long grass, the young mothers didn't see what happened next." The Wanderer paused. He took a sip of water and chewed a piece of meat.

"The four hunters hid in the tall grass and waited with patience for the herd to draw close. Finally, when their bodies hurt from staying still, a cow and her calf neared. When Donon judged the moment right, he rose from the grass and speared the calf. Ross, Chor and Tsutse rose as well and screamed at the cow and waved their arms so they wouldn't be trampled in a stampede. Just when they were cheering the success of the hunt, a spear from the sky came down and took Donon from the back. Tsutse helped him to sleep as the pain was tremendous and the wound, well, there was nothing any could do for that.

Donon's clan are thin now. They are afraid to hunt. They do when they must, but I fear they may not survive the winter. Ross and Chor are tense. Both want to be chief which should be Tsutse of course but she is too numb with grief. Chor is very young, but Ross is…" The Wanderer didn't finish the thought. There was a fine line between news and gossip, and he tried not to cross it. "Let us hope no more of Donon's clan are lost."

The clan was quiet for a long time while they thought of Donon, and his strength now gone. Some turned their thoughts to their own clan. What would happen if Ches were gone?

"When I told this tale to Hor's clan, Hor decided that the mother of all Elk has given the clans warning. Her children are to be left alone. Other clans agree and will not hunt elk." Heads nodded around the fire. Ches's clan would not be hunting elk either.

The following evening, it was the clan's turn to share news. The pall from Donon's tale was quickly shed as they delighted in being the storytellers of such a wonderous tale as theirs.

Change of Plans

The Wanderer retreated to his own shelter after the clan had finished sharing their news. It was early still, and the clan exchanged confused looks when he retreated, but, as always, they respected the privacy of their guest.

The Wanderer needed to think. He had been barely a man when he started his journey and became the Wanderer. Col, he thought. That's who he had been a lifetime ago. He was well into manhood now, grey hair and all. He thought of how he had left. He hadn't said goodbye to his mother, his father, or the rest of the clan. Only Bet. Year after year, the regret of that had grown. He didn't know what had become of any of them, just as they didn't know of him. He recognized his young pain for what it was. The pain of being different. Of growing up and finding his own path. He owed them something. An apology. An explanation. Something.

He had planned to go back this year. Or try. He wasn't sure he would know how to find them. As he sat and thought about these plans, he realized that his return to his roots, he could not think of it as home, would have to be delayed, perhaps forever. He had a role to play here and now. An important one. These were his people now, and they might need him, and if he was honest with himself, he had to admit that he could not resist what might be the greatest bit of news he had ever heard, and he would be in the thick of it. His heart beat a little faster at the thought.

The Wanderer poked his head out of his shelter. Now that his decision was made, he was too excited to sleep. It was too early anyway. The others were still by the fire, so he came out with a broad smile and started to play a tune he had written just for dancing while he pranced around them. Ches laughed at him, as did Ono. None understood what he had been thinking about, but it didn't matter. They all joined him.

When the tune was finished, all he said was, "You must introduce me to these people!"

Introductions

It was the bone flute, two weeks later, that alerted the *chaga* hunters to the clans' presence. They had been about to set up their shelters for the night when they heard it. They thought it was Moke of course, which brought out mixed reactions. Sele had hoped he'd seen the last of the strange ones. Triven was more realistic. They lived somewhere on this side of the mountains, and he thought it likely their paths would cross again. He would rather they be friends than enemies. After a tense discussion, the hunters carried their poles further into the trees. The notes of the flute carried a long way, and the sky was a dusky grey by the time they found Moke.

They waited until the song finished before calling out. By this time, it was full dark, and they were a voice from the forest. Moke was sure he recognized Triven's voice. His heart pounded in anticipation. He stood and called, "Good Morning!" The *chaga* hunters approached and Moke' eyes looked for Sola. His heart sunk when he realized she wasn't there. Until that moment, he hadn't known just how much he missed her. Not the *chaga*, and the challenge of language, or the other new things they taught. Sola. He missed Sola. He didn't have time to dwell on that. His attention was pulled by this first meeting and so it sat at the back of his mind, coloring his mood just a little bit blue.

The Wanderer put his flute away and watched and listened to everything with keen interest. He felt as nervous as he had the first time he met Donon. The Wanderer had a reputation for talking. He delivered the news after all. He, in fact, listened far more than he talked, and he was a fine reader of emotions. He watched the strange faces around him. At first it was overwhelming and then he realized that tension showed in clenched teeth or fists, the same as for the clans. He read the openness in Bron's face, the contempt in Sele's, the acceptance in Triven's.

He cast his eyes around the fire and caught the look of the one they called Ponu. A shock of recognition went through him. Ponu was like him! Thoughts he had never had before came to him as he stared into those eyes. In that brief glance, he saw himself sharing tears and laughter. He saw naked bodies. Joy and belonging. Abruptly, he got up. He didn't know what to do with the thoughts and emotions crashing around so unexpectedly inside so he just left. It was dark and moonless. He travelled a few steps before realizing he couldn't see and turned around awkwardly to disappear into his shelter. Images, thoughts, and emotions roiled through him until he was exhausted and finally slept. When he woke, he was just as confused but a little calmer.

Ponu sought him out almost immediately. With gestures, he insisted they go for a walk and the Wanderer was unable to resist. He shook with emotion, his earlier calmness gone. It had been an illusion he realized. They walked for an hour and that helped to settle him. Ponu seemed to see the tension in the Wanderer and waited for it to ease before stopping in a small clearing.

Ponu took the Wanderers hand and pulled him to a log. Then began the long, difficult task of learning each others language. He pointed to the log and said "log". The Wanderer said "utta tem" which meant fallen tree. They did this for hours. Soon they were sharing smiles and then laughs. When it was time to go back to camp, Ponu turned to the Wanderer, pulled him close and held him. The Wanderer hadn't been held like this, ever. Maybe when he was a babe, but he had no recollection of it. He almost wept with the feeling. He felt accepted and cared for. He felt like he was home. Ponu stepped back, smiled quietly, took his hand, and led him back to camp.

The group camped together for one more day and night. Moke kept hoping to see Sola. He would glance up from whatever he was doing, and his eyes would scan the horizon in all directions, even though he knew she must come from the south were she to come at all and then he would look down again, momentarily saddened.

Triven, too wished that Sola was with them. Ponu understood more than any other, but Sola was the most versed in their language. He thought he had agreed to meet Moke's clan when the leaves turned orange and the white geese went south. They were to meet close to here. Moke had taken him out to the steppe and pointed to a spot there. They would have a feast. Triven was a little nervous about how much of this he misinterpreted but then he shrugged inwardly. If he got it wrong, his own *chaga* could still come here, still have a feast. It would not be a catastrophe.

On the final morning, Moke and the Wanderer packed up and said "Goodbye" in Triven's language. Ponu stood next to the Wanderer and spoke. "I'm going with them. I'll learn more of their language and ways. I'll come find you when it's time to go to the gathering."

Triven thought this was a great idea and nodded his approval. He completely missed the chemistry between the two, but Privon saw and approved. He loved Ponu like a brother and was pleased for him. Ponu, for his part really had no idea of the journey he had agreed to. He thought he would be travelling with Moke's clan. The Wanderer, however, was taking him to meet all the clans.

The Gathering

They were late and so they ran. All of them. Even *Chagama*. Or she did until she turned her ankle on a rock. After that, the hunters took turns carrying her on their backs except for a short time in the morning and another after midday break. Most of the *chaga* walked faster than *Chagama,* but it salved her pride. Fortunately, they weren't so far from the gathering site that they needed to do this for more than two days.

They were late because as with everything to do with the strange ones, dissent reigned. Not everyone wanted to go and not everyone wanted not to go. So, there had been *chaga* talks that were not resolved in a day or even two. Finally, the entire *chaga* agreed. They would go. They would meet and assess these people. See if they were a threat or a friend. Sele decided he needed to understand his enemy better and he convinced the other hold outs with that logic as well. Triven rolled his eyes when he thought about it. By this time, he was so sure that they were just people, he was blind to any potential danger from them.

And so, in a hurried and somewhat careless way, the *chaga* arrived at the edge of the forest near the gathering site on the afternoon of the third day of travel. Each and every one of them gazed open mouthed at the tableau before them. There were dozens of shelters. A couple of hundred or more people. And the noise! Screams and squeals as children ran past. Music, some of it discordant, loud, and unapologetic. Men's voices raised in competition and camaraderie. Women singing, talking, or yelling. A pack of wolves were pacing nervously on the opposite side of the site, drawn by the smells of meat roasting and blood and offal from the kills made to support the feast.

Triven had thought they were meeting Moke's clan. He was assured by Sola that they were 'few'. The word they used for more than three which was as high as they counted. A small herd would be 'many' and 'few' was less than that. Just as he gathered his wits enough to contemplate leaving, they were spotted. Once one person spotted them, the rest stopped what they were doing and turned to look. Suddenly, there was silence. Even the wolves stopped yipping long enough to see what was happening.

Triven stepped out of the trees, walking tall and proud, unsmiling but not frowning either. *Chagama*, Sele, Sola and the rest of the *chaga* watched him with pride. He looked splendid in the new wrap that Reta had made for him. After a moment, the rest of the *chaga* followed. To the clans who gaped with both awe and fear, they appeared tall and proud but no matter how much dignity they displayed, they were still scrawny and funny looking. Triven would have been horrified had he read these thoughts.

Moke was the first of the clans to move. He pushed through the crowd and was about to continue forward to greet the *chaga* when Ches grabbed his arm and held him still. The Wanderer stepped out and met Triven on the field between the trees and the camp. He bowed to him, said "Good Morning", and waved his arm expansively to the clans behind him. The clan chiefs all moved forward next. There were eleven of them. An unprecedented turnout.

The Wanderer introduced the clan chiefs while Ponu interpreted. Ponu was far from being fluent in their language, but they had practiced this bit ahead of time in the interest of adding ceremony and flare. The *chaga* was told where to setup their shelters. A prime spot, dry and large, near the creek and the shade of trees, had been reserved for them. Once they were settled, Ponu told them there would be food, music, and a fire. They were not to contribute anything this first night as they were honored guests.

The *chaga* turned to setting up their shelters, most relieved to have a chance to digest their first impressions. Olin disappeared, curious and eager to explore. Nobody noticed. Slowly, the children of the clans gathered around. At first, they peered around shelters or hid in the grass at some distance, but curiosity got hold of them and with the fearlessness only children possess, they began to approach. Some smiled shyly, others touched things and still others asked questions that nobody could answer.

Flin was tucking bags of food into her shelter when a small hand reached past her and grabbed a bag. Not known for her patience or good judgment, she slapped it away without thinking. In fairness, she would have done the same to Grady or Olin, but this wasn't Grady or Olin. The boy had had his hand slapped before. This was not the first time he had reached for something uninvited but the shock of the stranger doing it caused him to snatch his hand back and wail to the heavens.

Triven, who had been setting up a shelter next to Flin's, turned to look. Flin put her hand to her mouth. She should not have slapped the child and she knew it. The boys mother ran forward and scooped him into her arms. She glared at Flin and stormed away without waiting for the apology Triven was anxious to give.

Triven called out to the *chaga*. When they had gathered, he said "You MUST NOT hurt these people, no matter the provocation." He was furious with Flin but didn't single her out. "We would be in a dangerous situation were we to alienate them. There are many more of them than there are of us and that isn't why we came. We came, to build relationships with these people, our neighbors. As is the tradition of our people for countless generations."

"You may have come for that. I came to assess our enemy."

"Grey Horn's turd Sele! Let's walk." Triven's ground this out. Sometimes he wanted to thrash Sele so soundly he wouldn't be able to move. Or talk. For a month. And this was most emphatically one of those times.

Moke was finally able to get away and sought Sola out immediately. Sola hadn't seen him in months, and she was surprised at how happy she was to finally see him now. He had grown taller. He looked like a man, not a youth. She herself had changed more. She too was a woman full grown and had filled out. Her waist was still tiny, but her hips had broadened, and her breasts grown. She was taller as well. As tall as Moke, she thought.

Sola looked around her. The people of her *chaga* were busy erecting shelters and sorting things. She decided she wouldn't be missed. She pulled Moke's hand and the two disappeared into the crowd.

Wherever they walked, people stopped talking and doing and just stared at them. Moke smiled and Sola did as well. Some smiled back but most were too busy gawking for even that. Soon, they were trailed by a pack of children. Sola turned around every minute or so and they scattered. They had all heard about the slap and were cautious. Moke weaved his way through the shelters and people until he reached the camp of his own clan.

"Ches," he called. A burly figure came out of the shelter. He looked like Moke, except for his coloring. Sola stared quietly. She felt suddenly shy and uncertain. Moke nudged her and she said "shoso", the word for greetings in their language.

Moke introduced her to the rest of his clan and then invited her to sit by the fire. They couldn't really talk. The children that had trailed them were back and braver. Hands reached out to touch Sola's hair and her clothes and then darted away. Just when Moke was getting angry, Ponu found them and told her she should go back to the *chaga*. They were going to eat and dance, and she should be with her own people for the first night.

The Wanderer began to play and Sout and Gurn, two peers of Moke's from other clans, rose and danced on the edge of the light from the fire. When Moke looked for them a few minutes later, they had disappeared. Moke wondered if they were mating. And if they were, was it for the night? Or would Sout go with Gurn's clan when the gathering was over? Others got up and danced around the fire too, mostly young people. Kor danced, limbs shooting out in tune with the music. Cheel bounced and made people laugh. Moke got up and scooped Cheel up in his arms and spun her around. She squealed in delight, and he smiled happily. Ono saw his smile and was grateful for its reappearance. Her glance slid to Sola, and she wondered if she was the reason.

The people of Sola's *chaga* watched with interest. They danced too of course but when they did, some of the *chaga* would pound the ground rhythmically while others chanted and still others danced. Their dancing had more to do with rhythmic pounding of the ground with their feet than with moving their bodies. This moving to the bone flute was different. Joyful, more abandoned. All limbs were involved. Maybe because the flute provided the music, the people were free to just move. Or maybe that was just the clans and who they were as people. Suddenly, or so it seemed, Moke was standing before Sola and holding his hand out. She glanced at the dancers and back at him and something shifted inside her. She smiled widely and jumped to her feet with glee. With the same abandon she saw from the clan's people, she threw herself into the dance. She looked as awkward as Cheel, limbs flying in every direction, but nobody cared. She certainly didn't. She felt happy and free.

Triven pulled Reta to her feet and joined the dancers. Brella tried to engage Sele but when he refused, stubbornly, she dragged her son Bron up. Soon, all the *chaga* children were smiling and moving. It was a good night for those who joined in.

Wrestling Match

Traditionally, the second day of a gathering was for wrestling matches. Clan gatherings were informal and lacked organization and that meant the wrestling matches rarely resulted in an overall 'winner' or even any kind of tournament. Pairs of people, men, and women challenged each other and then took turns in an area set aside for matches. For large gatherings, the matches could go on for days as winners were challenged by other winners and occasionally an ultimate winner was decided. Often though, if things went on too long, spectators disappeared, and so did the challenges.

Ponu relayed as much of this as he understood which was most of it. He didn't quite understand the part about spectators disappearing but decided they could figure it out later. It turns out he didn't really understand that men *and* women participated, and this would come as a shock to the *chaga's* gatherers later on.

The wrestling match area was a large swathe of steppe grass that some people of the clans had flattened in preparation. They'd also removed rocks and sticks for the safety of the participants. With some reluctance, Triven approached the area with the rest of his *chaga*. He suspected, and rightly so, that he would be challenged. He wasn't a coward, but he had noted the thick muscles on the people of the clans. Their burly chests and corded legs. He was taller but he doubted that would make a fig of difference in the arena.

One of the chiefs, Ches, he thought his name was, approached him. From Moke's clan, he recalled. He had a huge grin plastered across his face. Wide and inviting though it was, Triven cringed at what he knew was coming. Ches shoved him softly and tilted his head to the arena. Triven sighed. This was going to hurt was his final thought.

The crowd cheered as the two wrestled. Ches took it easy on Triven at first. He could have beaten him in the first minute but chose not to. Ches was a sensitive, jolly man and keen to let this stranger save face. The onlookers knew Ches wasn't really trying but it didn't matter. They watched and cheered and eventually, Ches put Triven onto his stomach and pulled his arms back and crowed in triumph. Triven went limp in defeat.

Ches rose and then helped Triven to his feet. Triven bowed deeply and the crowd roared. Ches slapped his back and the pair left together, both pleased for different reasons. Triven, happy it was over and Ches happy he'd done his clan proud.

Flin had been watching with the rest of the *chaga* and a small part of her was pleased to see Triven beaten. She wanted Sele to be chief and despite her encouragement and manipulations over the years, Sele refused to challenge him. The smile that lingered on her face was wiped clear an instant later as a clan woman challenged her. At first, she thought there was some mistake. Surely, women didn't wrestle, but the woman pushed her again and tilted her head to the arena. All eyes were on Flin and the tension was palpable. Flin realized with sudden fear that this was the woman whose child she had slapped the day before. Flin shook her head and the crowd exploded. They jeered and booed and hissed. Not those from the *chaga* but the people of the clans.

Suddenly, Triven was beside. "You must," he whispered. "Maybe you will think before striking a child next time hmm?" Flin stared up at him. His eyes were hard and merciless. Not an expression she saw often in that face. "Those women will find you and beat you I'm sure if you don't, and then I will be forced to do something, and this will all have been because you couldn't control your temper for a tiny moment." Flin looked into the angry faces around her and knew he was right. These women weren't just angry. They *hated* her. If they didn't get satisfaction here, they would get it somewhere else. The woman shoved her a third time, hard, causing Flin to stumble. This time she went. She was soundly thrashed. Like the match with Ches, the woman drew it out. Not, to save face this time, not gently, but to inflict punishment. At the end, Flin was left in a huddle in the middle of the arena.

It was Ches who helped her up. He was shamed by the behavior of Hupu, the woman who had beaten Flin. The crowd was hushed now. They shared in the shame. Hupu had gone too far. Who of them, after all, had not slapped a child's hand who was reaching where it shouldn't? Tsutse joined Ches in the arena. She looked for injuries and applied a salve to one of Flin's scrapes. Flin soaked up the sympathy and when she'd had enough, she limped out of the arena and hid in her shelter for the rest of the day.

Triven sent Ponu to challenge Moke. The two were friendly and he thought maybe that would go far in easing the tension. Ponu, always sensitive, and somewhat of a showman, made much of the challenge. His gestures exaggerated and comedic. Moke laughed at him and joined him eagerly. Ponu was no match for Moke of course but Moke had picked up on the humor and made much of it. The match ended with him placing one foot dramatically on Ponu and cheering while Ponu moaned in exaggeration. The crowd loved it and Triven relaxed a tiny bit.

Sout approached Moke at a slow walk afterwards with a slight smile on her face. She looked relaxed and Moke thought her previous evenings mating had done her good. "How about a match?" she asked him.

Moke was shocked. This type of challenge was usually issued to indicate an interest in mating and the resulting match would be more erotic than anything else. Pairs often disappeared right after to appease whatever feelings they aroused. Some spectators did the same. Moke blushed, shook his head 'no' and hurriedly walked away. Her laugh taunted him as he went. She knew he was tempted, and he hated that she knew.

"Good choice," said Ches, coming up beside him. "That girl is trouble, and I would prefer you not bring her home with you." Moke had his second shock of the day with those words. Mating was rarely interfered with by anyone. Couples chose who they wished, and the clans accepted it. If mates caused tension, then a pair would strike out on their own. This wasn't unusual. Clans were small for a reason.

An hour later, he got his third shock of the day. Sout and Bon were wrestling while Gurn looked on with a miserable expression. Sout made no real effort to fight back but arched her back while in Bon's arms and slid down his length. Both were naked and for a moment, Moke thought they would mate right there and then. Moke was unable to hide his own arousal. He wasn't alone in that feeling and couples began to slip away. He didn't notice that as he was too engaged in the display in front of him. Sout cast him a sultry look and he groaned. He was pretty sure that he would have not been able to stop himself from mating in front of the crowd had he accepted Sout's earlier offer.

"Come," said a voice in his ear. He startled and turned to find Hupu, Gurn's older sister holding her hand out to him. "Just for today," she clarified. Moke was unable to think of any reason to refuse her offer. In truth, he was beyond thinking anything and he followed her eagerly. The moment he had been dreaming of for almost two years was at hand. His eyes glazed and his mouth widened in a smile he didn't know was there.

Suddenly Sola was in front of him. She had seen everything. How Sout propositioned Moke, and then wrestled with someone else. She saw Moke's arousal and now him leaving with still another. It made her furious. She didn't quite understand why. She just knew she found it all intolerable. Her emotions felt crazy and out of control inside of her and she had to act, and so she stomped over to the couple and placed herself firmly in front of Moke, her craziness, jealousy, and anger, displayed for all to see.

A moment before, Moke was unable to think of anything but mating. Now, his dearest friend was obviously upset, and all thoughts of mating fled. He found it hurt to witness her anger and pain.

Hupu slinked away. Neither noticed as they stared at each other. Moke didn't understand why Sola was angry, but he was driven to find out. He grasped her hand and looked for somewhere they could be to figure it out. There were so many people! Although most were of his clans, they got together so rarely that even Moke was overwhelmed by them all. His eyes landed on his shelter, and he dragged Sola along behind him.

Love Story

"Po tot?" Moke asked Sola. This wasn't a phrase she knew but she understood him anyway and still was at a loss to explain. She shrugged her shoulders. Whatever made her mad had disappeared with the clan woman. Suddenly she understood. If he mated with someone else, he wouldn't be hers. She didn't know when she had started to think of him as hers, but she calmed as soon as she recognized it.

She pointed to him and then to herself and then she folded her arms together in the universal sign of a hug. Moke tipped his head as he looked at her, puzzling out her message. Sola watched him struggle and then pulled him close.

Desire which had faded when Hupu slinked away jumped back to life in an instant. Moke pulled away and looked into Sola's eyes. Is that what she meant he wondered? It had never occurred to him, for even a moment, that their two peoples could mate. He was surprised to find that he hoped it was. He loved her completely and unconditionally. He didn't care that she was a little funny looking, only that she was her.

Sola smiled shyly at him. She had noticed his physical reaction. And yes. That was exactly what she wanted. Neither knew what they were doing. They had seen it before but doing, as they quickly discovered, was very, very different.

It didn't take them long to figure it out.

Afterwards, they lay side by side, grinning at each other like a couple of fools. They stayed in Moke's shelter for the rest of the afternoon. It was hunger that eventually drew them out.

Feast

"Where have you been!?" demanded Flin. She didn't seem at all humbled by her earlier experience. Nor did she wait for an answer. Her hand flew, faster than Sola could duck and landed with a crack on Sola's cheek. "With that stinky Moke I bet. We needed you. Get those parsnips ready." It looked as if she might continue but then she noticed the quiet stares of the other women. Flin glared back. Brella turned away but Reta held her stare. *Chagama* stepped forward and put her arm around Sola.

"Never mind the parsnips. I need help with the mix mash. I remind you Flin," *Chagama* said with iron in her voice, "for the last time. I have claimed Sola. You will not strike her. Ever. Again." *Chagama* held Flin's gaze as she spoke, daring her to interfere. Flin dropped her gaze and turned away.

Sola hugged *Chagama* and then stepped slightly away. "I remind you both," she said firmly. "I am a woman full grown. Neither of you can claim me. Flin, if you ever strike me again, I will beat you so soundly you won't be able to walk for a hand of days." With that, she turned her attention to the food *Chagama* had been preparing. Flin drew back at Sola's words as if she had been struck. She assessed Sola, the girl she rarely bothered to look at and for the first time, noticed the muscles in her arms, the strength in her legs and the full-grown height she had reached. Sola could do what she said she realized. Flin turned away and the other women smiled quietly to themselves.

Mix mash was the best dish. It was different every time because it depended on what was on hand. They made it often in the winter when food got old and boring and tasteless, and it was good. But, in the fall, when the ingredients were fresh and full of flavor, there was nothing better. Sola squatted beside *Chagama*. *Chagama* had been cutting rabbit into small pieces when she had rescued Sola and she was now finishing it up. She passed some potatoes to Sola. They were small and could be added whole, but they needed washing so Sola took them and walked to the river. It wasn't hygiene that worried her, it was the knowledge that dirt added an unpleasant grit to the dish, and she wanted it to be perfect.

The mother of the child that Flin had slapped the day before was there. She stared so hard at Sola that Sola shivered. She was the same woman that had been leading Moke away Sola realized with a start. Sola gazed at her steadily and then nodded her head in acknowledgement. The woman sighed and turned to walk back to the gathering.

Sola bent to wash the potatoes and noticed some wild onions growing at the bank. She pulled them out happily. There were so many, she barely managed to carry all she found.

Chagama added thyme, parsley, and mustard seed to the mash as well as some of the onion Sola had brought. Sola saw her reach into a bag tied to her waist and sprinkle something else. When she tasted the mash, she looked at *Chagama* who stared back with determined innocence. Salt was what she tasted. She had thought they didn't have any. She grinned at *Chagama* and took another taste. Delicious.

Brella was making a sweetbread out of ground acorns, oats, pine nuts, and water, fried up on a hot flat stone and covered with fresh honey. Brella always managed to make a fabulous bread with whatever grains could be found. Sola was salivating, just thinking about it.

Flin and Reta were preparing galloper and twin horn meat for cooking later. They were slicing the meat into small pieces and seasoning each piece with thyme and rosemary. Sola handed them some onions. She noticed they didn't have any salt but kept quiet about *Chagama's* stash. Later, the women would fry the meat and serve it rare.

Alli was preparing parsnips. She rubbed them with some rosemary and a whole ton of twin horn fat. They would be good like that although salt would be better.

Maret had cooked some brassica and she was now stuffing them with a mixture of pine nuts, dried bison, blackberries, garlic, and onion.

They hadn't been prepared for the huge crowd of people, so they made tiny portions. Most could have a taste.

As the women worked, clans people walked by, curious. Some stopped and sniffed the air, others pointed, some even smiled, but not at Flin.

Word had travelled. They chatted amongst themselves mostly and it was probably good that the *chaga* women didn't understand what they were saying. "Look, they eat leaves!" one exclaimed as she watched Maret roll the braccia leaves. "And roots too." another said of the parsnips. They were keen to taste despite their words.

When the preparation was finished, the woman started cooking. By this time, there was a huge crowd around their camp, all eager to watch and taste. As the food became ready, the *chaga* women waved the people forward to come take a taste. They didn't have things like plates or serving platters, so people just lifted pieces off the stone that they were being cooked on. Or, in the case of the meat, pulled it off the cooking sticks. The stuffed brassica was served cold and the sweetbread warm. People jostled for a taste.

Sola watched with interest as the clans tasted their food. Everybody seemed to like the sweetbread. The honey she thought as she remembered how much Moke and Kor had enjoyed that. The parsnips, though, most spit those out. She laughed at their faces when they tasted them. The mix mash had mixed reactions. The meat was palatable, but Sola knew that Moke and Kor had hated the potato, so she wasn't surprised when many of them didn't enjoy it.

The women of the *chaga* weren't the only people preparing food of course and that was good. They had enough for everyone to taste but not for all to feel satiated. Triven was pleased. It didn't matter that the clans hadn't liked all the food. Everybody had enjoyed trying it and the mood of the crowd was relaxed and fun.

Music by the fire ended the day. Many people were exhausted, children most of all so there wasn't nearly as much dancing as the previous evening. As the day sputtered out, and people relaxed by the fire, a clan man jumped to his feet and ran to the bushes. Soon after, a few more jumped up, and then there was a rush. Clan people were not used to so much fiber in their diet.

The Bow Show

Ponu found the *chaga* in the morning. "There will be a spear throwing contest today," he said. "But Triven, Ches and Frome want to see the bow and arrow. Moke told them about it, and once you show them, I'm sure others will want to see it too."

"Well, we need to redeem ourselves today after being so soundly thrashed yesterday in the wrestling matches." Others had been challenged besides Flin and Triven and not one *chaga* person had won a match. "Who wants to toss spears? Who wants to shoot arrows?" Unlike the clans, only the males of the *chaga* would participate in either of these activities.

Bron and Fabe, not yet full hunters, chose bows. The spears required greater strength, the bows skill. Both had been practising for years and were eager to show off. Besides, the clans didn't use bows so they couldn't lose.

Ras wanted to go with the bows, but Triven encouraged the rest to throw spears. "You are great with the spear," he said. "We came to make friends and part of that is respect. We must show them that we are a force." Ras nodded. He, Sele and Privon would throw spears.

The women hurriedly prepared more meat. Enough for the day. They would take turns at the fire but otherwise enjoy a day of leisure, watching the contests, wandering amongst the other camps, and gossiping. They were as eager for the day as the men.

The children had no rules. They ran, they played. They made friends with the strangers as easily and quickly as only children can do. Even Grady, young as he was, toddled after Olin instead of staying with Flin. This freedom and abandon would bring terror to their mothers later in the day.

Triven, Bron and Fabe headed to the edge of the steppe where it met the forest. To really demonstrate the bow, you needed a target and trees were perfect.

Triven started the demonstration by shooting a tree. He chose one that was a few hundred feet away. Just far enough that he was sure he could make the shot. He was out to impress. Although Moke and Kor had told of the bow, Ches and Frome hadn't really believed him. Now the two gasped in amazement. And then they tore after the arrow to see for themselves. When they tried to pull it out, it was so deeply embedded that it broke.

Triven hated to waste arrows. They could all fashion arrow heads with speed although Sele made the best ones and therefore made most of them for the hunters. Still, crafting an arrow took time. Straight branches had to be found and smoothed out. Then they needed to be notched on both ends for the arrowhead and the feathers. Feathers had to be found and fashioned. Any old feather wouldn't do either. They needed to be of a size. Glue had to be made. The *chaga* usually made a large batch of pitch in the winter by heating pine sap and mixing it with charcoal. It would harden but they could reheat it to use it when they needed. They also needed to make cord for tying the feathers and arrowhead on, otherwise they separated after a single use. It meant that they didn't have an endless supply. They would make arrows throughout the winter months and carry as many as they could. By this time of year, they rarely had many left, if any at all. Triven decided today's display was a worthy way to use the ones they had.

Ponu and the Wanderer joined them. Triven could see others watching with interest and sure enough, some of them turned away from the spear contests. Their curiosity great.

Bron and Fabe each shot arrows into the trees while Triven stood next to Ches and Frome and demonstrated where to place the arrow, how to pull back and then release. The Wanderer listened and watched with keen interest. He was hoping his penchant for detail would allow him to describe the tool to all the clans so they could replicate it.

Ches tried it first. He pulled back as Triven had shown him and with great excitement, released. The arrow flopped to the ground in a disappointing anticlimax. Frome laughed hysterically and so Ches handed him the bow to try. With a flourish, Frome took it, notched the arrow, and watched it fall to the ground a mere foot away. Ches clapped him on the back and said "huh!"

By this time, others had come to watch and wanted to try. None met with success. One clan woman managed to hit a tree although it didn't pierce the bark. They had a lot of fun trying and laughed at each others' follies. Many studied the arrows and the bows carefully. They were the ones who would try to make one of their own.

That none were successful pleased Triven. He wasn't convinced that sharing this weapon with these new people was a good idea, but he was even more worried about not showing them and causing offense. For the first time ever, he was grateful for the many hours of practise that went into becoming a master of the bow.

A low hum drew his attention. Something was happening over at the spear contest. He couldn't tell what it was. He could just hear the combined voices of the crowd. He frowned. What was going on?

Spear Contest

Ras, Privon and Sele watched as the clans' people threw their spears. For the first time, Sele realized just how arrogant he had been in regard to these people. They had beat them soundly at the wrestling matches. All the *chaga* hunters had a turn in the arena and none came close to beating the clan people. Ras had been beaten by a female and still smarted over the insult to his ego. He was eager to throw his spear and redeem himself. Sele though, knew that there was a good chance he wouldn't win. Height gave the *chaga* hunter an advantage, but the sheer power of their opponents made that advantage dubious at best.

With a sigh, Sele stepped forward. He was next to throw. He took a breath to center himself before lunging forward and throwing with all his might. The spear landed inches short of the farthest spears thrown yet and surpassed many of the others. Sele was relieved. They wouldn't be trounced at least.

Privon was next and his throw was also respectable. Not as good as Sele's but close. He stepped back with a smile to make room for Ras. Ras had disappeared though and Privon looked around in confusion. Then he saw him running back from their camp area. He was carrying something, but Privon couldn't see what it was.

Ras was panting by the time he made it back. He bent over, breathing hard and clutching his knees for a moment. When he straightened, he looked determined. He stepped forward and Sele could finally see what he held. An atlatl. A spear thrower. Triven had specifically told them not to use it. He had to show them the bow because the clans already knew about that weapon, but this one was unknown to them and Triven, in the interest of caution, was keen to keep it that way. Sele thought about stopping him, but he was so eager to see them win the contest that he didn't.

Ras didn't look at Privon or Sele. He wasn't about to give them an opportunity to stop him. He wanted to show these strangers how powerful they were. He wanted them to be afraid of their *chaga*. He shook his head, his dreadlocks flying wildly and then he stepped forward with his thrower and prepared to toss. The hunters usually used the atlatl to add power when hunting large game with thick hides. It could and did make spears travel farther and with greater force. Accuracy was difficult as it was even harder to learn than the bow and arrow. Ras was by far their best hunter with this tool having practised for many an hour over the years.

Ras stepped back, careful to hold the spear between his fingers and the spear thrower at the same time. With a powerful forward thrust, he let loose the spear. A loud 'zip' sound accompanied the throw and then it was gone. The spear landed so far ahead of the other spears that it was the clear winner. Ras was pleased and a grin covered his face as he did a victory dance, his feet pounding the ground in rhythm and his arms moving to the same beat. He looked as intimidating as he had intended to.

The onlookers were quiet. The *chaga* men thought it was because they were stunned by the feat of Ras's throw. Then the crowd began to whisper. Again, the hunters misinterpreted the crowd. Sele and Privon forgot about Triven and enjoyed the shared triumph of Ras. They danced around Ras and whooped in triumph. The whispers turned to angry words and looks that weren't open to misinterpretation. Dozens of faces were turned toward them, and the three hunters at last understood. These people were angry. Furious even. Dangerous. They didn't understand why, just that they were. They looked around and saw Triven, far in the distance. The low rumble of the crowd had carried and drawn his attention.

The hunters looked around for Ponu or even the Wanderer as they gingerly backed away from the spear grounds. Other people came from their camps and cook fires to see what was happening. Playing stopped as even the children, both clan and *chaga,* turned to watch.

Triven ran towards them, followed by Bron and Fabe. The Wanderer, Ches and Frome were right behind them.

"I don't know," was Sele's curt response to Triven's question. They were still backing up, slowly and calmly but desperately afraid. Angry words were tossed at them. One man picked up a stone and threw it. It was a warning shot though and came nowhere near them. Triven, Bron, and

Fabe notched arrows but Triven had warned them firmly against firing unless someone was actually attacked. Not approached. Not touched. Attacked. "Ras threw a spear and then they got angry." Triven turned to look at Ras and saw the atlatl in his hands. He pushed aside his irritation at that to ask him if he had used it.

"Yes." Ras answered, after clearing his throat.

It still made no sense. Out throwing them shouldn't make them angry. The bow didn't anger them. And then the Wanderer and Ponu were beside them.

"We have to go," said Ponu. "Now. We're protected by the sanctity of the gathering, but the Wanderer isn't sure how long that will hold. He says we should leave everything and just go." Ponu's voice was laced with fear, and he shook as he spoke. Something had gone horribly wrong. "Go to our camp. I'll round up the others and tell them to meet us there." Then Ponu and the Wanderer were gone.

Run

Clan people, armed clan people, surrounded the *chaga* camp. They were restless and unsmiling. The rumble of the crowd was unsettling. A low and angry hum that carried far. One jumped up and down aggressively. Another lunged with his spear but didn't throw it. One of them was speaking. Ches, thought Triven, and he hoped he was speaking for them.

Triven had never in his life been this much on edge. Flin was pacing and fretting, her eyes wild. Olin and Grady hadn't returned. Reta too was a mess. Triven didn't think she could bear another loss and there was no sign of Cark, her youngest.

"Pack as much food as you can carry. We can leave the shelters and hides if everyone is back before they're packed. But start taking them down. We'll take whatever we have time to bring but we leave the moment everyone is here. Sele and Ras, you will lead. The rest of us will follow with bows drawn. To shoot though is to draw this entire crowd down on us. DO NOT shoot unless you absolutely have to. It will be certain death for many of us if you do. Are we clear?" He looked to each of the hunters holding a bow. "Give your spears to a gatherer to carry for you. Gatherers, keep your knives ready." Triven governed by consensus. That he was tossing orders like a man used to doing so was a little disconcerting to the others but also reassuring. None understood what went wrong but all of them, even the children, could feel the tension. They were glad to follow orders and do as Triven asked.

Cark, Olin, and Grady ran through the crowd of clan people, who thankfully let them pass unharmed. Reta collapsed to the ground and pulled Cark to her. Flin yelled at her boys, but she cried too.

"Is everyone here?" asked Triven. He looked to the gatherers in turn. It was they who kept track of the *chaga* people. Each nodded yes. He breathed a sigh of relief and then *Chagama* spoke angrily. "Sola is missing. Ponu too." She glared at Flin.

"Sola is no .." she began.

"Save it," said Triven angrily. He hoped the Wanderer and Ponu could find her. He didn't think they could wait much longer.

Triven turned to *Chagama*. "Can you walk? At least a little way?" he asked. She nodded and he sagged with relief. The *chaga's* very existence seemed as if it was suspended on a frayed rope above a pack of hungry wolves. A sudden jerk, a breeze blown to hard, or simply just hanging there too long would drop them into the midst of it. Sure, they'd hurt a few wolves, but the likelihood of any of them surviving was nil.

Ponu and the Wanderer were desperately searching for Sola and hadn't found her. Ponu worried that she had been harmed, and that if she had Triven would feel compelled to react. If that happened, the whole *chaga* was at risk. In rising panic, he increased his pace and looked in places he had already been. He wasn't thinking any longer and he knew he was on the verge of hysteria but couldn't seem to pull himself back.

The Wanderer grabbed his arm. "Breath," he said in Ponu's language. Ponu stopped and listened to the compelling tone of the Wanderer's voice. "What Sola like?" he asked when Ponu had calmed. Ponu shook his head, at a loss and then he remembered. "Moke!" he exclaimed. "She likes Moke!"

The Wanderer took Ponu's hand and ran towards Moke's clans' camp. When he got there, he peered into all the shelters and finally, he found them. They had just finished mating and were nestled happily in the pelts.

"Sola!" exclaimed Ponu. "We must go now. Hurry. We're all in danger." With a rush the outside world blew into Moke's shelter like a tornado. The hum of the angry crowd entered their consciousness. The fear on Ponu's face. The anxious movements of the Wanderer. The pair rolled to their feet, their contentment shattered.

Sola and Moke dressed quickly and followed the Wanderer and Ponu through the crowd. It was fortunate the Wanderer was with them and that he was so revered. The people they slipped past were so filled with anger, it is unlikely that even Moke would have been allowed to pass unharmed.

Chagama pulled her close in a fierce hug when she got to camp. "Grab some meat she said and whatever pelts you can carry." That's all Sola had time to do before they were leaving.

They moved slowly, the clans letting them pass, reluctantly, it seemed. Many hissed at them. Some shouted or waved their spears but they didn't harm them. Triven kept the archers ready anyway. He wasn't taking any chances.

Kor pushed through the crowd and waved at Sola. She was crying and then she was grabbed roughly and pushed back by someone Sola didn't know. Sola couldn't see Moke anywhere and she cried inside. They hadn't even said goodbye. Would she see him again?

Posse

"We should go after them!" someone shouted.

"We should not have let them go at all," said another.

"We can catch them. That old woman will slow them down. And they have small ones too."

"Their women are weak. They are as nothing to beat."

"They have those bows," came a reasonable voice.

"And did you see how far they can throw a spear?" came another, quivering with fear.

The people were standing around the central fire. The children had been chased away and told to stay in their own camps. Nobody sat. They were too tense for that.

Ches stepped forward. "They are under the protection of the gathering. We will NOT be harming them. Not today." Tomorrow was another story. Tomorrow, the protection of the gathering would be no more. Ches had no authority. Nobody did. Each clan governed themselves. The gathering was special. Hostilities of any kind suspended for its duration. The only reason that law held was because gatherings were so infrequent. People of the clans often fought with each other, physically and violently. It was why they were so small. Ches could only hope that his words would hold these people. These people who were not known for restraining their emotions.

Moke was confused and upset. The Wanderer had insisted he let Sola go alone. Now was not the time he said. Moke had reluctantly followed that advise and was now regretting it. He followed the angry hum to the fire, and he still had no idea what this was all about. "What is it they have done?" he asked in a strong voice. Ches was proud of him. He had some idea of what it must have cost him to stay so calm.

"Donon," replied Tsutse, venom dripping from her voice. She had been Donon's mate of many years. "When we were hunting in the grass and a spear came from the sky, it came with a 'zip' sound. The sound that their far spears make. It is THEY that murdered Donon. Them and their 'zip' spear." Her voice had been strong until the end when it cracked. She turned her face away but didn't leave.

Moke was shocked. Could it be he wondered? Sola would never do that. He couldn't imagine Triven would either. Or that he would sanction it. But Sele. And Flin and even some others had never accepted him and Kor. Could one of them do something so awful. He didn't want to believe it was possible, but he had to admit it could be. To himself anyway. To admit that out loud would be to sentence the entire *chaga* to death. And so, he shook his head.

"Those people saved me. And Kor. We would be dead without their help. And now you say they murdered Donon? No. They would not do that." And then he sat.

The crowd quieted at Moke's words. Unfortunately, that peace was to last only a few seconds. Tsutse's grief was too new, her anger too strong.

"I am going after them tomorrow," she said. "I will respect the laws of the gathering only until then. Who is coming with me?"

The crowd roared on around Moke as he broke a little inside. He didn't know what to do. How to stop them or how to help Sola's *chaga*. Or how to save his own people who would surely die in the face of the *chaga's* horrible weapons.

In the end fifteen people agreed to form a posse and go after the *chaga*. Tsutse would lead them. She came to Moke and begged him to join her. He knew where the *chaga* lived, she argued. They can't be trusted she insisted. He just shook his head and eventually retreated to his shelter, his words useless and unheard.

Tsutse then came to Ches. "We would like to bring Kor to guide us," she requested. Ches was horrified at the suggestion. "Kor is a child. You cannot take her to war." He was so angry that Tsutse did not pursue it.

"It doesn't matter." She told the others. They were all expert trackers after all and the *chaga* people would not be able to hide their passage. There were too many of them.

Moke didn't just sulk in his shelter. He gathered up his knives and his spears, his warm shirt, and a sack to carry food. He left the shelter and pelts. He would be uncomfortable, but the weather was still below freezing at night, and he would travel faster without them. Moke stepped out of his shelter and right into the Wanderer.

"Ponu and I are going to warn them," he said. The Wanderer had seen Moke leave the crowd and disappear into the shelter and suspected what he might do next. Moke frowned. He couldn't see Ponu anywhere. "He's waiting in the trees," said the Wanderer. "I stayed in the hopes of swaying them not to do this, but I've failed. If you go, they will follow you." The Wanderer nodded his head in the direction of a clansman, sitting close by, staring at them. "They won't think to follow me. Can you stay?" The Wanderer waited sadly for Moke to answer.

With reluctance, Moke nodded. The Wanderer and Moke embraced and then he was gone. Moke wondered if he would see him again. He wondered if he would see Sola again. He wondered if the clans would kill her. If they would kill all the *chaga* people. His heart broke a little.

On the Run

The *chaga* travelled late into the night. The moon was full but still, the going was dangerous and tiring. They set up two shelters and the entire *chaga* huddled under them uncomfortable and squished. Only their exhaustion allowed them to sleep.

Ponu and the Wanderer had caught up with them late that afternoon and explained to Triven what went so terribly wrong. Triven hadn't yet had time to digest the information or question the *chaga*. He was too concerned with their immediate safety. He was relieved to know that the gathering laws forbade the clans to go after them. Until this morning anyway. That meant they had a head start, but the posse wasn't burdened with old and young like they were. They wouldn't catch them today, but they might the next, or the one after that, and their winter cave was days away. They needed a plan. Triven didn't have one and until he did, they would move as quickly as he could make them.

Triven woke Ponu and the Wanderer first. "The Wanderer needs to go back to his own people," he stated emphatically. Ponu looked like he would protest and Triven continued, "I don't know what the future holds. What happens if he has to choose? What will he do? He may not want to, but he may have to betray us if it comes to them or us. I'm sorry Ponu, but he has to go."

Triven watched for a moment as the pair retreated a distance. They cried and they held each other. What words they shared he didn't know but their grief was plain to see. He felt terrible but knew he had done the right thing. The safety of all the *chaga* had to come before the happiness of one.

"Let's go," Triven called. He didn't wait for sleepers to wake. He started pulling poles down immediately. Grady cried and Olin grumbled. The young girls did too but their mothers shushed them harshly, gave them a bite to eat and started helping. They would eat on the run.

"I need someone to scout behind," said Triven. "They might send a scout ahead so you must be fast, and you MUST stay hidden. We will be able to move faster if the men can carry children instead of bows."

"I will scout," volunteered Privon.

I will too," said Bron.

"Bron, I need you to carry shelters." Bron was too young for scouting, his legs too short and his judgement not yet mature. Triven wouldn't risk him for his own sake as well as the *chaga's*.

"I will scout too," said Ras.

Triven paused as he looked at Ras. "No. It must be someone else." He offered no explanation and was clearly angry with Ras. Triven didn't trust him. He had showed poor judgement by using the atlatl. The stakes were just too high.

"I will scout," said Ponu. He offered this with reluctance. Could he actually betray the Wanderer if it came to that? He wasn't sure he trusted himself. There was no one else though.

Triven was relieved and he nodded. If one scout was taken, they could all be taken unawares. Two were better odds. "You head slightly east. Privon, you go slightly west. Not too far apart, just enough that you can see each other. Just. We will travel through the trees. It will be slower but if we travel the steppe, they will be able to spot us too easily, and they will be faster. Right now, the only delay we can put in their path is that they must pause to track us."

The *chaga* were ready and Triven was grateful. Sometimes, everybody pulled together. He didn't think he could deal with dissent on top of his other worries. Fortunately, as it turned out, Triven was able to deal with more than he thought he could.

He watched the scouts run out and then he turned to the *chaga* he had sworn to lead with wisdom and convinced to follow him with promises of safety and full bellies. "Come," he said to them. They were on the edge of the forest and in a moment had disappeared into it.

For three days they ran much as they had the first. They were slowed by their burdens, and tree stumps, boulders, streams, and the weaving through the forest they had to do. People were tiring and Triven was worried about how long they could keep it up. There was no sign of the scouts, another worry. The moon would not be in the sky this night. They would have to setup camp at dusk, loosing precious hours. Maybe it was just as well he thought. They needed rest, and if they couldn't travel, neither could the posse.

In the morning of the fourth day, the *chaga* woke to a fog so dense and thick and wet it gathered on the tree branches and rained down on them in slow thick drops. Direction was impossible to discern. Visibility was less than the length of a man. Triven knew they shouldn't be travelling. They could too easily go in the wrong direction or lose each other, but they had no choice. The clans could follow their tracks. They didn't need to see anything but what was right in front of them to do that. He wished now that he had taken a stand instead of running. The clans outnumbered them, but their own weapons were far superior.

"We have to push on," he said. "We'll travel single file, and we'll all hold on to spears so that nobody gets lost. Sele, would you go last? Bron, I need you to travel away from us. If they DO follow our tracks, they won't be sure of which are the right ones. Fabe, you too. Don't get lost!" The two young hunters nodded, eager to help and rejoined the group late in the afternoon.

The fog didn't lift that day and it greeted them the following morning, thicker and wetter, it seemed. The eeriness of it frightened the children. If they whimpered, they were slapped or pinched. Quiet was essential. They seemed to understand and quickly exhausted themselves with tension and fear. A blessing of the harshest kind.

Just as they were getting ready to push on, there were muffled footsteps in the distance. A branch broken. A leaf stepped on. Triven froze and listened. The others froze as well. Triven drew his bow forward and notched an arrow. He could only hear one set of footsteps and he sent a silent prayer to the Earth Mother requesting she deliver Privon or Ponu and not a clansman.

The footsteps came closer, and a shadow figure appeared. "I found you!" exclaimed Privon. He made his way up the line to Triven. "They're close," he said. "They'll catch up by tomorrow afternoon, assuming the fog lifts.

The day after if not." Although they could track in the fog, it was slow going.

"Any sign of Ponu?" Triven asked.

"I could see him in the distance sometimes until the fog came. I didn't see him captured if that's what you're asking. They don't send scouts either," he said.

Triven was relieved. He himself was not at all experienced in conflict. It seemed they weren't either. Despite how badly things went at the gathering, Triven clung to the hope of redeeming the situation. He didn't know how but he wasn't ready to give up. The *chaga* would want to go back south and he knew that wasn't the answer for them. There were just too many people where they came from and their *chaga* too small. Conflict was in their future no matter where they went it seemed.

All day Triven thought about what they could do. He concocted a plan, discarded it, and then came up with another. Finally, he settled on one with a heavy heart. If it failed, the hunters might survive but the gatherers and children could possibly perish. He shook his head to shake that image away. Failure was not an option.

The Trail

For the third day, the fog hung over the clan people in the forest. It muffled sounds and blinded eyes. Their ears came awake and none of the clan liked what they heard. Twigs snapped. Leaves rustled. Sometimes things went thump. It was eerie and they were frightened.

Tsutse overheard Diky and Uvo talking about their winter stores the night before. They had none and it was fall and time was wasting. Ensuring their clans safety in winter was beginning to seem more important to them than chasing strangers through the eerie fog.

Tsutse was not a patient woman, but she wasn't stupid either. She would have to sway them with self interest.

"These people murdered Donon for no reason," she reminded them. "They could do the same to any of us. We must wipe them out and ensure that can never happen."

"If they murdered him, then why were they so eager to be our friends?" asked Diky.

"Yes. And why did they allow their daughter to mate with Moke?"

"Their weapons! They could pick us off, one by one and we wouldn't even see them in this fog." This is what everyone was really thinking. At that moment, something went 'thunk" and they huddled nervously.

Tsutse had no answers. These were reasonable questions, but her own feelings were beyond reason. What could she say? What could she do to make sure they followed her?

"If it was your mate, Diky, that was murdered, I would go. And Uvo, what if it were your daughter? Would your son be next? Will they pick us off one by one as we quiver in fear because of a little fog or a winter storm? What good will storing meat do any of us if we're all dead?" She couldn't tell what affect, if any, her words had, and she didn't wait to find out. She had nothing else to offer. She picked up her spears and started to follow the strangers' tracks.

She pretended indifference but sighed in relief when she heard them following. There were more mutterings throughout the day, but she ignored them. They were with her and that's all she cared about.

With no warning other than a 'whoosh' that fluttered her hair, an arrow landed with a thud on the ground in front of her. And then another 'whoosh' and one landed beside her. A third whoosh saw one land behind her. Then a flurry of sound and arrows were all around them. Everyone froze. Their worst fears playing out in front of them. The arrows came from above and Tsutse peered up. Between the fog and the branches, the most she could make out were vague shapes that might be the strangers. They were out of reach of her spear and for the first time, she really took in just how powerful their weapons were compared to her own. Bravado and anger and determination would gain her nothing in the face of them. Then she remembered how much she loved her people. Ross and Chor, her sons were with her. Had she brought them to their death?

Ross, as if following the meanderings of her mind, hefted his spear in his hand, leaned back as far as he could, to add as much force as he could muster to his throw, and stepped forward to release. An arrow found him a second before he stepped forward. The spear dropped harmlessly to the ground. Ross dropped on top of it. Tsutse was shocked into stillness. It was Chor who bent to check on Ross. The arrow had pierced his neck. He stared up at Chor for a brief moment and then was gone.

A young voice spoke out. "No turtu," it said. The words meant no argument with words, but the clans people understood. These strange ones didn't want to fight.

"You murdered Donon!" Tsutse declared. "And now my Ross!" She tried to make her voice strong, but fear and pain laced it as she fully comprehended their vulnerability for the first time.

"Wom," insisted the young voice. It was telling them to go home. An arrow flew. It pierced the sleeve of her Chor's coat and Tsutse knew fear like never before. She had yet more to lose.

Nothing moved. The wind was still. The birds were quiet. Clan people and *chaga* people alike waited tensely for Tsutse to respond. A tear slipped from her eye, and she turned away. Her shoulders slumped in defeat. She bent to lift Ross and Chor helped her. Two other clan people helped as well, and then they disappeared into the forest. Tsutse went only a few feet before turning back and lifting her shoulders again in determination. The fog hid her. This wasn't over she vowed. It was only over for now.

Chagama's Story

The *chaga* breathed a collective sigh of relief. The cave was just ahead. It offered sanctuary and rest. The weary travellers were in need of both.

Triven posted scouts after their first night back. He couldn't spare the hunters, but neither could he spare the scouts. He only posted one hunter after the first night. He insisted a gatherer watch from the cave mouth. They could see both trees and steppe from there. *Chagama*, still recovering from her twisted ankle, did it most days.

"*Chagama*. You have been silent throughout all our discussions about these strangers," said Triven gently. In the months since they had first met Moke and Kor, *Chagama* had not voiced an opinion, told a story, or otherwise participated in *chaga* leadership. She had never been shy in the past and in fact had often needled Triven to the edge of sanity when she felt strongly about something. He had let her be this past year. He didn't understand but he could see she struggled. He needed her now, more than ever though. Her time for retreat had to end. He waited. All the others had left the cave this morning. The hunters were after a herd of gallopers they had spotted far in the distance. The gatherers were bringing in the last of the nuts and digging up parsnips and potatoes. The children with them. Triven hung back, determined to talk to *Chagama*, and now, the two of them sat by the fire, no sound but it's crackling.

Sola climbed the path to the cave. Her steps were heavy, reflecting her thoughts. She worried about Moke. She worried for *Chagama*, who was even more withdrawn since their return to the cave. She worried for the *chaga* and for the clans, and she worried for the life she knew grew inside her. Would he be accepted? It seemed that clan and *chaga* despised each other and he would be both. Welcomed or shunned? Would it be better to take some pennyroyal and try to abort?

"If you don't have a story to guide us, could you make one up? I fear the *chaga* will splinter like a lightening struck tree if we don't show them a path."

Sola stopped at the top of the path. Make up a story? Did *Chagama* do that? Wouldn't people be angry if they found out?

Finally, Chagama spoke. Her voice crackled with emotion, echoing the sound of the fire. "I have searched and searched for a story to guide us, but I have only one." *Chagama* paused for long enough that Triven thought she might not continue.

Sola peered into the dark cave. *Chagama* and Triven sat together quietly. Sola was about to leave when she saw a lone tear trace a path down *Chagama's* cheek. For a moment she stared. She had never seen *Chagama* cry and so she came into the cave and sat beside her and without a word, took her hand and squeezed it.

This happened to my mother's mother's mother's chaga, began *Chagama's* story.

My mother's mother's mother was not yet a woman but would be soon. Her breasts were but beestings, Her mound bare as a babe's bum. They were not a large chaga, but they weren't a small one either. It was a clear day, the sun warm on their skin as they trailed a herd of gallopers. Their bellies were full, and they weren't in a terrible hurry. They rested often. My mother's mother's mother played with the other children. She was a galloper as were the other girls and they pranced about while the boys chased them with their spears. They screamed in delight and pretended fear. Oh, what fun they had that day. Chagama paused for a long time. Sola squeezed her hand and waited.

'Chaga!' called someone. My mother's mother's mother paused her game. Another chaga was always fun. There would have new people to play with and news and often a feast if food was plentiful which it was. With excitement, they waited as the other chaga waved and drew close.

They couldn't see who they were at first and the adults puzzled about it. They knew the chaga's who roamed the steppe with them. It was odd that nobody called out 'there's Bot!' or 'it's Tatu's chaga'. Soon it became apparent that they didn't know them at all. The children thought that was even more exciting.

The chaga had met strangers before. Not often. But often enough not to fear them. Their Chagama had many stories that told of strangers, and except for those small bands of men that roamed and had no chaga, they were not dangerous.

At first things went along as they always do. The children played. The adults chatted. Their chaga setup shelters and built a big fire and shared their food. They had no Chagama and so our mother's mother's mother's Chagama told stories. Happy ones that were for entertainment and not lessons.

My mother's mother's mother dozed off and woke to one of the boys pulling her. A hunter really. Just. He tugged her arm, and she followed him willingly enough, and then suddenly he was on her, and his penis was in her. She was shocked, afraid, dry, and unready. She screamed of course. He was finished by the time her mother found her, but it was obvious what had happened. Her thighs were covered in blood, his penis still hard and dripping. My mother's mother's mother's mother grew blind with fury. Had the child been a woman, she may not have been so upset but she was a child still and mating with a child is forbidden, and so, she pulled her knife out and stabbed the boy which is a right thing to do in such circumstances. The young hunter's mother screamed and pulled her hair as he bled out on the ground beside my mother's mother's mother, and then someone killed the child's mother, and everybody in the chaga was fighting. Chagama, ever wise, called out and tried to calm the fighting. A spear struck her silent.

My mother's mother's mother lay in that spot, blood dried on her thighs, dead hunter beside her, as it went on around her. She stared, not comprehending, seeing, or hearing anything that went on. Eventually she slept. Even as the screams filled the air. When she woke, she thought she might be the only survivor, it was so quiet. She got up, dazed, and looked around. Two men and a woman saw her and pleaded for help. Their wounds were dire but not fatal. She didn't help them. They were from the other chaga. A babe cried too, but she did not know him and did not help him. She found one boy from her own chaga and took his hand and they walked away.

"So, you see," said *Chagama*. The only story I have of strangers is a terrible one. Everything in me screams KILL THEM before they kill us, and my reason tells me that is the very course that will bring our ultimate destruction, and theirs. My wisdom, hard earned, says there is a more reasonable course, but my fear paralyzes me, and I cannot think of it.

Triven, I cannot help you." Sola's beloved *Chagama* shook with tears and could not be comforted.

Grief

Mor stood at the entrance of Tsutse and Donon's cave, the place she had called home for the last few years. The place where Tsutse had helped her deliver her son. Her back was loaded with shelter, pelts, and babe. Ross, her mate was gone now and Tsutse was bitter and full of hate. Mor had shared her grief at first but could no longer stand it. She would go to Ches's cave. Her sister Neti was there. Their boys were of an age and perhaps, next gathering, she would choose a new mate. She was young and only had the one child. She was determined her life would be more than sadness and hate. Mor wiped a tear and stepped out of the cave. Chor and Luco, Tsutse's other son and his mate, had whispered their goodbyes the night before and watched now, silently. Tsutse was angry and kept her gaze on the fire.

"Goodbye," Mor said anyway. "I have loved you," and then she was gone.

Tsutse was lost. Her life with Donon, raising her sons, had been so happy. She had barely survived her mate's death. It was her grandchildren that saved her then, but even they couldn't find her now. All that was left was a woman that looked like Tsutse. Her sound, her scent, they were gone. The children were afraid of her which is why Mor left. Luco would go too, Chor feared, if Tsutse didn't come back, and then he would have to choose. His mate. His mother.

Decisions

They had been back to their cave for days. The business of taking care of immediate needs was tended. They had hunted and gathered and collected firewood. Despite full bellies and home comforts, people were tense.

After Triven's talk with *Chagama*, he spent days walking the forest and the steppe. Thinking. People looked to him for leadership, and he was at a loss. *Chagama's* story played over and over in his mind. Maybe things were destined to devolve into war between strangers. He rejected that thought but it kept returning to his mind, nipping at his peace, and then he saw the answer. It was right there in the story all along.

"We have two big topics to discuss," Triven said, by the fire that evening. "The first is 'What happened to Donon'?" He looked to Ponu, who understood the conflict the deepest. Did he have the name right? He nodded. "The second is 'What do we do next'". He waited a long time after these words. The chatter was loud as people discussed these things amongst themselves. Finally, he pounded the ground, as *Chagama* did when she was calling for a story.

"I want to go back home now!" insisted Flin. She wasn't reasonable at the best of times. Fear made her less so.

"You know we can't go back over the mountains now Flin. It would be certain death for all of us. We can, however, make plans for the spring. Do we want to go south in spring?"

"Yes," said Flin. A few others joined her.

"No," said Sola, Bron and others.

The 'no's' had the majority but that isn't how the *chaga* worked. Triven tried to get everybody to agree to a plan. It led to better harmony amongst them.

"I have to remind you all of why we came over the mountains in the first place. There were too many people. The herds disappeared. Friction between *chaga's*, virtually unheard of in my youth, is becoming common now. If we go back, we face those problems again. As before, I don't have a solution for them other than to join a larger *chaga* which brings a new set of problems.

Here," continued Triven. We have plenty of food. The clans are spread out. We have to travel many days to see one whereas in the south, it seemed we were always seeing others. We have shelter. We have superior weapons which doesn't make us invulnerable, but they do make us a force to be wary of.

If we stay, we must make peace with the clans. Otherwise, we live under threat and that will be unbearable. I have an idea for that…" Triven trailed off while discussion broke out again amongst the *chaga*.

"What is your idea?" asked Reta. She, of course, had lost the most on the journey north. She had a new babe now and would not willingly risk it again.

The rest of the *chaga* were quiet as they waited for Triven to respond.

"When we see another *chaga,* we greet them happily. Maybe it is Bata's chaga, and as Bata's mate is Brella's sister, feasting with them is a pleasure. Or maybe it is Siv's *chaga*. Our sister, Sele, and we hug her happily. It is the ties to these other *chaga's* that make our relationship with them secure.

We don't have ties with the clans. Yet. But what if we did? What if when we came across Moke's clan, we met them with joy because our Sola lived with them, and we were happy to see her? What if Bron chose a girl from another clan and she had a babe and her mother felt pleasure to see her? What if we forge ties with these people? What if we make them our family?

If we did that, we could stay here. We wouldn't need to worry about being ambushed, or if there was enough food, or if our *chaga* was big enough to stand the pressure of a larger *chaga* being near us. We could be safe. Fed. Happy. What if we could have all those things?"

"I would rather be hungry than mate with one of them," cried Flin, and she shuddered in horror.

"But wouldn't you be happy to see Sola?" asked Reta.

Flin looked at Sola for a long moment before answering. "No," was all she said before turning away. "We should go back across the mountains to where we belong."

Sola fought back tears at that response. She hadn't ever been close to Flin, nor could she remember any kindness from her, but the stark, shamelessly bald response cut her deeply, nevertheless. She took a deep breath and hardened her heart. She had *Chagama*, Reta, Triven, Ponu firmly in her court. She didn't need Flin.

"I don't like the winter here," said Alli, "and I don't want a mate from the clans. I would have to hunt if I lived with them, and I don't want to hunt."

This last was something that Sola hadn't thought about. She didn't know how to hunt. Would she want to if she did, she wondered? She didn't think so. Would Moke expect her to if she were his true mate? She didn't know the answer to that, and if he did expect her to hunt, would she want to be his true mate?

"I would take a mate from the clans," said Bron. He had someone in mind already.

The discussion went on for a long time. In the end, there was no resolution or agreement from the *chaga* on what they should do next. Triven was tired. Too tired to bring up the other matter.

"We'll talk more tomorrow," he said and then he retreated to his bed at the back of the cave.

Triven again wandered the steppe and the forest for the entire day, thinking. At the fire that evening, he decided to change tactics.

"Tonight, we talk about Donon. Even should we agree that we'll stay and have the clans as our family, it won't work unless we figure out what happened to Donon and fix that problem."

"We had nothing to do with Donon," insisted Flin.

With patience, Triven responded, "Flin. It is a hunter that killed Donon. The options are one of theirs or one of ours. As a gatherer, I think it fair to say that you would not be able to determine that. This discussion is really for the hunters. The gatherers' role here is to listen."

Flin flushed but retreated in silence which was a relief to more than just Triven.

"The clans have accused us of murder," Triven continued. The words hung over the *chaga*. There was no larger crime. "It had to be the spear thrower that killed him. That's the only thing that makes that 'zip' sound. I don't think it's possible to throw a spear without the thrower, hard enough to make that sound."

"It's not murder if they're not people," came Flin's retort. Once again, Triven regretted allowing her into the *chaga* those many years ago, but then his eyes fell on Sola. She was a blessing he could never regret.

"Quiet Flin!" came a chorus of voices. Triven smiled inwardly but carefully kept his expression bland.

"I don't think they have spear throwers. Ponu, Sola, anyone? Have you seen them use a tool like that?" None had. "I think then, we can be sure it wasn't one of them that killed Donon." Triven had suspected that was the case, but it hurt him deeply to say that with certainty.

"Did anyone here throw a spear at one of these strangers?"

Ras and Sele exchanged a glance but were silent. As were Ponu and Privon.

"What about you two?" asked Triven as he looked at Bron and Fabe. He didn't think either had near enough skill with atlatl but had to ask. They shook their heads.

"Has anyone seen sign of others like us?"

At that, there was a great deal of excitement. "I would stay here if there were!" from Alli. When the excitement quieted, Triven repeated the question as it hadn't been answered, but none had seen others like them.

Triven didn't know where to take the discussion next and gave up again with a sigh.

For the next few days, the hunters and gathers and children spent long hours preparing for winter. They had tasted the winter of these parts and had no interest in worrying about food again. In the evenings, Triven strived for consensus on what they should do come spring. And he continued to ask about Donon but got nowhere. Eventually, he left the decisions for another day, far into the future.

Reta

"*Chagama, Chagama*!" cried Sola.

Chagama was sitting by the fire. The last days before winter brought frosty mornings and freezing nights. *Chagama* was feeling her age and waited for the warmth of the sun to warm the air before venturing out. Her ankle had healed but it bothered her on cold or wet days. She would not be going back over the mountains if that is what the *chaga* decided but she kept that decision to herself.

Sola appeared at the cave entrance, panting and frantic. The light of the day momentarily blinded her as she sought out the shape of *Chagama.*

"What is it?" *Chagama* asked as she pulled herself to her feet. Her knees groaned in protest, but she could tell by Sola's tone that whatever it was would require her presence, and that meant a trip down the path and into whatever patch of steppe or trees Sola had been searching for food.

"It's Reta!" panted Sola. "We found her unconscious and bleeding from her legs. Her vagina I think."

By the time Sola and *Chagama* got to Reta, she was waking. As soon as she was able, she cried "Bale! Bale!" and the other women passed him to her. They had found him sleeping nearby. Whatever had happened to Reta, it seemed that the young babe had slept through it. Reta clutched him to her so tightly it caused him to scream in angry protest.

Chagama squatted beside her. She could see that Reta was hurt but not greatly, so she waited with patience and wisdom for mother and babe to calm down.

"What happened?" she asked when they had. Tears came to Reta's eyes and *Chagama* squeezed her hand while the other women petted her in comfort.

"It was strangers. Men from the clans. Two of them. I was pulling these onions," Reta waved to the scattered onions on the ground beside her, "and they were just there. Standing in front of me. They weren't like Moke or Kor. They hated me! I could see it in their eyes. They held their spears so tight; I was sure they were going to kill me, and I think one of them might have but for the other. He held him back and pulled out his penis and rubbed it until it was hard. I knew what they were going to do then and all I could think was 'please don't wake up Bale'. And I prayed to the Earth Mother and the river spirits and when they threw me back on the ground, I pleaded with the sky spirit too. It hurt so much! I could feel the blood and I thought 'Earth Mother, I give it gladly. Please, let that be enough.' And it was. I passed out before the other raped me. I assume he did, but I don't know. I think all the spirits answered me and kept me and Bale safe."

Chagama examined her. She was torn and bleeding, but the abrasions were shallow. She would be fine. Physically, at least. *Chagama* found some moss and gave it to her to pack in her belt and the women helped her back to the cave.

It was a subdued *chaga* that sat by the fire that night. They had all just been reminded of how vulnerable their position was.

"Did you recognize them?" asked Triven.

"Aside from Moke, they mostly all look the same to me," said Reta. Others nodded. It was hard to pick out individuals amongst the many strange faces. It would take much more than a single gathering to learn their distinct features.

People who had previously argued to stay, like Bron, Ponu and Sola were quiet now or, in the case of Bron, voiced their change of mind.

It was decided. The *chaga* would go back over the mountains in the spring.

Sola and Ponu both retreated to their own beds, turned away from their *chaga*. Sorrow and regret their companion for the night.

Nightmares

The sun was high in the sky, its rays casting no shadows of relief from their unrelenting warmth. The trees were tall by the river and the mist trapped between their branches the night before hadn't completely dissipated though it soon would. For now, the trees were a dubious haven.

The boy crouched low in the grass. It didn't grow very high amongst the trees, but it was late summer, and the grass was at it's tallest and he was small enough to hide in it. He was pretending to be a long tooth cat and he had his eye on prey. His mother. She was picking berries not too far from him. She knew he was there and smiled to herself, but the boy didn't notice that. He was circling around so that he could surprise her. So intent on his own movements, he didn't notice the rustlings of grass or breaking of twigs that signaled the presence of someone, or something else in the trees.

His mother heard. She stilled, her head tilted, listening. She was about to call for him when three men stepped out. They were unkempt, their loin clothes tatty and stained. Their hair in matts or missing altogether, and their skin blackened with dirt. She had heard of men like this. They had no *chaga* of their own and they travelled in bands, taking what they could from unwary people. Like her. In a flash, she was regretting her decision to strike out on her own this morning, seeking respite from the gossip and petty disputes of the other gatherers.

She took a deep breath. She put her bag, made of hides carefully stitched together, on the ground beside her. At her waist, she carried her knife and she reached towards it but before she could grasp it, one of the men had crossed the clearing and clasped her wrist roughly.

"No need for that," he said as he reached for the knife with his other hand and tossed it into the river behind her. The other two approached more cautiously. They moved slowly and peered through the trees. "Who is with you?" one demanded. It was very rare for anyone to be on their own.

"Nobody," she answered quickly and loudly. A message to the boy in the grass. She squeezed her eyes closed and quietly asked the spirit of the grass to hide him well.

One man reached for the bag of berries she had set down and casually tossed a handful into his mouth. The purple juice dribbled out the side as he chewed and the look in his eyes frightened her. The one holding her arm pulled her closer. She could feel his hard penis through her loincloth. It was all she wore in the heat. Again, she breathed deeply. She could survive a rape, she told herself. If she screamed, she feared it would cause her son to come to her and she didn't want that.

The man holding her threw her to the ground. He pulled his loin cloth off and dropped down between her legs. The other squatted on either side of her. They grinned and she shut her eyes tight, unable to look at the evil she saw in their eyes.

The boy watched from the grass, wide eyed and terrified. He wanted to scream but his voice didn't work. He wanted to run but his legs didn't work either. He watched in helpless terror as his mother was raped, again and again by the strangers.

When the men were done, his mother lay quietly like she was sleeping. He could see her chest rise so he knew she was alive. Young as he was, he was well familiar with death. He saw it all the time and knew what it looked like. This wasn't it.

The three men casually put their loincloths back on. They stood for a moment and looked at the woman on the ground and then they picked her up and tossed her into the river with a laugh. Then they were gone as suddenly as they had come. Silence hung over the clearing.

The boy stayed in the grass. Night fell and he didn't move. Eventually, he slept. He awoke in terror at dawn. He had dreamed that a long tooth cat had pounced on his mother and dragged her away.

He got up and went to the bank of the river. He couldn't see his mother anywhere. He called to her until his voice cracked and his throat hurt. He sat down and he waited. There was no answer. He was hungry so he went to the bushes where his mother had been picking berries. He found her bag there and thrust his hand in and pulled out a handful of berries which he pushed into his mouth greedily. The purple juice dribbled from the corner of his mouth, and it was fortunate he couldn't see what he looked like.

He ate nothing but berries that day and slept with the bag clutched in his arms that night. And the next. He woke to the sound of voices the morning after that. He froze in terror.

Zin found him when she tripped over him by the berry bush. She saw his terror and the streaks from tears on his cheeks and she picked him up and held him close. He latched on tight and wouldn't let go. He was of an age as her Triven, and she decided in that moment that she would raise him as her own. She asked him what his name was, but he wouldn't answer. He didn't speak for weeks. Unsure if he ever would, Zin decided to call him Sele which meant 'found one'.

When he finally began to talk, Zin asked him what had happened to him, and why he was alone, all he said was "Cat". And then the tears fell quietly down his cheeks, and he didn't talk for days. Zin never asked again.

Unmasked

Sele called out in his sleep, "Stop, Stop!" and a while later, he called out "Satu!" *Chagama* woke and went to him. She didn't know who Satu was, but she had a suspicion. Sele was still sleeping as tears ran down his cheeks, and he tossed and kicked.

Chagama lay beside him and held him as best she could. When he finally woke up, he felt her arms and lay for a moment before nestling his head against her breast like he had when he'd been a child.

"I remember," he sobbed. "It wasn't a cat. It was strangers. I hid. I did nothing as they raped her and then tossed her in the river. I just watched. I couldn't move, I was so afraid, and I couldn't call out. I just watched as they raped her and tossed her into the river."

"Oh honey, you were so tiny. You couldn't have saved her any more than Bale could have saved Reta. It's not your fault. Not at all."

The rest of the *chaga* had woken to Sele's cries and they listened quietly as he cried in *Chagama's* arms. When morning came, Brella handed him some meat for breakfast and Flin filled his water bag. Brella heated some potatoes in fat for him and Triven slapped him gently on the back. The *chaga* was there for him.

That night, by the fire, a quiet and humbled Sele relayed his memory of the loss of his mother to the *chaga* who had adopted him and loved him. When he was done, he was quiet for a time and then he continued.

"I was wrong about the strangers. I think I became that little boy again when I saw Moke and Kor and they were so different and unknown. It was a feeling I had that they were dangerous, but that was wrong. Yes, two, who attacked Reta were dangerous, but that isn't all of them. It is two of them, and they were provoked by the death of their Donon. I would kill those strangers who threw my mother in the river easily and without regret but the strangers who saved me?" He looked at *Chagama* as he said this. "To them, I would give my life."

"Did you kill Donon," Triven asked formally, sure of the answer.

Sele didn't answer for a long while. A tear rolled down his cheek when finally he responded. "I didn't. But it could have been me and it was an accident. It was that day you sent us out to look for others. Ras and I were together, and we had travelled far north and east. A herd of elk were on the steppe. We watched them for a while and then we thought, 'we haven't seen any other people, but this is a gift from the earth mother.' And So Ras got ready with his atlatl and spear while I prepared to fire with the bow. Just as we were ready, Donon stood up. I was surprised and my arrow landed in front of me. Ras's atlatl struck true. We hadn't even known they were there. They were hidden in the grass, and we were too far away. We just watched in shock. We only got a brief look at them, but we knew they were different. They all hid in the grass after we, Ras, threw the spear. We waited. The elk fled in a thunder of hooves and the dust hung in the air, but those people didn't move again. Finally, we just left.

Ras and I never talked about it. Even when you started asking, but it was an accident, and I told myself they weren't people, and it was no different than if he had hit the elk instead. Then Moke and Kor came. They had to be not people. Do you see?" Sele turned to Sola. "I'm sorry Sola."

Sola was crying. She felt like her heart was breaking. If Sele had just been braver. More honest. Maybe she wouldn't have to lose Moke. She couldn't be angry with him. He was too sincere in his regret. Sola reached forward and squeezed his hand in forgiveness.

"I see that I have made things worse by clinging to the idea that their death didn't matter because they weren't people. His eyes slid to Ras. "And I have been proud of the deed. Pleased it was done." He hung his head and tears he had thought dried up welled again.

Triven hadn't missed his glance at Ras. Nor did he miss the paleness and shock in Ras's face.

Ras jumped to his feet. "You said they were evil!" he screamed at Sele. "You said they all needed to be killed!" He ran from the cave and into the night.

Both Ras and Sele knew that Ras had, in truth, had time to refrain from throwing his spear. A moment only. But enough. Triven could read this too and suspected the truth of things.

It was Sele who found him and brought him back a week later. He was half starved, and his eyes were crazed. He had frostbite on two toes and *Chagama* thought she would have to cut them off. Ras refused to speak to anyone except for Sele. He would only eat or drink if Sele stayed with him and encouraged him. *Chagama* shook her head mournfully when she looked at him and encouraged the others to let him be.

Decisions Made

The snow was melting. In some spots, the ground could be seen. It was a warm day and Sola stepped out of the cave with a heavy heart. The *chaga* had already started preparing for the journey across the mountains and Sola didn't want to go. Every morning she rose and looked past the trees to the distant steppe, hoping to see Moke. He would come. Sometimes, she was sure of that. Other times she thought it might be wishful thinking. If he did come, would he come in time? What would Sele do if he saw him first? Or Ras?

Sola headed to the creek to fill her water bag. Bending was already becoming difficult, and the babe wasn't even due until late spring. She had no mate to help her and her mother, well, her mother wasn't likely to and *Chagama* was showing her age. Sola worried about travelling over the mountains. It would be difficult for both her and *Chagama*. With her water full, Sola decided to walk. She made her way through the trees and found the spot where Kor and Moke had camped the previous winter. Signs of them were hard to see. Even the blackened earth where they had kept their fire had partially recovered, the black washed away by snow and rain so that only grey remained. Tiny grass shoots were showing and soon they hide it completely. She smiled as she remembered being naked in the snow with them. How carefree they were that day!

Sola heard noises from the trees, and she was suddenly reminded of why she had been warned not to walk alone. Predators were always hungriest at the end of winter when game was scarce and what could be found was lean with hunger. She froze and listened. Often, she could tell what it was by the sounds it made while walking through the forest. All her people were skilled at this. One animal she decided. She listened more. A person! Trying not to get too excited, she shifted so that she was hidden by the trunk of a large tree. She hadn't forgotten what had happened to Reta. Whoever it was, was getting close now and she risked a peek around the trunk. It wasn't Moke and she was suddenly completely and utterly deflated. She had so hoped. Quietly, she sunk to the ground.

The Wanderer was just as skilled at identifying sounds in the forest as Sola was. He made his way to her and ignored the mushy ground as he sat beside her.

"Good morning," he said. This made her smile as she was reminded of Moke. She shook off her disappointment and clasped his hands as she gazed into his face. His eyes had dark circles that hadn't been there in the fall. And bags too. There were more grey hairs. He seemed older. As if all the cares of the clans rested with him alone.

"Good morning to you! Come, Ponu will be so happy to see you." The Wanderer smiled at that, and Sola saw the man she was used to seeing. Being with Ponu would be good for him.

A flurry of activity met them as they returned to the cave. The hunters had just returned and brought a deer back with them. The women were slicing the meat, as the younger *chaga* members gathered firewood so that it could be smoked in preparation for the journey home. *Chagama* was sorting through pelts, deciding which to bring and which to leave. She had yet to tell anyone that she wasn't going. She slipped some good pelts into the back room of the cave for her own use. Ponu was resting by the fire, spent from his day's activity. At the sight of the Wanderer, he jumped to his feet, all vestiges of fatigue sliding off him as his face lit up in joy and surprise. The two embraced and then disappeared into the trees together.

By the fire that evening, the Wanderer did what he always did. He relayed news. He was, however, careful in what he chose to share. Although he, himself bore no ill will to the *chaga* and loved Ponu fiercely, he would not betray his people.

"Tsutse is still intent on driving you out," he said through Ponu. "You have time. But not much."

"Moke...," he began and then trailed off. He was staring at the cave wall behind the fire. Ponu frowned in confusion, but the Wanderer was oblivious to him and everyone else. He got to his feet and walked as if in a daze, to the cave wall. He turned around and held up a small skull, burnished brown with age.

"Where did you get this?" he asked through Ponu. It was *Chagama* who responded.

"My mother passed it down to me from her mother and her mother's mother's mother."

The Wanderer listened carefully to her words. He was sure he understood but looked for a translation from Ponu just the same. He frowned in concentration as he rolled the skull over in his hands, examining every aspect of it. Finally, he looked up and said, "Ches has one just like it."

Bone Hearth

"Their wise woman says she has a story she must tell you. They beg your ear and your protection until the tale is told."

Ches regarded the Wanderer for a long, long time before stepping to the cave entrance to peer outside. He couldn't see anything except the odd shadow by the light of their fire. He suspected their hunters had their weapons close and ready though. Just in case.

Ches was well aware that his own hunters, even with the women, were outnumbered by theirs, and that the *chaga* weapons were so superior that a fight may as well be suicide. He appreciated the courtesy in the request but that did nothing to soothe the well of fear that sat in his belly.

Moke waited breathlessly for Ches to respond. He wanted to run down and find Sola and ask her to be his true mate. Frome held his arm and although he could shake it off, he didn't.

"In the morning. When they have rested," said Ches finally.

The *chaga* arranged themselves behind *Chagama*. Triven sat at her right, Sele her left. The hunters sat on the outside of the group, even young Bron and Fabe. The gatherers and children sat between them. Aside from the knives that everyone carried at their waist, they had left their weapons in their shelters. A show of faith that Triven had insisted on.

Ches descended first from his cave. His family behind him. He arranged a pelt that he had brought with him in front of *Chagama* and then lowered himself to sit on it. His family mirrored the *chaga* and arrayed themselves behind him. They had brought their spears but placed them at their backs, as they would if they were meeting friends.

Moke's eyes sought out Sola, but she was hidden behind her *chaga,* and he vowed he wouldn't let them leave without seeing her, no matter how this turned out.

This story is from my mother's mother's mother. Who got it from her mother's mother's mother. Who got it from her mother's mother's mother. It is our first story. Our oldest story.

Chagama told the story in short sentences with long pauses in between so that the Wanderer and Ponu could translate. Their language wasn't perfect. She hoped it was good enough.

Corb and Bella were born on the same day. It was a time of great difficulty for their chaga. Food was scarce. Their chaga small. None in their chaga thought the babes would survive. Nevertheless, the women brought Momo many gifts and cared for her while she cared for the babes. They were the same and yet not the same. Corb had large brows and deep-set eyes, hair the color of the sun, eyes the color of the sky. Bella was dark of skin and hair and eyes. They were the opposite to each other in almost every way.

They were very close, often to the exclusion of the rest of their chaga. They spoke words to each other that none in the chaga understood and with their secret language, they caused much mischief. Momo loved them even when others in the chaga did not.

On the day the twins were to mate, Momo gave them each a bone hearth. The bone hearth was made from the small skull of an animal. Perhaps a monkey or maybe a rabbit or an otter. The hearth had holes bored into the top of it where hide strips were strung through. This allowed the bone hearth to be carried easily. Inside, the hearth was an ember from Momo's fire. They could carry it with them and always have fire. Momo's chaga knew nothing of flint and so this beautiful bone hearth was in fact a precious gift.

The twins hugged their Momo with tears in their eyes. All three knew they would not see each other again. Each child was going with a different chaga and each chaga was going in a different direction.

Although the twins were sad to say goodbye to their mother, they were even more desolate at the thought of loosing each other. No others knew their words. None in their new chagas would understand them either. Even as they looked forward to their new lives, they were facing a terrible loneliness that only the other understood.

They stood together and promised to teach their children their language so that they would know each other when their chagas met. The twins were convinced that although they would not see each other again, their children would.

The first word they must learn was "Momo". And then "fire". And finally, "ember". For when their children met, they should know each other as family by these words.

Ches was shocked at those words. 'Fire. Ember. Momo'. They were the same in both their languages.

Chagama had tears on her cheeks as she finished her story. From the bag at her side, she pulled out a small skull so old it was of deep burnished brown. The inside was blackened from carrying embers and the skull itself was thin and frail. The hide strings had long since been replaced, and the clan and *chaga* could see that *Chagama* kept them in good repair.

Chagama looked to Ches expectantly for a long moment. Ches stared back at *Chagama* without moving. The *chaga* and the clan looked on. They seemed to understand that something important was happening, but none quite knew what. Finally, Ches rose. He went into his cave and after some time, returned to the circle by the fire.

Ches held up his own bone hearth for all to see. It too was ancient and burnished. The hide strips also in good repair. "Sister," he said.

"Brother", *Chagama* replied.

Reconciliation

Both Ches and *Chagama* were crying. They, more than any understood the significance of the bone hearth. They embraced warmly and would forever more recognize each other as family.

The meeting wasn't finished yet. There was one more matter to resolve. Triven stood and he called Ras to his side.

"This young man is responsible for Donon's death. He deeply regrets his actions because of the cost the *chaga* has paid. It was an accident, but one that likely could have been prevented. He has agreed to go back over the mountains and join others of our kind." Triven paused while the members of the *chaga* gasped in shock. They hadn't known about this.

"The rest of us would like to stay. If, that is, we can have peace. We have no desire to war with your people."

Ches turned and spoke to his family. Moke was quick to agree to peace, but the others were more wary. Ches looked across to Sele, a man he knew to be a problem from the tales that Kor and Moke had shared. He knew there were others too and he wasn't sure that Ras leaving was enough.

"I will escort Ras," said Sele. "See him safely gone from here." Triven nodded.

"I want to go too!" said Alli. Triven was surprised. He looked at this girl, who he thought might be a little wrong in the head. He had seen people without a *chaga*. They were always desperate, thin, hungry. A girl would be ill used by any who found her. He shook his head no. "There is no life for a young girl without a *chaga* in the mountains or over them." He thought Flin might want to go, but she looked away when he glanced at her.

"As a symbol of our commitment to peace, we gift you with this bow." Triven brought forth a finely crafted bow. He, himself had spent hours on it, making sure it was perfect. "Privon, our finest bowman, has consented to stay and teach your clan how to use it."

"We will agree to peace," said Ches finally. His fingers itched to hold the bow, but he forced himself to wait. He had spent the winter trying to recreate the weapon but had not met with success. "We are not your biggest problem. You will have to convince the other clans. And then you will have to convince Tsutse."

As soon as Ches spoke his final word, the clan people and *chaga* people alike, jumped to their feet and whooped in joy. The tension of both had been so fraught that a release was required, even from those who didn't feel joy. Flin. Mor. Sele, Ras and Alli.

Clan's people, and *chaga* people alike threw wood on the fire. Meat quickly followed. Moss and spring mushrooms were mixed for a side dish. The feast was nothing like the one at the gathering, but the absence of fear and uncertainty carried a delicious flavor all their own.

Moke had no interest in food or fire. He forced his way through the throng, intent on only one thing. Sola. When he found her, he lost his voice. She was so thick with child; he could only stare in shock.

Sola was struck by his silence. Did he not want her now? Did he find her ugly? Her chin tilted. This child was the future. If he was too blind to see that, she was certain she could… and then she was held in a fierce embrace. Moke was crying and laughing. He let her go, looked down at her stomach and pulled her close again. Sola smiled. He was as smart as she thought him after all.

"I will not hunt," Sola said firmly when Moke settled down. He laughed. "Fine," was all he said.

Peace

The Wanderer paused on the hill overlooking Tsutse's camp. He had been to all the other clans. Told the story of Corb and Bella. Of Ras and Sele. He had given each a bow, not as fine as the one Ches had received, but beautiful, nonetheless. They had all agreed to peace, but they warned they wouldn't go against Tsutse. Peace must be made with her. This was it. His words here would decide the future of both peoples.

It was late in the day, a greyness settling in already although it wouldn't be full dark for an hour or more. He could clearly see Tsutse by the fire. She was hunched over, her shoulders stooped. There was meat on a stick beside her, but she didn't even glance at it, much less eat it. Perhaps she had eaten already. She was alone. He knew Mor had gone to Ches's clan. Had Chor and Luco left too? His mind turned to the young Tsutse, full of laughter and life. A fierce hunter and generous mother. The woman who'd been his first friend. The one who'd helped him become the Wanderer. For her to come to this was unbearable.

Tsutse had her back to him and couldn't possibly know who stood on the hill behind her. "Come down and stick me or join me. Just decide," she called without looking to see who it was.

He walked down to the fire and sat beside her without speaking. He didn't know what to say. She reached past him and placed a stick of meat on the fire. Once it was seared, she offered him a piece which he gratefully ate.

"Tsutse, I am so, so sorry for all you have lost." She cried at his words.

"I have nothing left. Nothing but my anger and my grief. It has cost me Chor and Luco as well as Mor. They have all left. They say I'm too full of hate. They are right, but I don't know how to get rid of it!" Tsutse cried.

"I have an idea." Tsutse looked into his face. Hope. The first she had felt since Donon had gone.

The Wanderer took Tsutse home with him. They travelled far and the going was tough. Tsutse was quiet for most of the journey but gradually, she noticed the fauna, the landscape, the sky. Slowly, she came back to herself. Maybe not completely, but enough that he knew her.

The Wanderer wouldn't stay amongst his people. He planned only to visit. Let them know what happened to him and say a proper goodbye. He had Ponu to return to, and the clans that were his true people now. But Tsutse. Maybe she could build a new life with these people. Or just heal.

Over the Mountains

Sele and Ras didn't talk much as they made their way through the mountains that they had come over almost two years ago. Ras was old enough to understand his way would be rough. A strange *chaga* would not welcome him. That he had left his own *chaga* was all they needed to know. The best he could hope for was to join a band of men. Men like him. Who had no *chaga* and took what they needed when they could. Men like those who had raped Sele's mother. A part of Ras thrilled to that idea. The part that had brought him to this.

The going had been rough. Spring came later to the mountains than it did the valley. Many areas were too packed with snow to travel. Some paths were covered in ice. When they came to those spots, they had no choice but to wait it out. Rain or heat had to clear the way. Despite their lack of communication, Sele was careful to write of this time in his memory. It would be the last he would see of his first born.

They were almost at the pass where part of the path was missing. Sele and Ras had spent two days cutting saplings for a bridge in preparation. The camaraderie of the shared task was a treasure to Sele. When the sun set that night and Ras was snoring beside the fire, Sele allowed himself to remember his last conversation with Triven before they left.

"The *chaga* can't afford to lose two hunters Sele," said Triven with all seriousness. He was afraid that Sele would stay with Ras, who he knew he loved, rather than return to the *chaga* who needed him.

Sele had rolled that idea around in his mind, but he couldn't see a way where he and Ras did not become the men who killed his mother. That he couldn't bear.

"I'll come back," said Sele. He didn't suggest that Ras stay too. Ras would have refused even if he had. He couldn't seem to reconcile his actions. He clung to the belief that Moke's clan weren't people and his taking of Donon's life was not a crime. He would not be happy on their side of the mountains.

"You first," said Sele as he laid the poles across the path. He didn't look at Ras as he stepped out on the makeshift bridge. Tears glistened and he didn't want Ras to see them. Ras stepped out, gingerly, slowly, so as not to shift the bridge. Sele shoved the poles with all his strength and the side he was supposed to be anchoring slid off the path. Ras screamed in surprise and terror as the bridge disappeared from under him. His hands reached for the path on the other side and briefly grasped them before slipping away.

It was a kindness.

Sele didn't look down. He got to his feet and started the journey back.

Epilogue

The fall air was cold. It would snow soon. Ponu paused at the top of the path to the cave to look out across the steppe. The Wanderer wouldn't be back before winter. He knew that but he always looked anyway. The grass was empty. He sighed and entered the cave.

Chagama was sitting by the fire alone. She did that a lot lately. Her ankle had never completely healed, and it bothered her. She missed Sola too, he knew. He wondered if *Chagama* would come with them when they roamed in the spring.

Ponu sat beside her and took her hand. There was something he had been meaning to ask her for months and now seemed like a good time.

"The story," Ponu said. "The one of Momo and the twins."

"Yes?" replied *Chagama*.

"It's not quite how I remember you telling it before."

Chagama smiled a secret smile. "No. But it will be how it's told forever more."

Ponu wasn't quite ready to let it go.

"Why Corb?" He asked.

"It was Sola's idea. The whole thing was her idea, in fact. The clans have a lineage. When they find their true mate, they will speak of it. Ches is son of Corb. So is Moke."

Ponu nodded. "And I suppose you found the common words from Sola too?" he asked, although he already knew the answer.

"Yes, she knows quite a bit of their language."

Again, Ponu nodded. He got to his feet and turned to the back of the cave. He'd come for arrows.

"Ponu," *Chagama* said. Ponu turned back to look at her. "The bone hearths. They are real," was all she said.

The End

Printed in the USA
CPSIA information can be obtained
at www.ICGtesting.com
LVHW020013260923
759270LV00002B/194